SHADES OF SAVAGE

SARAH URQUHART

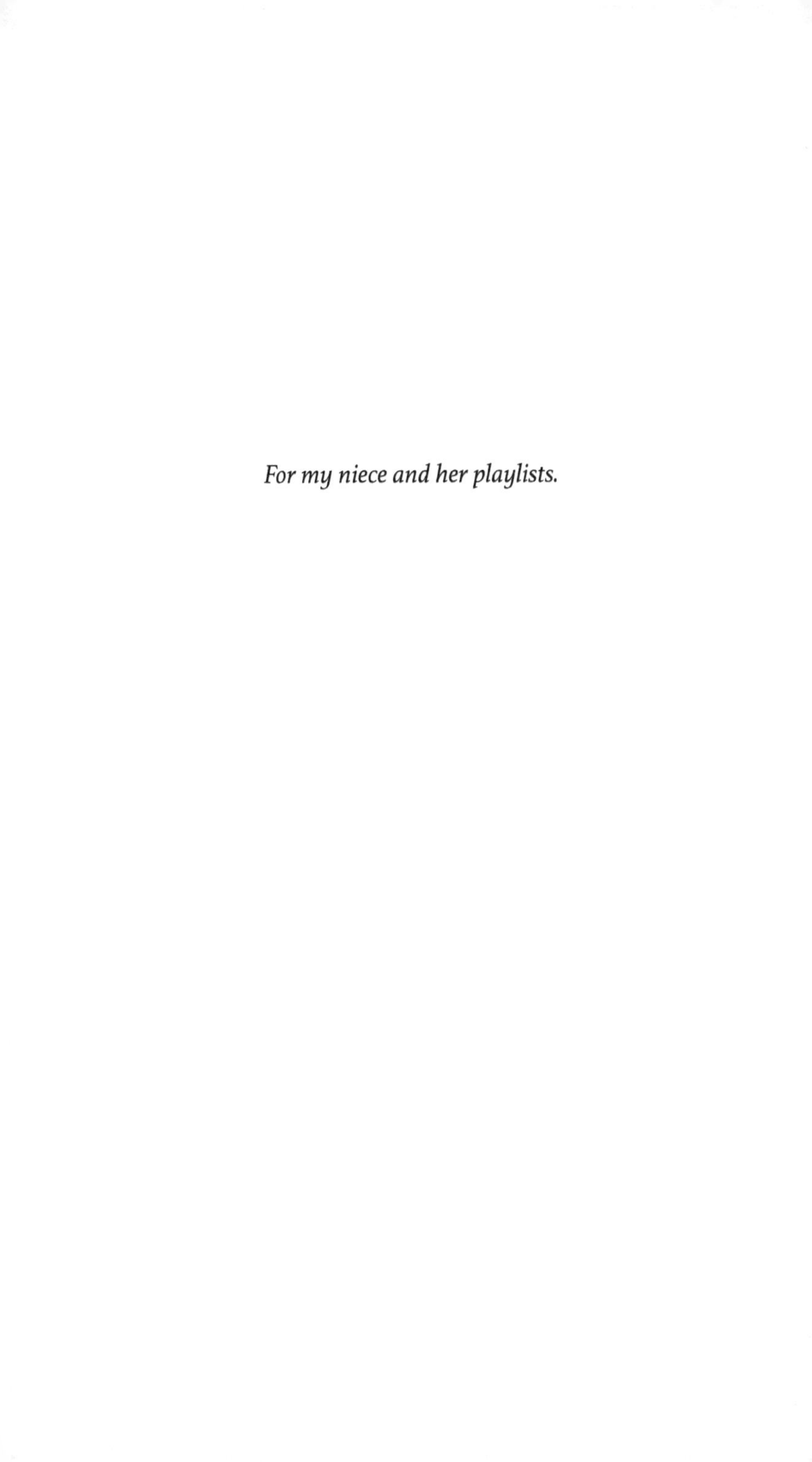

For my niece and her playlists.

$$1$$

Sophie kept her eyes on the teller and not on the faces standing in line.

"Ms. Lee, you're sure you want everything transferred?" The powdered face of the early sixties teller turned downward, her glasses catching on her nose. Suspicion froze in her eyes, keeping the look straight rather than narrowing.

"Yes." Sophie gave the woman a single nod and straightened her shoulders. Holding herself stiff kept the ache away and out of her expressions.

"There are two names on the account, Ms. Lee." The condescending tone lashed at the panic tethered in her system. Sophie pinched her lips, holding tight to her patience. She couldn't afford for this to go wrong.

"I'm aware I share an account with my husband. But I am the primary account holder." Her only saving grace was that her husband had terrible credit. When they married, he'd needed her name on everything. For a little while, he'd allowed her to maintain their finances, and she'd been able to keep him from burying her credit six feet under. But now her name was no better than his. At least she wouldn't have it for much longer.

The teller's oddly even brows rose.

Sophie's fingers twitched against the counter, and she had to pull them back so no one noticed her nerves. The room heated, but Sophie knew it was her. Everyone else was cool and calm, or irritated and bored. But clammy skin crawled under her clothes. The other tellers gave both Sophie and Miss Condescending side eyes. Sophie smiled when she caught them staring. Maybe they thought Sophie was crazy, or they thought the teller was rude.

The woman tapped away on her keyboard, pausing every few seconds. "Ms. Lee, I need to speak to the manager. I'll be right back."

Sophie choked back her retort. Causing a scene and demanding the woman do her job wouldn't help her. The bank had no reason to deny her request. It was a simple transfer, after all.

The woman came back with her hands folded and her nose up. "The manager is waiting for you in his office, Ms. Lee." She pointed around the corner of the long counter. "Third door on the right."

"Thank you." Sophie's gratitude was low and dry as she eyed the hall. Holding tight to her purse, she moved around the counter. She tapped on the third door and poked her head in. The man waited with his hands clasped on the desk.

"Ms. Lee." He nodded. "Please have a seat." It took all her strength not to show any concern, but her eyes landed on the phone beside the manager's elbow. Had they already called Alan? Her husband would be here in minutes and charm the pants off everyone in the bank. They'd practically drool at his feet for that side smile that made his one eye twinkle. Everyone except her.

The cushion in the chair had worn away over the years and she winced as she dropped into it. "Is there a problem, Mr. Walters?" She tilted her head to read the name plaque on the edge of his desk.

"Not necessarily. We want you to be certain of the transfer. The amounts in your accounts exceed the threshold allowed for the tellers to handle and needs managerial approval."

"I see." She didn't. She didn't know how much money was in the accounts, but Alan never made that much. While he had let her manage their finances once upon a time, Sophie hadn't seen the accounts in almost two years. So many times when coming in here to squirrel away what little she'd earned into her own account, it had been tempting to inquire the status of the shared accounts, but if Alan ever found out she'd even looked, he'd dig until he found her account and would force her to close it. She had little in it, but every cent she could sneak away from her part time job at the library went in there. He never noticed the odd five dollars missing from her pay. Despite not having more than a couple hundred in that account, Sophie couldn't wait any longer. She'd only hoped what he had in the shared accounts could help her disappear.

"These are significant sums to transfer all to one account from shared ones. Are you sure we shouldn't call your husband?"

She first wanted to reel at him for such an absurd question with his tilted head and sympathetically pursed lips beneath his mustache. But if she showed her true feelings, the fear and panic at her husband finding her here, the red flags would slap the manager in the face. As hard as her blood pumped in her ears, Sophie barely heard her calm response. "If that would make you feel better to waste the time of a man who doesn't hold the same sexist views as you and your staff, by all means."

"Ms. Lee, that is not..."

"But it is." Even her soft tone cut him off. "Consistently asking a woman if she's sure of her decision diminishes her value, and questions her intelligence. I received the same judgmental treatment from the teller at the front as I have from you, Mr. Walters. If you have no other objections to the transfer from the accounts of which I own to another account, still within your bank, that I also own, other than the need to consult my husband, who only has signing authority I might add, then please continue to waist your time." Sophie set her purse down in the seat beside her. Crossing her legs, she leaned back and stared at the bank manager.

"My apologies, Ms. Lee. Of course, there are no objections." The manager turned to his computer and made several clicks over the screen before printing something off. He slid three pieces of paper over his desk and tapped at them with his pen.

Sophie took her time retrieving her purse and leaning forward.

"These are the balances of the accounts we transferred funds from." He pointed to the zero at the bottom of the first page and flipped it over to tap on the zero on the second page. "And this is the new balance in your account."

Sophie nodded at the exceptionally large number while her breath did barrel rolls in her lungs instead of racing out of her to keep her alive. "Thank you." *That sounded normal.* Where the hell had Alan gotten all that money? And what was she going to do with it now? After the experience she just had with the bank manager, Sophie didn't trust leaving it in her account. She pulled the papers together and folded them into thirds before tucking them inside her purse. "Have a great day, Mr. Walters."

"You as well, Ms. Lee." The manager stiffened behind his desk. Sophie hovered near his door long enough to see his hand reach for the phone. He thought she was stealing from her husband. Which she was, but that wasn't his business.

Sophie marched out of the bank. As soon as her shoes hit the pavement, she picked up the pace. Not a run. Running would draw attention. And as she was sure the bank manager was on the phone with her husband, she would no doubt have a tail soon.

She called the cab as she continued to walk, instructing him to meet her at the next intersection. The timing was perfect. The two-toned car pulled up as she hit the cross-walk. She called out the address and met the driver's eyes in the rearview mirror with a smile. He pulled back out into traffic and stopped at the red light in front of them. A familiar dark blue convertible sped through the changed light.

Her element of surprise had vanished.

***

DAK NEEDED to hire more guys. Cursing, he ran his fingers through his hair, while he scrolled through his messages. A kidnapping. Victim recovery. Money retrieval from an idiot employee. And at the bottom of the list, an assassination. It wasn't a bad thing. It meant this business was doing better than he imagined. Both the legitimate and illegitimate sides. Finding and training guys to do both types of jobs was difficult. Legal bodyguard and security specialist by day, deadly assassin by night.

The front door opened, sounding off the low chime on the entire first floor. Hunched shoulders flattened as she caught sight of Dak. The woman blinked and looked at the floor before lifting her chin. She kept her hand on the door as it closed until it connected with the frame.

Stepping forward, she held her purse at her side. "Hello."

He nodded and pointed to the chair on the other side of the desk. Dak didn't ask if she was in the wrong place. He'd learned a long time ago that the surface meant nothing. And Dak recognized the way she'd rushed inside with fear squeezing her shoulders.

She eyed the large windows with only her neck turned and her stiff torso facing him.

"No one can see inside."

She jumped at his scarred voice. "Oh." He'd had all the windows and doors tinted in a way that reflected from the outside, allowing for complete privacy.

"What can I help you with?" Dak wasn't the one to sit at this desk on a regular basis. They didn't have a receptionist. He made the other guys take rotations to work out here when not on a job. The odd time everyone was out, he hired temporary employees to answer the phone and take messages while keeping the front door locked.

"I need to disappear." She released the words with relief. Straight, dark blonde hair framed rich blue eyes that met his. He waited to see how long it would take her to turn away. No one caught his gaze for long. But this woman didn't look away.

"Disappear?"

"A new identity." She pulled in a long breath as if to let it out with a sigh, but winced. She worked the air out of her with soft, shallow puffs. But her face remained confident. She did well to hide whatever pain she was in.

On the surface, *King Security* was a legitimate company supplying personal security, private investigations, and security system installations. But if one inquired in the right places, they'd find the multitude of other jobs not listed on the company website. Dak tried to imagine this woman researching where to get a new identity. The image of her sitting in a seedy bar talking to someone with very little morals made his lip curl.

"That is something you can do, right?"

"Why do you need a new identity?" He didn't want to answer her question just yet. Authorities knew what this place was, who owned it. Who it was named after. They were careful how they ran that side of the business. Customers looking for illegal hire rarely walked in the front door.

"I don't believe that information is necessary to do the job." A chin firm with pride tilted toward him. A simple summer blouse and jeans gave her a prim look with an air of authority. Such an odd mix for her soft features.

"But it is."

"I can take my business elsewhere." She pulled her purse tighter, as if preparing to leave. The rings on her left hand caught the light, shifting as her fingers turned white. But she didn't move, stamping a firm denial on her bluff.

"You don't have time for that." As slight as they'd been, Dak caught the side glances she'd made out the window on her left. She had one arm tucked tighter against her side than the other and since she'd sat down, her entire upper body hadn't moved. This woman was on the run.

Her confidence left the line of her lips. "I need to get

away from someone." Her face, neck, and wrists were all free from marks or bruises and she carried herself with bravado and clear eyes. But he'd bet his sharpest knife that someone had abused her.

"Lift your shirt."

"Excuse me?" She stood from the chair, her body moving as one. With every move she made, Dak made one of his own. "The only form of currency I have is money. If that doesn't interest you, I'm leaving."

"I don't repeat myself." People listened the first time he spoke.

In preparation to run, the woman flattened her arm against her torso and took a large step backward. Dak caught her before her foot hit the floor. He rushed her against the wall behind her, pinning her wrists in his hands. Her purse fell to the floor as soon as he took hold.

She hissed and whimpered as she struggled against him. That had to stop. Dak pulled her arms above her head and pinned them together with one hand. With his thigh between her legs, he took away some of her purchase on the floor. He used his free hand and body weight to hold her still.

"Please, don't." She closed her eyes and turned her head.

"Easy, princess." Dak let his breath brush against her cheek. Once she'd stilled, he reached for the hem of her shirt. "Look at me." Telling her he wasn't going to hurt her wouldn't be enough. She needed to see it for herself.

He let his fingers brush the bare skin of her stomach until, with a clenched jaw, she turned her head. Dak gave her a single nod when she'd held his gaze long enough, then tilted his head to watch what he revealed beneath her shirt.

He lifted slowly. Fading greens and yellows blended and swirled together over an elongated oval on her ribs. The size of a fucking boot. He hooked her shirt over her breast to keep it up and traced the shape and swirls of the bruise. How the fuck was this woman walking?

She winced when he applied pressure to her ribs.

"Who did this?" The same man she was running from was his guess.

"My husband." Her whisper rose and fell.

Dak gentled his touch and soothed his thumb back and forth over the large bruise. He was about to ask her name when she rolled her head against the wall. Her eyes widened, and she thrashed between him and the wall, getting nowhere.

"My husband!"

Dak looked out the window and saw a man walking towards the door, glancing up and down from his phone.

"Hendrick!" He released her from the wall and grabbed her purse from the floor. Hendrick charged out from the back. "Take her. Find the tracker."

"Tracker?" She tried to reach for her purse, but Hendrick took it from Dak and grabbed her elbow.

"Do as you're told, princess." Dak circled the desk, but didn't sit down.

Hendrick had her out of sight just as the door opened and her husband walked inside. The man was as tall and broad as Dak with a shoe size to match the bruise on princess's ribs. He'd tucked his polo shirt into his slacks and the belt he wore to hold them up had an extra shine. He searched the room before landing on Dak.

"Hello. I'm looking for someone." His consonants clipped through a smile that he forced into his eyes.

Dak crossed his arms and waited. He'd found the longer he stayed silent, the more information he could get from people. They'd spill everything and more when silence stretched into tension.

"Right. It's my wife. We were supposed to meet for lunch, but I think she may have gotten lost. She does that often." He shook his head with a half smile. "I thought I saw her come in here."

"Lost or not, I doubt anyone would mistake this place for a restaurant."

A flat smile and tightened eyes stared back at Dak while the man lifted the phone he still had in his hand.

"She's the friendly sort and has no trouble asking for directions." He turned his phone around, holding up a picture of the woman that was in the back with Hendrick. "Did she come in here a few minutes ago?"

Dak studied the picture, appearing to give careful consideration. He shook his head. "Sorry."

"Right. Well." He looked around the small lobby once more, his eyes lingering on the hall leading to the back. "If she comes this way, tell her to meet me across the street. I'll be waiting."

Dak didn't move while he watched the door shut behind the woman's husband. He stared while the man walked across the street, taking a table outside at the small bistro.

This job just moved to the top of the list.

"I'll be waiting." The familiar threat in Alan's voice that kept Sophie awake at night echoed back. Hendrick told her to be quiet when they stepped out of sight. Hearing Alan had been more than enough for her to shut up. She'd planned this escape out months ago and only felt foolish now that he'd caught up to her so soon.

Hendrick led her to what looked like a break room with a long table, sink, and refrigerator. Even a stove. He searched her purse and scrolled through her phone, never asking her to unlock it.

The man from the front appeared, and Sophie stepped back. Shivers raced over and through her. He'd terrified her, yet even when immobilizing her against the wall, his touch had been gentle. When he'd forced her to stop fighting, she stopped hurting. The bruise over her ribs hummed with the memory of his touch. His dark eyes were a stark contrast to the blond hair. The man in his soul wasn't a mystery.

"Tracking app on her phone." Hendrick waved her phone back and forth. He scrolled for another few minutes, then tilted his eyes up to look at her above the phone. "You have anything on here you need?"

Sophie's skin warmed. The slow crawl of her blush filled her neck and up to her hairline. "He knew where I was all morning. And every day." The bank manager never needed to call him. Alan already knew everywhere she'd ever been. Known she'd gone to the bank regularly to deposit into her private account. He'd known when she went to work or when she stayed home.

"Only if he was paying attention. This one doesn't record. Only gives real time information." Hendrick set her phone down on the counter beside him.

"Do you need anything off there, princess?"

"I already backed everything up onto a flash drive. I have to get a new phone after today." Her carefully laid plans drowned and died. Hendrick tossed her phone into the sink and pulled a knife from his hip.

"Don't do it, Hendrick." Dark Eyes shook his head. Hendrick looked back with a grin that set a spark in his eyes, and for a moment, the man looked a little crazy.

Raising his arm, he held the knife between his fingers. He whipped his wrist and a shatter and clunk echoed back. Hendrick grabbed a tin cookie sheet and covered the sink while Dark Eyes covered her. Facing her, he looked down. Sophie couldn't look away. She wanted that darkness holding her. As he'd held her against the wall and forced her fear of him away. Forced all her fear away.

Flames spurted out from under the thin tin.

"That never gets old." Hendrick leaned beside the sink and crossed his arms while he admired the flames. A few minutes passed before he removed the tin and turned on the tap.

"It does," Dark Eyes said to her rather than turning to speak to Hendrick. "Especially when you could have just turned the phone off." Sophie's lips twitched at the boredom in his tone. His lids lowered until they settled on her ribs. "Set up a decoy loop to bring her back here." He stepped back. "Dear hubby is out there watching. He knows she's in here. He needs to see her get taken away."

"I hadn't hired you yet. I'm only looking for a new identity." Although she was sure that what now sat in her account would cover whatever security she needed.

"Right now you don't have a choice, princess. But you'll have to tell me a lot more than you need a new identity."

Sophie blanked. She couldn't get out of here on her own. Everything crashed and burned in a matter of minutes. Dark Eyes was her only option to get away from Alan.

"Get her a coat. I'll walk out the front with her and put her in the car. You drive off, get lost, then bring her back."

"Won't he see us leave?" Her eyes followed Hendrick as he turned off the water then left down another hall.

"That's the point. He knows you're here. He'll watch you leave, but he doesn't know you're coming back."

"That seems almost too simple." He'd called it a decoy loop. Pretend to leave, but end back where you started.

"What's your name, princess?" Dark Eyes took a step closer.

"Yours first." She lifted her chin as he took another step toward her. His heat invaded her space.

"You're going to learn that isn't how I work." His voice, already rough and scarred, dropped to a husk.

"But you've adopted a moniker for me. I have nothing to call you."

"I bet you could think of something."

Sophie shouldn't challenge this man, but that's what she did. "Nothing appropriate."

His stern face hadn't moved up to this point, but she swore she saw his upper lip twitch with his brow. "Dak."

"Sophie."

"That wasn't so hard." Hendrick stomped back into the break room. "Here you go, Sophie." He held out a fine wool coat. The garment would stand out in this weather despite the plainness of it. Which she supposed was the point.

She slid her arms into the sleeves and held it closed in front of her.

"I'll be out front in a few minutes." Hendrick left again.

"While we wait, you can tell me your plan to escape your husband. And how the hell you're able to walk with that bruise on your ribs."

"It's not as bad as it looks, and I've been working hard for the past almost three weeks to rebuild my strength to disappear while Alan thought I was still stuck in bed."

"You're in pain." Those three words were like listening to thunder roll beneath her feet.

Sophie ignored his observation. She hadn't felt this bad since the first week. "My first stop this morning was the bank. I emptied his accounts." Not because she wanted the money. Sophie would escape him with nothing as long as it meant getting away. This was her own piece of revenge.

"You stole all of his money?" What did she hear in his voice? It hitched, ever so slightly, that she might have imagined it.

"No. They were all joint accounts. It was as much my money as it was his."

"Where is the money now?"

"In my personal account. He didn't know I had one. At least I don't think he did." She couldn't be that lucky that he'd never looked at the tracking when she'd been at work or at the bank. "I need to get that money out of there. I don't trust the bank."

"Why?"

"I think the bank manager called my husband after I left."

Dak pulled a phone from his pocket. "What's your last name?"

"Lee."

"Husband is Alan Lee?"

"No. Alan Morgan." She'd fought him to keep her last name.

Dak tapped on his phone. "You'll have a new account with the money transferred by the time you get back here."

"How?"

"You understand what kind of business you walked into or you wouldn't have come in looking to disappear."

He was right. If you wanted something illegal done and done right, you went to *King's Mercenaries,* also known as *King Security.* Sophie came across an old classmate from high school several months back. They hadn't been friends, but she remembered him to be friendly enough. He wasn't doing so well now. One night sitting at a sketchy bar with him and she'd learned what she needed to know.

"Time to go, princess." Dak pulled the hood up on her coat and slid his hand beneath it, pulling out strands of her hair to settle against the front of the coat. An identifiable feature. He rubbed her hair between his thumb and fingers before letting it fall. Sophie retrieved her purse from the table before following him to the front.

"What happens when I get back?"

"That depends. But this is buying us time to figure out what needs to be done and how long it will take." Dak unlocked the front door. "Ready?"

"Yes."

Dak opened the door and ushered her out with an arm around her back. He made a show of looking left and right. Sophie caught Alan's stare from across the street. A large hand cupped the back of her head.

"Head down."

She huddled closer to his body. Hendrick parked a few metres away. Far enough for someone watching to see what was happening. Dak opened the back door and put more pressure on the back of her head to tuck her inside. He shut the door without another word, and Hendrick pulled into traffic.

For the first time in years, safety crept around her.

2

———

Damn, that woman had a spine made of steel. Her unorthodox approach to escaping abuse impressed him—taking the steps to control her future.

Roen's name flashed on his buzzing phone. He wasn't the only employee with computer and hacking skills, but he was the fastest.

"Dak."

"Boss. Money transfer is done. But I don't think that money was legit. After transferring the ridiculous amount, I dug into the history of the joint accounts."

"Any idea where it came from?"

"I will soon." Roen spoke with the confidence he deserved. The creak of the chair leaning back echoed through the line.

"Send me the new account information."

"Should already have it. This for a new case?"

"Yes." The princess didn't have a choice. She'd walked in here with a tail after stealing possible dirty money. She'd hired him when she walked in the door. "Don't only dig into the money. Find out what you can on Alan Morgan.

And send his face to the others. He isn't allowed in the building."

"Way ahead of you." Roen clicked off.

Dak pulled up the account information Roen had sent. The balance had way too many zeros and commas for the slicked back man who'd walked in wearing off-brand, mis-sized, and wrinkled clothes. Whoever owned that money was going to miss it.

Cole walked into the main lobby, his hair dripping from a shower after spending a couple of hours in the gym.

"Take the front. I have a case to deal with." A pretty blonde case. *Fuck.*

"What kind of case?" Cole finger combed his hair and sat on the edge of the desk. Cole and Roen had been two guys Dak trained himself. He trained with all their employees, but Cole and Roen had been green three years ago when Dak had found them.

"One that my instincts are telling me is more complicated than it appears." But would that hinder Sophie's plans to disappear? How far would they have to bury her identity?

"And what does it appear to be?"

"A woman on the run from an abusive husband." Helping her disappear from Morgan would take them a day, maybe two. But that might not be sufficient after they followed the money.

"And you're working the case?" Cole cut off his surprise before it reached the end of his question. Dak's home was in the shadows. And he only worked the jobs that needed the shadows.

"I was working the front when she came in."

"Huh. Didn't know that was a rule." Cole moved around the desk and plopped in the chair, ignoring the deadly glare Dak sent his way.

"Roen should have sent you details on the husband."

Cole gave Dak a two-finger salute. Dak left to meet Hendrick and Sophie in the parking garage. This building didn't only house *King Security*. The upper levels were apartments with Dak's at the top and the other half of the ground level housed the lobby. Dak owned the most secure building in the city. He knew everything there was about each of his tenants, and he kept the top floor to himself. There were two apartments on that floor. His and a spare that had only been used once.

Twice, once Sophie returned. The safest place for her was beside him. And that was the only reason he was going to put her in that apartment.

Hendrick pulled into the parking garage, driving a half ton four-door pickup truck rather than the SUV they'd left in. Peering through the windshield, Dak saw which side Sophie was on and went to the back door to open it for her.

"Any trouble?" Dak asked as Hendrick stepped out.

"None. He never caught up to us until I let him after we'd switched vehicles. He zipped past us with his head on a swivel." Hendrick leaned on the roof of the car.

Dak looked at Sophie as she stepped back. Her face had paled and her pain glowed in contrast. "Upstairs."

"Boss?" Hendrick asked.

"She'll be in the spare beside mine." Dak shut the back door and closed the distance between him and Sophie.

"Got it." His lips formed an 'o' to whistle, but he didn't make a sound. With high brows, Hendrick shut the driver's door and disappeared toward the gym.

"The spare what?" Sophie rubbed her thumb back and forth over the handle of her purse.

"The spare apartment. You're staying here." Dak took one step closer to her, but she matched it to back away.

"Shouldn't that be my choice?"

"You came to me, princess."

"To disappear. Not for a place to stay." Her lips quivered and while she tried to push her shoulders back, one slumped either to relieve pressure or from exhaustion. He wasn't sure, and it didn't matter.

"Sophie." Dak laid his hand over the bruise, cursing the fabric covering her skin. "You're safe here."

Her eyes tightened, and she stared up at him. The question of if he was right or not played back and forth on her face. Eventually, she caved and her other shoulder dropped to match the first. Breaths, short and harsh, rushed out of her.

"This is the longest you've been out of bed since he kicked you, isn't it?"

"How did you know he kicked me?"

"Sophie," he growled, making it clear he was unwilling to talk around in circles. Dak wanted his answer.

"Yes. I haven't had any pain for over a week. But I've spent as much time in bed as possible to heal and to make Alan think it was worse."

Dak bent and scooped her up against his chest. She held her breath until he had her settled. At the private elevator that would take them to the top floor only, he bent his wrist beneath her knees so he could punch in the security code.

"You don't have to carry me." But she didn't struggle or stiffen in his arms. She let her weight rest against him, her hands holding his shoulders.

"I'm not an asshole."

"You sure? You did pin me to the wall and force my shirt up. I'm pretty sure that's something an asshole would do."

"I can do it again. But this time it won't be to look for injuries."

Her bright pink lips parted.

Why? Why did he say something so suggestive? The woman was pure beauty, but the problem was, she was barely a woman. Too young for his blood. Yet, the words spewed out of him as the thoughts ran rampant through his head.

He let his face turn hard and stepped into the elevator, staring at the closing door.

"Dak?" That breathless curiosity clutched at him—like long fingers running down his chest and straight to his...

"No, princess." He didn't look down at her. The elevator ride was quick and opened into a long hallway with three doors. Two entrances for his apartment and one for the spare. The spare apartment also had an entrance into Dak's.

Dak set her down to unlock the door, then guided her with one hand on her elbow and the other around her back. Too much contact, but he wouldn't let her fall.

"I'll send someone up soon with supplies." He continued to lead her through the apartment to the bedroom. Pulling the coat from her shoulders, he tossed it over a chair.

"We still haven't discussed business." Sophie lowered herself to the bed. "I thought I was well enough to escape."

"You did good, princess." She made it to where she needed to be. Where she had the best chances. Here.

"But all for nothing. He would have found me if it hadn't been for you."

"Maybe. Maybe not. Where did your husband get that much money?"

Surprise brightened her eyes. "I don't know. I was expecting to be lucky to find a thousand in there. I would have run without the money, but I wanted my pound of flesh."

Pound of flesh? She took everything he had out of

revenge. More than her spine carried steel. "How did you intend to pay me?"

"I'd hoped it wouldn't be more than the few hundred I've squirreled away."

"It would have been." But he wouldn't have let her walk back out into danger.

"What am I going to owe you for all of this and a new start?"

"We'll talk payment later." Hell, she could afford it and more. But Dak didn't feel right taking her money. She could live a comfortable life off that sum. As long as they kept the original owners from ever finding her.

"No." Sophie pushed herself to sit up straight and folded her hands in her lap. "We'll talk about it now."

Dak kept his scoff internal. He hadn't thought that steel spine had any strength left. Stalking toward the bed, he leaned over, placing his hand on her chest and his other at the small of her back. Applying pressure, Dak laid her down. "I'll be right back."

He turned away from her and left, shaking his head. He wouldn't take the warrior princess's money. But he wondered if he was strong enough not to take something else from her.

<hr>

THE DAMN MAN IGNORED HER. Sophie didn't want the stress of payment hanging over her. This wasn't to come cheap and while she hadn't yet decided how she'd use her newfound riches, she didn't want all of it to go toward her escape. An escape that should be simple. Alan wasn't smart enough or motivated enough to find her. At least not past the initial few months.

It hurt to sit herself upright to face Dak. Gratitude grudgingly took hold as she relaxed. She closed her eyes with a deep, slow sigh as she heard a door click shut behind Dak. Her abdomen trembled. Just something else to be embarrassed by. Sophie hadn't expected her escape to set her back after having little to no pain for so long. Small aches around the bruise on her skin weren't enough to deter her. But if she'd waited any longer, Alan would have wondered why she'd still been stuck in bed. She'd milked this injury for more than it was due to make him believe she could barely make it to the bathroom on her own.

If her plan had worked, Alan wouldn't have known she'd left until he got home from work—if he came home from work. More than enough time to make her run to the bank, buy a new identity and then hit the road. She should have left her phone at home that morning. But if she had, she wouldn't have been carried in the arms of a sexy savage and surrounded by the softest pillows and blankets she ever imagined.

Being out of Alan's reach now left her feeling half her weight. The effort it took to make it through a day with that man in her life was astonishing, and something she hadn't seen until Dak closed her in the car. She'd carried the physical pain of his abuse, but also the pain of her life.

It fled. Streams of it had poured out of her as Hendrick drove away. She must have had adrenaline pumping, because her body had throbbed and her blood flow slowed. The effect of the past three years showed.

A door clicked again and soft thuds sounded off the wood floors of the apartment. Tilting her head, Sophie listened to the steady beat. She thought he was making noise on purpose. He was so graceful and purposeful.

She'd bet he could keep himself utterly quiet if he wanted to.

She opened her eyes when he walked into the room. Tall, broad, and hard. If it weren't for his dark eyes, he could be mistaken for someone kind. Her breath caught and she replayed their exchange in the elevator. He'd been as surprised as she by what he'd said. Sophie forced a shaky breath into her lungs.

"Do you ever wear coloured contacts?" She rolled her head to track his progress.

"Why would you ask that?" He sat on the side of the bed.

"Your eyes give you away. I assume there are times when you need people to think you're something you're not." Blue eyes and smiling and Dak would have queens and kings eating out of his hand.

"No one can see my eyes from where I stand." He held out his hand and placed two pills in hers. "Take those."

"What are they?"

"Pain killers. Good ones."

She looked at them suspiciously.

"You're safe, princess. Take them." Dak wrapped an arm around her shoulders and helped her up. Since he'd laid her down, her body lost every ounce of strength. He pressed a glass of water into her hands and held her up while she took the pills and swallowed them down with a drink.

Dak held her there a few minutes longer than needed. He splayed his free hand over her ribs. He didn't need to touch her. Shouldn't touch her. But this wasn't a man that worried about what he should or shouldn't do. His thumb swiped back and forth. His strength and heat wrapped around her and for the first time in years, Sophie felt cherished.

Again, the fool. Cherished by a man who'd forced her against the wall and lifted her shirt. But what about the man that carried her up here, swearing he wasn't an asshole? Or the man who suggested he'd lift her shirt for another reason? But he'd shut her out the moment that suggestion ignited. Dark Eyes didn't cherish.

It had been so long since Sophie felt good about her body. And even the small slivers of interest from him fed the ache inside her.

"Dak?" He'd been harsh when she'd used that same curious tone earlier in his arms.

"Get some rest." He looked away and lowered her back to the bed. Standing, he pulled a phone from his pocket and set it on the nightstand. "A temporary burner. It has my number in it. Call if you need anything."

"Thank you." She watched him leave and turned her head to the clock on the nightstand. Four in the afternoon. And he'd left her like she was going to bed for the night. But her eyes were heavy and drifting closed after only a few minutes. Whatever was in those pain pills was a doozy. Her body hummed.

You're safe, princess. That rough voice echoed over and over in her head while sleep took hold.

HIS COCK THROBBED and his insides tightened. Dak took the elevator straight down to the gym. This wasn't the same gym he'd built for his tenants with rows of treadmills, ellipticals, and mirrors. This was the private one where King's mercenaries trained. The building was massive, housing separate amenities for the tenants and the business.

Stripping off his shirt, he tossed it in the corner and stalked toward the bags. He measured each punch and kick so that the others in the room didn't see something was wrong with him. Didn't know how hard he'd fought the urge to devour Sophie.

Hendrick was working with weights and Roen was on one of the two treadmills. King, the master of all mercenaries himself, sparred with his now wife on the mats. Feminine growls followed every humph. King laid the small woman out on her ass within seconds of each round. But the little thing was learning. Just not fast enough for Dak's liking. If she's living a life next to King, she's living a life with a target on her back. None of them would sleep well until she defended herself with the same high standards as any of the men in their employ.

"No one will wait for you to recover from the first attack before going for the second, little girl." King held a hand out for Ember to help her up. She glared at the hand. Smart. She was learning, but she placed her hand in her husband's anyway. King did as Dak expected. Pulled her up and kept her momentum going to swing her behind him.

Dak had to feel a bit of pride as Ember did what he'd taught her the last time he'd sparred with her. She dropped her weight to the ground and swung her legs sideways with one in front of King's feet and one behind, doubling her grip on his hand so she pulled his arm backward. No matter which way King moved to counter the twist in his shoulder, he'd trip over her legs.

Unless he'd anticipated what she'd done. Lifting a leg higher than hers, King stepped back.

"Good. For most people, that would have worked."

Ember didn't look pleased with the praise. With his grip still on her hand, King pulled her to her feet and against his chest.

Dak blocked out the couple and moved on from his rhythmic warm up.

"Heard the new case is staying upstairs." King held Ember to his side and walked over to the bags. Dak didn't want to stop. He needed to expel the energy inside him somehow. It was the bags, the man standing next to him, or Sophie. And he'd rather no one saw the state he was in. So each hit, elbow, and kick were all perfectly timed patterns.

"You heard right."

"How many guys do you need on it?"

"Don't know who we're dealing with yet. I might need you." There were some in the underbelly that upon hearing King's name, even since his retirement and subsequent return, made their ankles quake. If the original owner of that money was one of those people, getting Sophie out of trouble would be easy. If not, then Dak would be stuck with the steel-spined beauty. The too young, *she's-a-job* beauty.

No more touching. No more holding or helping. No more holding his hand over her ribs, as if he could heal her with sheer will.

"I'm taking the victim recovery job. Shouldn't take more than a few days."

"Is Ember going?" Dak nodded at the raven-haired woman.

"No."

"Yes." The couple spoke over each other.

King growled at his wife. He'd almost lost the woman to his own vindictive past. Then again, from his own stubborn beliefs.

"Right. I'll call if I need you." Dak picked up his pace

against the bag and blocked out his partner. The worn logo printed on the leather of the bag morphed into Sophie's husband. He wanted to make the man bleed. Each strike hit dead centre, demolishing the imaginary Alan Morgan.

Sophie hadn't been the first abused woman to walk through their doors and she wouldn't be the last. But never had Dak felt this need for revenge, the need to touch her, to do everything in his power to make everything right.

Heaving, Dak clutched the bag while his lungs burned. *Finish the job.* He pushed up and looked across the empty gym. The others must have left somewhere between King and Ember leaving and now. Never was Dak's focus not on the people around him. That pissed him off enough to throw another spinning back kick into the bag. The chains holding it in place tensed and groaned.

Dak snatched his shirt from the floor and used it to wipe the sweat from his forehead and neck. Roen and Henrick both stepped from the showers.

"Anything?" Dak stepped in front of Roen.

"I'm impressed with how well they covered the transaction trail. I have some programs running."

"Fine. Keep at it." Dak turned to Hendrick. "I need you and Cole to get supplies for the spare apartment. Groceries, toiletries, clothes. She's staying there until Roen tracks the money or we have someone other than her husband sniffing around. Do it in the morning and try not to startle her."

Hendrick nodded, and he and Roen left. Dak showered. Despite telling himself he needed to stay away from Sophie, he wanted to check on her. The pills he gave her should take away every ounce of pain and help her sleep straight through until morning. But in case they hadn't kicked in or she woke up, Dak planned to take her something to eat.

He grabbed a meal to go from the bistro across the

street. Chili, bread, iced tea, and water. Dak let himself into the apartment from his own, this time masking all sound he made.

The apartment was still and quiet. He'd shut the bedroom door when he left, but not tight so he could get inside without waking her. Peeking in, he opened the door further when he didn't see any movement on the bed. The pills had kicked in all right. Slow, deep breathing lifted the blankets.

Her bow lips parted and the lines of pain on her face had disappeared, making her age even more apparent. She couldn't be more than early twenties. What the hell would a man approaching forty who was not only raised on the streets, but born on the streets, do with a princess like her?

She hadn't eaten since before she'd walked through his door. But food wasn't what she needed most right now. True rest would help her heal faster. He set the iced tea and water on the nightstand and would put the food in the fridge for her to eat later.

A strand of hair had fallen over her face, crossing over her nose. His hand reaching out to her passed in his vision and he snatched it back.

No touching. He growled at his own reminder. Not only did he want to brush her hair back, but he wanted to run his hands down her body. She was fucking asleep. What was wrong with him?

Dak turned on his heel and left, putting the chili and bread in the fridge. He reached the door to go back into his apartment and paused. Her face swam in his vision. Soft. Supple. Lips ready to devour. And a strand of hair blocking it all.

Fuck him.

He stalked back across the apartment and slipped into

the bedroom. Sophie hadn't moved. Reaching out, he hooked the hair on his finger and moved it away from her face. The tip of his finger stroked over her forehead and behind her ear. She didn't stir and Dak hadn't expected her to, but he imagined what he would have done if she'd woken as he stood over her.

His gut twisted, and he closed his eyes. He left without another look back. *No. Touching.*

3

———————

Deep breaths brought Sophie awake. Softness engulfed her. She blinked, pushing the last of the sleep away. She'd run from Alan. This little adventure might not be over, but she was safe from him. Sophie tried to think through the events of the previous day, but her thoughts kept coming back to Dak.

Turning her head to look around the room, she saw a bottle of iced tea and a bottle of water sitting on the night-stand. They hadn't been there when Dak brought her in. Did he come back?

Her stomach growled and rumbled long. She'd been too nervous to eat much before leaving her home. Holding her ribs, Sophie pushed herself up in bed. They didn't hurt as she'd expected. A trip to the hospital would have clarified her injuries and told her what kind of recovery time she'd been looking at. But as her pain faded after the first week, she scratched her plan to sneak away to a walk in clinic. If she hadn't played the injury up for more than what it was, Alan would have expected her to be up out of bed by now. Sophie's plan depended on fooling him. Her pain from yesterday must have been agitated by the stress of her escape.

Despite the light ache and the call of the soft bedding, she planted her feet on the floor and tried to lift her weight. Whatever those pills were, they helped give her the rest she needed to heal properly after running away.

Wood tapping made her freeze as she reached for the bottled water. Another sound. Like a cupboard door. Someone was in the apartment. Had Alan found her? How did he get past the mercenaries?

A light knock sounded on the bedroom door. The sound was sudden, with no footsteps approaching, that it startled her. She dropped back onto the bed as the door opened.

Hendrick poked his head in, then came all the way in once he saw she was awake. He carried a canvas bag.

"Hey. Brought you some clothes." He set the bag on the end of the bed.

"Thank you." She should feel vulnerable. In a strange apartment. Men she was smart enough to fear. But moments like this one, like Dak leaving her the iced tea and water, carried more respect than her husband had given her since the day after their wedding. As the sun rose the morning after, it brought with it a mean man that he'd hidden from the world. Hidden from her.

"We brought some other supplies, too." Hendrick moved back toward the door.

"We?" Her foolish stomach leapt at the hope of seeing Dak

"Cole. You haven't met him."

"Which is a shame." A cheery voice yelled from the kitchen as the closing of cupboard doors got louder. The complete opposite of Dak as he sounded.

"I haven't had enough coffee to handle him." Hendrick mumbled and stepped out of the bedroom.

"Of course you haven't. I hid the coffee this morning just so I could put you on your ass in the gym." Cole's voice echoed from the hall.

"Because you know you can't take me otherwise." Hendrick's lips lifted with the same crazy lilt when setting her phone on fire.

"Nah, I was just lazy this morning." The cheery voice didn't match the tanned skin with dark scruff lining his jaw that stepped into the open door. "Hi, Sophie. Nice to meet you."

"Nice to meet you, too." Was it, though? Was the situation she found herself in *nice*? She supposed it could be a lot worse. She could be in a sleazy motel, hoping Alan didn't find her on her first night away while she mapped her route out of the city. Despite knowing how dangerous these men were, Sophie knew she was safer here. Maybe she should check her instincts. She'd already called herself foolish twice since her brilliant escape. She should add trusting mercenaries to her *Sophie's Foolish Thoughts* list.

But that list didn't matter anymore. Being away from her husband, she was ready for a do-over of the past few years. She decided where to go, get her new identity, pay Dak for his services, and check on her parents. Alan wouldn't hurt them, but she didn't want to have to stay away from them either. She would for a while, until everything settled. But in the meantime, Sophie didn't want Alan filling their heads with lies about her.

"If you two could give me a few minutes, I'll be out."

"Everything is all done, anyway. You take your time. Lots of groceries. Got you some shampoo and shit, too. And I put pain killers on the kitchen counter." Cole slapped the frame of the bedroom door.

"I'm not staying here."

"Yes, you are." Hendrick stepped up beside Cole and squared off his shoulders. "You heard Dak last night."

"And where is he now?"

Hendrick shrugged. "Don't know. But that doesn't matter. Stay put. Eat. Sleep. Rest. Watch TV. But that's it."

Cole's chipper disposition dwindled away as he matched the expression on Hendrick's face. Both men turned while Sophie stuttered over her words. She let them go. They weren't who she needed to talk to, anyway. Dak ruled this place, although her informant said she needed to ask for King. As in the king of mercenaries. Sophie didn't believe King and Dak were one and the same. But Hendrick and Cole answered to Dak.

Shuffling to the bathroom, Sophie took a much needed shower. A single, plain, unscented body wash sat on a shelf in the shower, but her priority was cleanliness over scent. And she didn't want to search the apartment for where Cole unpacked the *shampoo and shit.*

When she finished, she slipped her old clothes back on, minus the underwear. She'd save the new clothes for when she was on the run. The last thing she'd wanted to bring attention to had been a suitcase. She had a clean pair of underwear tucked in her purse, but nothing else.

She guessed since she was stuck here for at least the day, she might as well explore. She found enough food and supplies stocked in the cupboards and fridge to last her weeks. Not a day. Not two days. Not even one week.

No. She needed answers. She needed to hire *King Security,* or *King's Mercenaries,* whoever she needed for this, officially and get the job done. Alan might look for her, but his ambition would wane.

Sophie spun on her heel to find her way to the main floor. But when she swung open the door, a hand gripped her elbow and pulled her back. The door shut with the swing of her arms. Sharp panic jumped in her throat. Hendrick and Cole had left, yet someone was still in the apartment. She looked up to see who'd grabbed her.

Dak's grip tightened, and he pulled her arm against his chest. "Where are you going?"

"To find you."

"Here I am." His thumb moved over her arm before he let her go. But Sophie didn't move away from him. She wanted his hard heat and the reassurance it gave her. But she wouldn't have this when she left on her own.

DAK'S HAND BURNED. It was the only reminder he'd told himself not to touch her.

"Where did you come from?"

"The other entrance." He hadn't yet told her about the door between the two apartments. Her frown furrowed deep, and she looked around the apartment. "This one connects to mine."

"You have your own private entrance into your spare apartment. Why?"

"So I can sneak up on my guests." It was for security. Another way of escape in case of an emergency. But Dak enjoyed the glare she shot back at him.

"We need to discuss some things." Sophie squared off with him. Colour had bloomed back into her cheeks and her shoulders were no longer stiff. He hadn't intended to come back to her so soon, yet here he was.

"What is it we need to discuss, princess?" A husk threaded through his voice, adding to the roughness. Despite his rules for himself, he didn't want to discuss anything unless it involved his hands on her. But he'd come in here to talk, not tempt himself.

"I would like to hire you officially for your services in acquiring a new identity and escaping my husband." She folded her hands in front of her. Her formal speech made him pinch his lips. Dak wanted to rip her hands apart and flatten them against the wall.

"I'm not taking your money." He rarely did with abuse victims. They didn't deserve to lose what little they had while escaping. But with the amount of money Sophie now had, Dak wouldn't bat an eye. Taking money from Sophie turned his stomach.

"I told you, I don't have any other form of compensation." Her breath shook and Dak didn't think it was from pain.

"I'm not asking."

Sweet blue eyes widened. A moment of fear, but the steel he'd recognized the day before beat it away.

"I'm not taking, either."

"Then I don't understand."

"You don't have to."

"You won't help me?"

"I'll help you. What can you tell me about your husband?" Roen had dug up everything he could on the man. Work, finances, family. After Cole and Hendrick dropped off supplies for Sophie, he'd sent Cole to watch him. Some habits didn't have a trail. And Roen had found nothing to explain the money he'd had in his accounts.

"I can't tell you much. He stopped telling me anything a long time ago. And I stopped asking. I didn't care anyway, so why was I giving myself a beating for information I didn't want?" Sophie shrugged and moved into the kitchen. Pulling open cupboards as if acquainting herself.

"Can you tell me where he works?" He didn't need her to tell him, but her answer would help him gage how much she knew.

"I can tell you where he worked as of three months ago, but that's only because I was an image on his arm at events." Bitterness coated her tone.

"How long has he been abusing you?" Dak didn't need to know this, but he wanted to. How much did Alan Morgan need to suffer?

"Our third anniversary was three months ago." She shrugged one shoulder.

"That isn't what I asked, princess." Dak moved into the kitchen, close enough to reach for her, but he didn't. He didn't place his hand on her hip and pull her closer. He didn't wrap his hand around her neck to force all of her attention on him.

"I wasn't talking about our wedding anniversary." Sophie cast her eyes to the floor. Still, Dak didn't set his knuckle under her chin to lift those eyes to his. "That was six months ago."

"Why did you stay so fucking long?" He couldn't control the growl that gripped his chest. Sophie backed up, hitting the counter behind her, fear trembling through her hands that lifted toward her chest. He followed her and set his hands on either side of her on the counter. Not touching her. But he was so close now. Close enough to feel her warmth, her breath. Close enough to smell her.

"That doesn't matter."

"Wrong, princess. It matters." What was strong enough to stand against her and keep her from leaving her abuser? She took her revenge while running from him. Sophie didn't seem the type of woman to hang around without a reason.

"He threatened my parents, and it's taken me this long to realize there isn't much he can do." A flush traveled up her neck to her ears.

"Where are your parents?" Dak hadn't asked Roen to look into Sophie yet. Only her husband.

"They live in Ontario."

"His family is there too." The couple had likely met there. "He has access."

"His family is oblivious to the man he is. And he has little ambition."

"You said you're part of his image? And you stole from him. You've given him motivation, princess." Dak leaned closer. Their clothes touched. It was too much and not enough.

"No." Her whispered breath brushed his chin. "He doesn't care enough."

"Except it isn't just him to worry about." Dak could take care of the husband in a day.

"The money?" Wide eyes looked back up at him. She made the connection quicker than most. Hope that she was wrong narrowed her eyes.

"Yes. The money. It doesn't belong to him. People don't let go of that much money."

"They'll go after him. Maybe me, but I'll be long gone. They won't have any reason to go after my parents." Her features hardened as she tried to rationalize.

"Except to get to you when they can't find you and your husband can't give them the money. Think it through."

"That's unlikely." Stubborn princess.

"Not as unlikely as you'd think." Even Dak and King had gone after someone for less.

"I came to you for a new identity, and that's it. I appreciate the help to get away from my husband yesterday, but now that he has no way to track me, I'm fine. I can leave on my own and disappear. I'll look after my parents." Too stubborn for her own good.

"Not happening, princess." Dak leaned in.

"Excuse me?" Her attempt to step away from him only put her closer.

"Not until we figure out who the money belonged to. You're staying here."

"That isn't your decision."

"It is now." Because he made it his decision. And that's when he lost his fight. He pressed his body to hers and lifted her chin, exposing her neck.

"I told you." Short, heated breaths lifted her chest, pressing her breasts against him. "I'm not offering alternative payment."

"This isn't payment."

"Dak?" There it was. The question. The husky invitation and uncertainty. The sound that shot down his body and straight to his cock, filling him with a heat he'd never felt before. He was always in control. Never did his body, and definitely not his cock, decide for him. That thought should be sobering enough, but the scent of her skin washed it away.

He pressed his lips to hers, sliding his tongue along the plump flesh to taste her. Growling, he wrapped his other arm around her waist. She wasn't moving from this spot until he allowed her.

Dak listened to every movement she made, from the fluttering fingers to the light touch of her tongue. She had a hell of a war waging within her. And he wasn't gentleman enough to make it easy on her. But considering the marriage she escaped, Dak didn't slide his hand beneath her shirt. Everything else was fair game.

Tilting his head, he slid his tongue along hers. Slow, he drew out the motion for an entire breath. Sophie shuddered and her hands found a landing on his chest. Small and precious, he devoured her. He devoured her until his hands itched to take this another step further.

Dak lifted his head and stepped back, still holding onto her hips. "Stay here. We're tracking the money and following Morgan."

Sophie took several deep breaths and ran her tongue over her lips. An imperceptible shake of her head washed away the haze from the kiss. "Do you really think someone will go after my parents? I wasn't going to stay away from them for long."

And that's where they would have found her. "I'll send someone to watch your parents."

"You will?" Her hands dropped down his chest, landing on his wrists.

"Yes."

"Why?" She squeezed.

"So they're protected."

"But you won't let me pay you."

"No." He left his answer at that. Because saying more would mean she wasn't just a client. She wasn't just a princess. She was *his* princess. And that wasn't possible.

HER LUNGS HURT for another reason and her lips tingled. When was the last time butterflies tumbled in her stomach or heat bloomed between her legs? And the feeling had been nothing to what Dak filled her with. Pushing him away hadn't crossed her mind, but touching him, kissing him back, she hadn't known how.

Stupid. Foolish. Of course she knew how. But Dak wasn't just a man, a date, male company. He was deadly. And he'd kissed her like she was life.

"Stay here," he repeated and backed away, his hands letting her go. A chill raced over her.

"You mean in the building."

"No, I mean in the apartment."

Sophie pushed off the counter, but Dak placed a hand on her lower abdomen to set her back.

"Don't argue, princess." His fingers splayed and his thumb drew circles beside her navel. The barrier of her clothes did nothing to take away the impression of his hand or the strength behind him.

She did as he instructed. She shut her mouth tight and only focused on breathing.

"Good girl." Dak moved away from her. "Go back to bed." He left, but the imprint of his hand remained. Sophie watched his body move across the apartment with grace. Rigid, muscled grace. He reached the side wall and revealed a hidden door. She saw what his dark eyes tried to tell her, but she wondered if she had a naiveté she didn't know about. *King's Mercenaries* didn't just do jobs to get around the legal side of paperwork. Her source had told her a long list of jobs they'd do, including cold-blooded assassination.

Dak was dark and claimed the shadows as his own, but he wasn't cold.

Holding her hand over her mouth, Sophie rubbed hard to force away the tingling. He'd told her to stay in the apartment, yet this building was supposed to be secure. Stilling her quivers, and pushing away the memory of his touch, Sophie counted to one hundred before leaving the apartment to search the building.

The long, blank hall had only three doors. Her apartment only had the one leading to the hall, which meant Dak's must have two. One elevator was in the centre of the hall and a door leading to a set of stairs was on the right, past Dak's apartment. Sophie chose the stairs.

Slow and careful, she opened the door, reducing the noise it made as much as she could. She doubted Dak hung around home, but Sophie kept her eyes on his apartment as she slipped into the stairwell.

Only dim light allowed her to see half a flight down at a time. Traction on the stairs quieted her steps. With a grip on the railing, Sophie tried not to let the eerie feeling stop her. The feeling that something was closing in on her. Probably Dak.

Doors led to each floor, but required a password to open. An electronic pad sat on the wall beside each one with blinking red lights, politely asking her to input a password she didn't have. Sophie stuck her tongue out at the first three and carried on down the stairs, hoping they led to the back rooms she'd been in the day before. She counted the floors as she descended and tried to remember how many the building had.

Cursing when she reached the bottom level, Sophie pulled on the door while the keypad beeped at her. She couldn't get through to any level. And no door had a window to see what waited for her on the other side. But she assumed, being the bottom level, that it must be the parking garage. She guessed the next two levels up were a basement and the main level she'd walked into off the street. Banging on the door wouldn't put her in anyone's good graces. With a sigh, Sophie climbed back to the top, glaring at the keypads that kept her out.

A keypad at every level. Beside every door.

Including the top floor that led to her temporary apartment.

4

————

"What are you doing back?" Dak glared at Cole, who still sat at the front desk, his feet kicked up on the wood and his gaze out the window. Dak had sent him to follow the husband.

"Easy to watch someone who is watching us." Cole's eyes didn't leave the bistro across the street. Dak stalked over to the glass. In the corner of the outside dining area, Morgan hunched in his seat, dressed all in grey and brown, sipping a coffee every few seconds. "I slipped a tracker on his car before coming back in here."

"If he's here, it's less damage he can do elsewhere." But it didn't answer any questions or get him off Sophie's back. "Where's Roen?"

"In his usual hole." Cole hiked a thumb over his shoulder. Roen's usual hole was surrounded by screens. Not because that's what he preferred, but because he was the fastest. Dak walked out back and descended into the basement. Roen leaned back in the old chair he insisted on bringing himself. It creaked as he rocked and drank a coffee. Numbers and letters scrolled over the screen on their own.

"I'm still tracking the money. I'm trying to be patient."

"I have another job for you."

Roen rolled his head back and lifted both brows.

"Can you do that on the go?" Dak nodded at the computers.

"Yeah."

"I need you to watch Sophie's parents. See if you can get a bead on them from here and make sure everything looks clear, then hop on a plane. Don't make contact unless you have to. But you're boy scout enough you can charm them into letting you in their home if needed. Get to them before someone else does to use against her. "

"You know I was never a boy scout."

"But you look like one, and can act like one."

Roen conceded with a tilted head, then sat up, the chair screeching. He started clicking and typing. Dak watched, only to keep himself from pacing. He never worked these types of jobs. He couldn't sit still in the light. The shadows calmed him, filling him with more patience than he could handle. But put him in the light, give him a princess to handle, and his body tightened.

"Problem." Roen straightened.

"What is it?"

"Sophie's parents boarded a plane an hour ago." Roen stood, leaning forward as he continued to click through information.

"Going where?" But Dak knew where.

"Here."

"The husband," he muttered. Dak hadn't thought the threat anything more than empty and manipulative. But with the amount of money now sitting in Sophie's account, the stakes were higher than an abusive relationship. "Get ready to go to the airport. Call Hendrick too. And tell Cole the husband is about to move."

Dak moved to the elevator and punched in his code for the top floor. He needed to lock Sophie down before going after her parents. Letting himself into her apartment, he listened. A comfortable silence filled the space. Silence he preferred when entering his own apartment, knowing that no one was in there but him.

Despite his instincts telling him he was alone, he searched the apartment on silent feet. Back at the front door, he pulled his phone out and called Roen, interrupting his answer. "Find Sophie."

Where the fuck did she go? If anyone unauthorized got into this building, he'd know. At least it wasn't her husband. But how the hell did she get out without him knowing?

The tension inside him popped loose, thread by thread. Blackness engulfed his vision. Sophie was missing. His pr... No. *Fuck.* No, not his princess. His client.

Stepping into the hall, Dak took a breath. She was stubborn enough not to listen to him, and he should have seen that. He just hadn't expected it. The elevator wouldn't move without a passcode and he'd come up that way. The stairwell, however, let a person in, but not out. Each tenant had their own security code to use for the elevator and stairwell.

As he reached for the bar to push the door open, his phone rang.

"The stairs." Roen clipped over the speaker.

"Yeah." Dak slipped his phone back in his pocket, ignoring his premature panic, and opened the door. Sophie bolted up from where she sat on the top step. She took the few steps separating them and reached for the open door.

Dak's chest exploded with relief, and he shut the door before she could grab it, locking them both in. The panic, tension, and relief created a cocktail he didn't like the taste of. And the source of all of it stood in front of him.

"Got yourself stuck, did you?"

"I don't need to stay in the apartment." Her pointed chin lifted, but she took a step back. Wise woman.

"You don't?" Dak slapped on the act of surprise and frowned. "What makes you think that?"

"I should be safe anywhere inside this building, considering the amount of security you have here." She waved at the keypad beside the door behind him.

"Except I told you to stay in the apartment." One of those snapping threads whipped back, giving a taste of his displeasure. Sophie swallowed. *Good girl.*

"This wasn't my plan. I should be gone from here by now."

Dak reached forward and wrapped an arm around her waist, swinging her around to shove her back against the door. He settled his body along hers, a hand gripping her hip hard enough to bruise and his other hand wrapped around her throat. "You aren't going anywhere until I say so."

He searched her eyes for fear of him. Fear of his touch or fear of his words. Her chest heaved and her fingers gripped his arms. Her touch burned him, searing beneath his skin.

"Do you understand me?" The harshness in his voice changed. The demanding savage left, and in its place was another who wanted to devour her.

"I understand." She licked her lips. "I don't agree."

"Stop tempting me, princess."

"I didn't ask for you to do this. I'm not tempting you. If you can't control yourself, that's your problem."

Can't control yourself. Dak bent his knees enough he could thrust his hips against hers. Her gasp gave him an advantage to take her mouth. Plunging inside, he tasted her like he hadn't already had her flavour coating his tongue from their earlier kiss.

With her, he fucking had no control. Dak tore himself away and Sophie caught herself against the door.

"You are temptation." Temptation had never pulled him down before, but dress it with deep blonde hair and blue eyes, a bruise and steel, and Dak had his kryptonite.

"You're sticking with that? I've done nothing."

"You're too young to know any better."

"Fuck you. I've lived more than you know." She tilted her head to go nose to nose with him.

"Not in my world."

"Find another excuse for kissing me. I'm not tempting you."

Dak shook his head, but closed the distance anyway. He slid his hand up her arm until he reached her neck. Stretching his fingers, he gripped her chin. Dak leaned in, the barest touch of their lips tickling. "You accept my touch. Your body invites mine. Those lips part, begging me. I'm sticking with it. You're tempting."

Her breath carried the light sound of a whimper. He was fucked.

"But I don't have time to fuck you now. Your parents are on their way here. We're going to pick them up at the airport."

Sophie pushed against his chest, but he didn't release her. He wouldn't until he left her in the apartment. "You flew them here?"

"No. But we'll pick them up before someone else does." He let his hand leave her chin.

"I have to go." She tried to push him away again, but Dak gripped tighter, settling her against the door.

"No." He slid his knee between hers and lifted until only her toes touched the floor.

"If Alan brought them here to use against me, seeing me will help in keeping them away from him. I'm sure he's already spun some tale and they're worried about me. They wouldn't have gotten on the plane otherwise without talking to me first. Please. It will be the quickest way to get in and get out."

It wouldn't be the quickest, but the smoothest. They didn't need her parents causing a scene in the middle of the airport. Dak punched in the code on the keypad. The lock beeped. He wrapped an arm around Sophie's waist and opened the door behind her.

"You won't like the consequences if you disobey me." Dak led her to the elevator and lifted her as he stepped inside. He'd lost his damn mind.

SOPHIE'S HEART wouldn't stop. Her breath wouldn't stop shaking. Dak's arm held her against his side, and Sophie couldn't decide which feelings to allow to the surface. The nerve of someone to demand the way he did and then to blame her for tempting him. She should give him a big ole fuck you and run the first chance she had.

Fear held the hand of her anger. Warning her to be cautious after escaping her marriage to get wrapped up in the arms of a man like Dak. A man. An assassin. A mercenary. Someone whose touch gave her the first sense of safety in years.

Sophie took the moment in the elevator to lean into his hold. But once the doors opened, she stiffened. Men surrounded the exit. Leather jackets and black cargo pants.

All different, but they stood out when gathered together. She'd met Hendrick and Cole, but not the other two. Something was different about them. They'd been relaxed, playful or crazy. But they each had a hard face and a terrifying tension in their shoulders.

Dak lifted her out of the elevator and set her feet back on the floor as Hendrick handed him knives from a table behind him. One by one, Dak slipped the knives into place on his body, unseen.

"I don't think a sixty-some year old couple will give you guys that much trouble." Sophie pointed to the hidden knives.

"This isn't for your parents." Dak tucked the last knife at his back. "These are for your husband." A gleam sparked in his eye and anticipation lifted the corner of his mouth into a gesture of eagerness and nothing close to a smile.

"And any other trouble we might run into." Hendrick rubbed his hands together.

If she had just left the money alone and gone to her parents years ago, she wouldn't be in this kind of trouble. And neither would her parents. Avoiding their disappointment wasn't worth putting them at risk. Sophie had been wearing big girl panties for a long time. But when it came to her parents, Sophie had given them enough worry. A failed marriage didn't need to be another thing.

Pathetic.

"Plane lands in thirty. We're running out of time." A dark-haired man the same height as Cole stepped back, moving toward the front.

Dak nudged her forward. "You're going with Roen and Cole." He nodded toward the dark-haired man walking away.

"Why?" Not that she should care. She shouldn't. This possessive beast was letting her go.

"They're better with people. We need your parents to come willingly with us and to hurry. No questions. No luggage."

"That's a big ask." Her stubborn streak was all natural.

"It's up to you to make them understand, and it's up to Cole and Roen not to scare them." Dak nudged the small of her back again.

"I'll try."

Cole stepped aside to let her follow Roen. She tried not to look back at Dak. The door shut behind her. Cole and Roen flanked her to a waiting car.

"Don't worry, Sophie. Your ex won't even make it to the gate to meet your parents. And by the time he does, we'll be long gone." Cole settled his head against the back of the front passenger seat and closed his eyes. Roen drove, eyes focused forward and on all the mirrors.

"Where's Morgan now?" Roen tossed his phone on Cole's lap.

"You're tracking my husband?"

"Of course." Cole peeked at her with one eye. "I checked before we got in the car. He has a five-minute head start and heading for heavy traffic. We can beat him there."

Sophie bounced her knee as they drove. Roen always focused and Cole seemingly relaxed, but as she watched him more closely, she saw the twitch of his jaw every few minutes. That's when the reality of what she got herself into settled in her chest.

Over money. Money she hadn't wanted or didn't care about. She only took it from him out of spite. It would make getting away from him easier, but she also hadn't expected to find much in the accounts. She wanted to hit Alan where it hurt, but she put herself and her parents in danger. Enough danger she needed a knife wielding entourage.

It wasn't too late to give the money back, was it? Not to Alan. Hell no. She wouldn't do anything for him. But if they found the original owners, she might be able to give it back and be done with all of this. Go back to her original plan and just escape her husband. Disappear. Start over. Not marry the cute guy she met at her high school graduation.

The guy that had sweet-talked her into a date, swept her off her feet for months until she was so dizzy that the spark of a diamond made her say yes without thinking. That diamond turned yellow during their honeymoon.

Alan had charmed her, charmed her parents, and charmed her friends. Friends she didn't have anymore because she didn't have the energy to maintain them and survive her husband. And they all thought she was so madly in love that she wanted her entire world to revolve around Alan.

"Ready, Sophie?" Cole's voice broke through her thoughts, but he wasn't in the front seat. He held open the back door and leaned his head in. He had a boyish look and personality, but he was just as deadly as Dak. The glimpses of them all standing around the elevator and the tension he'd carried in the car while looking relaxed and still showed the hardness beneath that smile.

He could be a charmer. Alan was a charmer. Dak wasn't.

"Sophie?" Cole tilted his head, a hard line slashing down over his forehead. The emotion, the concern for her, broke through. Cole didn't wear charm like a mask. They could if they needed to, but he didn't need to charm her.

"I'm ready."

"Okay, Sophie." Roen stepped up beside Cole, blocking her from the entrance to the airport terminal. "We beat your husband here so we can get inside before he does. After that, the best way to stay out of sight is to blend in. Here's your bag."

"My bag?"

Roen handed her a leather backpack. It was full, but barely weighed a thing as she slung it over her shoulder. "Most people have a carry on when leaving on vacation."

"I can't wait to see where we're going." Cole wagged his eyebrows and threw an arm around her shoulders.

"Where we've been. We're walking through departures." Sophie slipped her arm around Cole's waist and leaned into him.

"This will go over well," Roen muttered and walked ahead of them. "I'll be in the crowd." It only took minutes and Roen disappeared.

"I can't see him."

"That's the idea. But he's right there." Cole made a quick pointing gesture.

"You can see him?" Sophie lifted herself onto her tiptoes, but Cole pulled her back down.

"Yes."

They weaved through the crowd and slipped into departures, hovering near the exit and pretending to check the signs for baggage claim.

"Hubby just arrived." Cole leaned close, his nose touching her temple.

"Did you see him?" Sophie leaned closer to Cole. She hated how she feared that man. Even knowing that any of the guys she'd recently met could keep her safe, the arm around her wasn't the one she wanted. And the body that would stand between her and Alan wasn't beside her. That body was hiding in the shadows.

"No. My phone buzzed."

"Right. The tracker."

"Passengers are exiting." Roen's voice whispered nearby, but Cole wouldn't let her turn at the sound. They moved to watch the passengers.

Her parents stepped through the doors, worry pulling down on their faces. Her father carried his duffle bag and her mother's purse. She'd put them through this.

Sophie bolted forward.

"Sophie." Cole's growl accompanied a swipe at her shirt. He missed his grip and cursed.

Roen stepped in front of her, but her parents had already seen her.

"Sophie?" Her mother gasped and shook her head. "What are you... We thought..."

Sophie stepped around Roen and grabbed her mother in a hug. Her father set the bags down and wrapped the two women up in his arms. A glance back and the act had left Cole and Roen. Fierce eyes searched the area and their hands lay ready at their sides. The knife wielding entourage was ready to attack. She wasn't supposed to move from Cole's side.

Pulling away from her parents, she took a breath. "Mom, Dad. It's time to go. These are friends of mine that drove me here to pick you up. I'll explain everything. I have a lot to tell you. But first we need to get out of here."

"Alan called us and said you were ill and that we needed to come out here." Her father looked over her head through the crowd. How difficult would it be to convince them of Alan's abuse? She was their daughter. They should believe her, but Alan had a way with people.

"Sophie." Roen stepped closer and the urgency grew.

"I'm not sick. I need you guys to trust me. Please. We need to leave."

"Mr. and Mrs. Lee, I promise we'll send someone back for your luggage. Please listen to your daughter." Cole's eyes softened, and he seemed to shrink himself when talking to her parents. There was no room for intimidation in his expression.

"Are you in some kind of trouble?" Her father glared at Cole and Roen before taking hold of her shoulder.

"Shit." Roen moved in behind her parents. "We've got company. No time for any more questions."

"Sorry, folks. Time to go." Cole and Roen each took a bag and an elbow, rushing them through the airport. Another body appeared next to Sophie. Looking up, she saw Hendrick, his sharp, crazy eyes focused.

"Is it Alan?"

"No."

The only other threat she had after her was who she stole the money from. And they showed up at the airport for her parents.

WHERE THE FUCK did they come from? Who did they come from? Suits stalked through the crowds and weaved around the cars in the parking lot. Gear had stopped Morgan, cutting off his trek to the building with his motorcycle and acting like a world class ass.

But when Dak spotted the suits, he called Gear off and sent him to secure a path out. Hendrick joined Cole and Roen to help with Sophie and her parents, while Dak followed the suits around near the entrance. The suits outnumbered them, but that was nothing new.

The public was to their advantage, until they stepped outside, then they'd be vulnerable. Dak tried to work through the situation. Had Alan set this up? Alan hadn't known Sophie would be here, hadn't known Sophie would discover her parents' arrival. He likely thought to use them to draw her out once they got here. The suits were here on their own. It was a win all around. Take Morgan. Take Sophie's parents as bait. Or take Sophie.

They could have Morgan, but Dak wouldn't let them lay a finger on Sophie or her parents.

Gear pulled up at the exit with the car, parking along-side two other cars who hadn't left enough room for a third, blocking them in and anyone else from passing. It was an obvious move, but it gave them a direct way out.

"Five guys moving in close behind us." Roen spoke through the comm link.

"Another five outside the doors." Dak spoke back as he took in the positions of the waiting suits. "Car is a straight shot out, waiting in the street. We'll stop them. You get straight to the car and drive out."

Gear hopped out of the car and reached for the end of the nearest suit jacket, pulling it up and over the guy's head like a high school bully. Dak let him create the scene and the distraction, getting the attention of three of the suits waiting for Sophie to exit.

"Coming out now." Hendrick's voice snapped Dak into action. He pulled on the back collar of a guy while firming his leg behind him, tripping him to the ground. A satisfying clunk of his skull hitting the pavement gave him a shot of adrenaline to take on the next guy. Seeing Sophie's terrified body shivering behind Cole, Roen, and her parents turned his vision black. He wanted to go to her.

Screeches and curses of other departing passengers filled the air and attracted a crowd.

Movement caught his eye, slipping away from Gear and

straight toward Sophie. Roen and Cole had reached the car with her parents. Dak jumped forward, cutting Sophie and Hendrick off to reach the suit before he could touch what was his.

He rushed the guy, slamming him into the pavement. Dak reared up in time to land a punch hard enough to knock him unconscious. When he turned, the car with Sophie and her parents in the back was pulling away. A black SUV lurched from the edge of the parking lot to follow. There had been more than the suits roaming inside and out. They had cars waiting to move.

Gunshots popped through the air. His vision tightened, the figures around him becoming sharp shadows as the ping off the metal echoed back. Dak tried to reach their other car, but the still conscious suits blocked him. Gear sidled up next to him, blood dripping from his lip and amusement lighting his pale eyes.

Dak wanted to beat it out of him. Nothing about this amused him. It should. Any other day. Any other job. Any other client.

He shook himself. Sophie was a client, not his. He put all of his attention on the men trying to crowd them. Two others dragged Sophie's husband away from the airport and across the parking lot. Dak found some of Gear's amusement to use against the suits moving closer. Despite their well-coordinated attack, they weren't a match for him and Gear.

They didn't wait for the suits to reach them. Gear cocked his fist and jumped, smashing his knuckles downward into a shoulder. Dak faked a lunge and ducked to shove forward, flipping the closest one over. They worked seamlessly, moving from one suit to the next, running them down until they lagged. Gear dashed for his bike and Dak made it to their other car as airport security ran outside.

He reached for his ear to check in with the other car and found nothing. Fuck. His piece must have fallen out. He tried to call Cole. No answer. The same with Roen and Hendrick.

The lie that Sophie was just a client hurt in that moment. Nothing had hurt him in a long time. Dak raced through traffic, zipping past Gear on his bike. He needed to catch up to the other car to catch his breath.

5

———

Sophie's spine bent forward as shots hit the car. Cole drove and Roen sat in the passenger seat, giving directions and watching behind them. Hendrick sat in the back seat with her and her parents. The four of them squished together had little room to move around despite the lurching back and forth as they drove, trying to lose the people shooting at them.

Her mother's and father's cries broke her heart. With a solid arm around his wife, her father's lips moved in a repetitive prayer.

Sophie trembled, but she forced herself to ignore her own fear. This was her fault and her doing. Her parents were terrified and suffering because of her. She didn't deserve to focus on herself with her parents beside her.

With shaking hands, Sophie straightened and wrapped herself around her parents. "Shh. It's going to be okay. They're going to get us away from them."

Rushed and unintelligible prayers fell from her mother in between sobs and screeches.

A shot winged the tailgate of the car. Her parents went

wild, hitting the back of Cole's seat and scrambling for the door handle as if they'd rather lunge from the speeding vehicle. Pulling on the latch did nothing as they locked them in from the driver's side.

"Sophie, hunny. I hate to put this on you, but you need to calm them down." Cole didn't sound at all like the same man he'd been earlier.

Sophie gripped tighter and tried to rock with what little room she had. Hendrick added his arm around the back of the seat.

"I'm so sorry. I love you both so much. It's going to be okay. It's going to be okay." She repeated it over and over, softening her voice with each repetition as her parents stilled and quieted.

The shots ceased, but the sharp turns and neck-breaking speed didn't.

She soothed herself with her mantra and rocking, falling into a safe space where she could block everything out.

"Sophie." Large hands settled on her shoulders. "Sophie." Hendrick pulled her away from her parents, who seemed to come out of the trance. The back doors were open, and she recognized the parking garage outside the car.

"It's over?" She put one foot on the pavement.

"It's over." Roen shut the front passenger door, and Cole held the other back door for her parents. She should be the one to help them out, but Cole's smile forced their lungs to breathe. Hendrick's heavy hand on her shoulder made her realize how much she still shook. Sophie needed the seconds to regain her composure.

"What have I gotten myself into?"

"Nothing we can't handle." Hendrick's eyes lit wide. He squeezed her shoulder before letting her go.

"You okay?" Roen moved in closer and spoke low so her parents couldn't hear from the other side of the car.

"I might be." She looked over her shoulder. Her father still had a protective arm around her mother, while Cole's slow-toned rhythm kept their attention. "I have to be."

Cole moved her parents toward the elevator. Hendrick grabbed her elbow to stop her from following. "Give yourself a little more time."

Cole hit the button to close the door and winked just before it shut. They waited for the elevator to reach the next floor before putting in the code again for another trip.

"Who were they?" The men dressed in suits had come out of nowhere and come from everywhere. One moment everyone around them had been normal travelers, then black clad and greased hair popped up—one, two, three, ten, fifteen. Sophie hadn't counted, but they'd outnumbered them.

"Don't know yet. But I will." Roen glared ahead, determination striking through his words.

"They grabbed your husband."

And whose fault would that be? Hers? Or his? She couldn't seem to summon any sympathy, but none of this might have happened if she'd just taken her bag and left. Revenge had been too tempting not to take a taste.

Lesson learned.

They reached the top and entered the same break room she'd been in the first day. Her parents pushed themselves up from the couch.

"Sophie. Thank God you're all right." Her mother took her hand and her father gripped her shoulder.

"Why have you hired a security team?" She didn't know what Cole had told them. She didn't think it was much based on the confusion on her father's brow.

All her insecurities about disappointing her parents flashed hot over her cheeks. Barely graduating high school, falling in with the wrong crowd a time or two. It didn't matter that she pulled herself away from those friends each time, the suspicion was always there. It didn't matter that she'd doubled down and worked her ass off to pass her final year, they always reminded her that she almost didn't make it. Her parents loved her. Sophie knew that in her core. It's why it hurt so much to disappoint them.

They loved Alan. Adored him. They thought their marriage had been the best thing to happen to Sophie. Something in them relaxed on her wedding day. Like knowing their daughter was safe. Sophie hadn't wanted to tell them. Bury her head in the sand and avoid all talk of Alan had been her plan. Run away with a new identity and show up to see her parents from time to time. Her identity wouldn't matter. Alan didn't have that much ambition. But there was something about starting over that had called to her.

"Sophie?" Her mother pulled on her hand.

"Mr. and Mrs. Lee, please sit back down. Can I get you anything?" Cole maneuvered himself in front of Sophie.

"Call us Matt and Carol. Mr. and Mrs. is long and cumbersome." Her father waved a hand across his face, but helped steer his wife back toward the couch. "Sophie, tell us what's going on."

She winced as flashbacks of her father standing with crossed arms in the kitchen while Sophie dripped mud onto the floor. Then standing at the bottom of the stairs when she came home from the school dance with a torn dress. Picking up broken glass from the living floor. Her father never yelled. He didn't have to when his voice carried so much.

The door leading from the basement bursting open and hitting the wall behind it prevented Sophie from answering.

In her next breath, she was sandwiched between a hard, rigid body and the wall. And the only thing that left her lungs was his name.

"Dak."

DAK HAD SKIDDED and parked sideways in the garage. Relief had eased his breath, but the organ pounding hard against his ribs drummed harder. Heavier. He had his hands on her, and that was all that mattered. Pinning her to the wall, he felt every inch of her body. It was the only way to satisfy himself that she was unharmed.

"Dak." His name on her breath sunk into his heart.

Not his. But no part of him wanted to listen to the warning in his mind. His hands cradled her hips and his mouth lingered over hers. Dak breathed her in while he realized people surrounded him. Mostly his employees, who had never seen him act in any other way than controlled.

"You have an obsession with pinning me to the wall," Sophie whispered. She didn't struggle or tense. Her hands landed in the crooks of his elbows and squeezed.

"Definitely an obsession with something." Dak didn't know what to do with himself. But now wasn't the time to analyze.

"Excuse me. What are you doing to our daughter?" A male voice with the crack of age echoed from the other side of the room. Dak didn't bother answering. He ran his thumbs over the bare skin beneath Sophie's shirt before letting her go.

"Sophie? Who is this man?"

"He owns the security company."

"And why did he have his hands on you?" The protective tone from her father threw Dak off, but he had to remind himself they didn't know about Sophie's abuse.

"Just the way he works." Sophie's eyes ran over him until they reached the floor by his feet. She had no idea how he worked, and it wasn't like this. The shock on her parents' faces said they didn't buy her explanation.

"Mom, Dad. I've left Alan."

"Whatever for?" Her mother slapped her hands together on her chest.

"He's been abusing me for years." Sophie's eyes pinched tight and still hadn't left the floor in front of his feet.

"Sophie, sweetie. A marriage takes work and there will always be fights and misunderstandings. Abuse is serious."

Dak had never thought her parents would need more than a single word from her, but they questioned what she said. Making it out to be something it wasn't. They didn't have time for this. Dak didn't want to make time for this and the blank stare on Sophie's face just about killed him.

He pushed her back against the wall and lifted the front of her shirt to expose the faint colours of the healing bruise.

"Does this look like a misunderstanding?" Dak didn't need to be so harsh, his rough voice slashing down. But they seemed to need proof. Shame filled her father's eyes and her mother's watered. Sophie shoved his hand away and pulled her shirt back into place, holding the hem down as if she thought he'd do it again. He made his point.

A tear rolled down Sophie's cheek. He'd embarrassed her. He should feel bad about that, and part of him did, but he didn't regret his harsh actions. Not when the result was for the best. Was the best for Sophie.

The tear caught on her nose. Dak leaned forward, his

back blocking her from her parents. With his index finger, he started from the corner of her eye and dried the trail. Those seconds stretched, giving everyone in the room time to catch up.

"Why were people shooting at us? What does all of this have to do with Sophie leaving Alan?" Her mother clutched onto her husband's arm as she searched each person in the room for answers.

"It's complicated, but her husband isn't the only threat." It wasn't up to Dak to give all the details. That would be up to Sophie. Another time. "Roen, take Mr. and Mrs. Lee to a safe house and work from there."

"And Sophie, too." Her father's voice croaked.

"No." Dak could give many reasons why Sophie wouldn't be at the same safe house. Even safety reasons for her to stay within this building. But none of them were why Dak was keeping her here. He'd wanted to use his tongue to take away that tear instead of his finger. That was why Sophie would stay with him.

"If this is serious enough that we need to be in a safe house, then why wouldn't Sophie?" Movement of the couple on the couch standing unsettled the air behind Dak.

"Say goodbyes, princess," he whispered and stepped back. Sophie stared back at him, but didn't argue with his edict.

"It's okay. They know what to do. This is all very sudden and confusing. I'm sorry to put you through this. I didn't think Alan would call you and tell you to come out. Not so soon anyway. I thought I had more time."

"He was worried about you." Somehow, her mother still seemed to believe that.

"No, he wasn't. He wanted to use you to get me to come back. Please listen to Roen and do as he says." Sophie clasped her hands together at her waist. Dak recognized the uncertainty in the grasp of her fingers. Not willing to reach out and touch them, but not ready for them to push her away.

"We'll have you all back home, safe and sound, as soon as we can." Roen stepped in to take over for Sophie.

Something seemed to snap. Sophie's hands flew apart, and she pulled her parents in, hugging them together in one. "I'm sorry. I love you."

Dak moved in behind her and urged her to let them go with a hand on her hip.

"This way." Roen gestured them ahead of him toward the elevator for the parking garage.

"You keep her safe." Her father pointed his finger at Dak. "And send me the bill for your security services." Her father earned some respect back from Dak for those comments.

"The bill has already been taken care of." He ignored the look Sophie sent him. A side glance her parents didn't catch. But smart people would conclude that Sophie was paying in a different way. Even Dak would make that assumption after the way he'd manhandled her against the wall.

Roen cut off further questions by moving in behind them. "We'll get anything you need while staying at the safe house. Make me a list."

The door shut, and all eyes turned on him.

"What the hell, boss?" Hendrick gestured to the wall.

"I lost my comm in the fight and no one answered their fucking phones." His ire should have them all cringing. But no. He'd trained the bastards too well.

"Difficult to do with the driving, the swerving, the shooting, the people freaking out in the backseat." Cole bobbed his head up and down as he listed off the excuses. This wouldn't be an issue if Sophie were any other client. They wouldn't be staring at him like he'd gone insane.

"Find out who the fuck the suits were. Start with where they took Morgan." Dak ignored them all and wrapped a hand around Sophie's elbow.

He had an obsession he needed to get rid of.

SOPHIE LET Dak pull her along. A sense of shock filled her as she took everything in. The fear she'd felt in the car settled the moment Dak first touched her. But it didn't take away the memory. Or the regret over her parents. Humiliation leached over her body when Dak pulled up her shirt. He had no right. But the sudden acceptance from her parents had never happened before.

The safety of the apartment helped her sort through her thoughts. But it wasn't her apartment. It was Dak's. Dark grey everything with random blue items that popped out. A white wall around a fireplace was on one end of the apartment and an open kitchen with black cupboards and appliances was on the other. The blue popped out of the rug, couch cushions, and the kitchen chairs. The place wasn't as cold as it should be. There was something warm and safe about it. And she supposed that had to do with Dak.

A man she still barely knew that lit her body on fire. It was one thing to put her own life at risk with mercenaries. But it wasn't just hers anymore.

"I'm forced to trust you with my parents' lives."

"You are." No platitudes or promises. Somehow, that made her feel better. She'd been surrounded by flowery fake words for years. Alan even had run-on sentences when beating on her.

"I don't know you." One day since she'd walked into the office of a known mercenary and requested his services to help her run away.

"Remember that." Those two words sounded more like a threat than a warning.

"Why?"

"Because I'm going to touch you."

"You're already touching me." She lifted her elbow, pulling his hand with it.

"That's not touching."

Oh hell. That word hummed from his chest. There was his promise. He didn't make his promise with words, but with a sound, a look. A touch.

Dak pulled her against him and wrapped his arm around her back. Her body reacted with heated trembles. Her state of shock melted away, passing over her fear and worry to Dak.

Leaning down, he caught every breath she released with one of his own.

"You said the bill had been taken care of and brought me up here. Dak..."

"This isn't payment. This is because your core clenches when I do this." He pressed his hips forward while holding her tight. His erection pulsed against her.

Sophie couldn't help herself. She leaned into him and closed her eyes, wanting to take in whatever he wanted to give her. She hadn't thought she could crave that touch so soon. Her focus hadn't been sex. Just running.

"You're supposed to be a client."

She snapped her eyes open. "I'm not?" Panic slid around her throat. "If I'm not a client, then what have you done with my parents? What are you going to do with me? Why won't you help me? I've offered to pay you."

"Shhh, princess." He almost seemed soft as he tried to soothe her. "I'm helping you. But I also want to do more to you."

"Oh." His words *to you* rather than *for you* didn't go unnoticed by her.

"What did your husband do to you?"

"You already know."

"No, I don't." His fingers slid along the top of her jeans. Back and forth.

"He yelled. A lot. Quiet was worse."

"I don't need you to go down memory lane."

"He hit me."

"Sophie." His fingers dipped lower in the waist of her jeans. Her skin burned with his touch. "What else did he do to you?"

"He hasn't touched me in that way for two years." Most of their marriage.

"Did he ever force himself on you?"

"He tried. Couldn't stomach it. Blamed me, and beat me for it. He hasn't touched me since." Even before that, he'd blame her when the sex wasn't good for him. She didn't do enough for him. She wasn't into it, so it threw him off. She went to bed too early or too late.

"Do I need to send you away from here? Away from me."

"Away from you? Why?"

"I'm a savage through and through. Especially when I fuck."

Her throat constricted, and her stomach trembled.

"Say the word and I'll send you off to the safe house with your parents until this is over. Otherwise, you're staying here. And I've told you what that means." As if she wouldn't remember, he cupped her ass and thrust against her again. Hard and slow—a taste of his savage.

"What word do I have to say?" She didn't understand why something so simple would surprise her. Dak was blunt and aggressive. He'd only expect blunt in return.

"There's only one."

"No?" She made it a question because Sophie didn't want him to misunderstand. She wasn't telling him no.

He nodded.

"If I don't say it?"

"You've made your decision." Dak bent his head. She felt his lips touch hers without the contact. "What do you say, princess?"

"I say..." Sophie questioned her sanity. What was she getting herself into? More trouble or perfection? "What's it like to fuck a savage?"

Holy hell. The man grinned. Barred teeth spreading sinful anticipation. "Deadly."

6

———

Almost every part of his being screamed at Dak to get his hands off her. This obsession that had taken over wasn't going away, and it was going to get dangerous. Dangerous for her and everyone around him that depended on him.

Yeah, he had people that depended on him now.

"You're in this now, princess." She deserved a fair warning. "You can always tell me no, but unless you do, I won't go easy. I can't. You're going to feel everything."

"I already feel more than I ever have with just your touch." Her voice caught as her breathing picked up.

"That can't be true." But as he looked into her eyes, he saw it wasn't a false platitude. Doing the math in his head, he realized the only other partners she might have had other than her husband would have been in high school.

"It is."

"I'm going to own your body." Dak moved his hand up to grip the back of her neck and put an inch of space between them. She swayed to get closer, but his hold stopped her.

"As long as you take away this ache." She gripped his chest.

"That ache is for me, princess. I won't take it away, but I'm going to use it." The reasons not to do this faded away one by one. Possibilities and desires flipped through his mind like pages of a book. The kitchen, the counter, the couch, the floor, the wall, the shower. He'd use them all, but for now, he needed a bed.

He used the grip on her neck to force her backwards, guiding every step she took with a hand on her hip. Sophie tried to turn around, tried to control her own steps.

They reached his bedroom, and he had to pause. Dak didn't bring women here. He fucked them where they begged. Older women were wise enough not to get involved with him, unless they were looking for danger. Dak gave it to them without harm and tried his best to warn them away from danger in the future. He stayed away from the younger ones when he could help it. But sometimes sex with a soft innocent helped him stay on the right track. Not the track of a good man, but he kept his morals intact.

Sophie was a whole cup of everything. To the brim with steel and a healthy dose of grey morals. Just enough to need to see the guilty punished. It took strength to face someone like Dak.

And Sophie rarely looked away.

"Where does it ache, princess?" Dak urged her closer to the bed and released his hold. Playing with the hem of her shirt, he lifted it. She raised her arms, and he slid it off her. A simple bra covered breasts he wanted to suck. Would she be sensitive enough to get off from her nipples alone? Fuck, he hoped so.

"Everywhere."

"No. It doesn't ache everywhere. It doesn't ache right here." Dak tapped her shoulder. "Or here." He tapped her elbow. "Here." Her nose. She gasped with each touch. "Where, Sophie?"

"My chest. My knees. And..." Her voice fell away. Dak reached for the waist of her jeans and undid the button.

"Tell me and I'll touch it." He was becoming a whole other kind of savage. Sex was sex. Dirty, rough, and delicious. He demanded. They obeyed. And he took. But with Sophie, he needed to hear her voice—hear her beg for him.

"My... in my..."

He lowered the zipper.

"You know where." The words escaped with frustration.

"But I don't think you do." Dak pulled her jeans down.

"Between my legs," she rushed out.

With her bottoms gone, Dak stopped. He stood back from her, waiting for her to calm down. Her breathing slowed and worry creased her brow.

"Dak?"

"That's very vague. Take your bra off and lie back on the bed. We're going to try this again."

"How the hell is that vague?" She reached for her bra and whipped it down, throwing it against the floor. Her outburst baffled him, making adrenaline surge. The good adrenaline. Excitement.

"Do as I said, princess." But that excitement wouldn't stop him from keeping his control over her. She snapped her mouth shut as he lowered his chin. Sophie backed up to the bed and centred herself on her back. Taking her ankles, Dak pulled them apart. "There's a lot between your legs. A lot to touch, to tease, to taste. Show me where it aches." He was dragging this out longer than he usually would, but with Sophie, he needed more.

Sophie closed her eyes and lifted her hand.

"No. You fucking look at me while you show me." Beautiful blues locked onto him, so much uncertainty reflecting back. But there was a need that matched his own. That had to be the origin of his obsession.

Her finger touched over the hood of her clit, then over her entrance before moving away from her centre.

"There's one more place, isn't there?"

She nodded and moved her hand back to her entrance, this time sliding her finger inside.

"Good girl, princess."

Sophie took her finger out. Before she could put her hand further up the bed, Dak grabbed her wrist. He slid his knees onto the bed and brought her finger to his mouth. Fucking sweetness. He sucked hard, ensuring he got every bit of her cream.

Dak looked down her body. Tight pink nipples, smooth skin, a bruise that could send him into a rage if there wasn't her willing wet cunt waiting for him just below it. Dak needed no more words, didn't want them.

He ran his fingers through her folds, reaching her entrance. He thrust one finger in, steady and strong. His. Sophie was his. Would this obsession ever go away?

HER BLOOD PUMPED AND RUSHED, making her dizzy with every touch and every word from him. That single finger was more bliss than she'd ever thought she'd feel. She never expected sex to be something good for her. Maybe one day, she'd be lucky enough to have a kind companion.

When hell froze over.

Dak knelt on the bed, still clothed while he kept an

excruciating slow pace with his finger. His eyes didn't stop. They raced over her chest and down her belly. They watched his finger thrust in and out, then traced down her legs, only to jump back up to her eyes to start all over again. That dark colour heated with every pass. Her heart soared, knowing someone desired her.

He stripped Sophie raw. This had barely begun and Dak forced her open, forced her to admit she needed him.

Each drag of his finger increased the sensation around those nerves. Her clit throbbed. But he already knew that.

This was more than she ever bargained for, and leaving all of this would be hard. But she'd do it and take this memory with her.

"I'm taking everything from you tonight, princess." Dak pulled his finger out and added another, stretching her further. And it was a stretch. A delicious sensitive stretch that only added to the climb of her arousal.

"I don't know if I have anything to give." She'd been escaping on her last beat of life. Rebuilding from scratch was her plan. Sex wasn't where she planned to start.

"You don't have to. I'll find everything you have and take it. Starting with an orgasm." Dak added his other hand and pressed his thumb over her clit. He stroked in upward motions and she clamped down on his fingers.

Zings travelled from her body to her centre. One by one, they hit.

"So silent," he scolded. "When I said everything, I meant it. Don't hold back, princess." He moved his thumb faster and curled his fingers.

Sophie gasped with a squeak. Her hips bucked up for more, then back to get away from the overwhelming sensations. He followed her hips and worked his fingers harder.

"It's right there. So tight. So wet. Mine, Sophie. Come,

now." His rough voice scraped over her skin and sunk deep inside her. Her core contracted and the sharp sensations of a climax took control. Dak took control. It was his will that pushed her there.

And Sophie would never fight it.

"Another." He bent to the bed, putting his head between her legs. Using his thumb, he pulled up on her clit. The first orgasm still wracked her as he placed his mouth over the exposed nub. It was too much. She was too sensitive. But Dak slapped his free arm around her waist and held her down.

She whimpered with every suckle and her hands buried in his hair. Sophie pulled. She needed him to slow down. But Dak growled against her and kept up his pace.

Seconds. It only took seconds to throw her into the next orgasm. As the first harsh contractions eased, Dak lowered his head and removed his fingers. His tongue thrust inside her, lapping at her entrance. She was way out of her element. Was this what sex was like for everyone?

Any sex she'd had before had a sequence—unwritten rules. Kiss, clothes off, touch here, touch there, insert until done.

Dak hadn't even taken off his clothes and she'd had two orgasms. Her entire body felt out of control.

He let her go and sat up. It gave her a moment to breathe, but a chill covered her with the lack of contact. "Better than I imagined." He thumbed his chin, wiping away her juices, then licked them off. "And I expected a five star dessert."

Those dark eyes melted when one side of his face pulled up into a grin. She shivered, now knowing what he could do to her.

"Want more, princess?" He pulled on the back collar of

his shirt. He was just as hard as whenever he pressed her to a wall. Hard edged tattooed muscles. This man could cause so much damage and as another convulsion from her orgasms spread through her, Sophie realized that he'd cause just as much emotional damage as physical.

"Yes. I want more." She wanted more, despite knowing she likely couldn't handle it.

He tilted his head. "You scared?"

"A little." Hiding it wouldn't do her any good.

"You should be. But I won't hurt you, Sophie." Dak undid his jeans and stepped off the bed to pull them off.

"I know."

He stood beside her, naked. Her eyes dropped, taking him in the same way he had her.

"Please, Dak. Don't drag this out. I need you to touch me." She needed his touch to feel safe. The only time she'd felt safe in the past several years had been the day she'd walked in here and he first touched her. Well, not first. Terror had slammed into her when he forced her against the wall, but when his hand hovered over her bruise, she knew she was safe with him.

"I'll take as long as I want. But I can do that while touching you." He lowered over her, positioning himself between her legs. Bracing himself on an elbow, he used that hand at the back of her neck to angle her for his mouth.

The kiss was fire. Electric blue flames that burned through her body. His other hand didn't stop. He said he'd touch her, and that's what he did. Everywhere. Rough fingertips ran up and down her side, over her breast to twist her nipple until she whimpered.

Dak spread his fingers across the back of her head and into her hair. Slowly, he gripped and pulled. He immobilized her while he licked across her tongue and supped at her lips.

"This is where you get the savage." He lifted one of her legs over his hip and lined himself up with her entrance. "Take a deep breath, princess."

As she filled her lungs, Dak filled her. His agonizing pace just about killed her.

"Let it out."

Again, he matched her. But her lungs stopped cooperating. Air rushed in and paused before rushing out. And Dak thrust once with every breath she took. His grip in her hair and on her hip held her so she couldn't move. The slow pace should have given her time to recover, but what he was doing to her was complete ownership. Harsh and slow, he set his forehead to hers as he moved in and out of her.

"Sophie." Her name didn't sound the same coming from him. He didn't sound like himself. With such controlled movements, she thought he had all the control. But the slight croak in his voice said otherwise.

"I can't, Dak."

"You can and you will." He broke. Tilting his hips, he slammed into her and his rhythm took a one-eighty. If he didn't have the grip in her hair, she'd be rocking beneath him. Her scalp tingled and her core clenched around him.

"Dak." She cried out his name. Never would anything live up to this.

"My princess." He growled against her lips and ground himself on her mound.

Sophie didn't want to read too much into his words. The implications of being his. He didn't give her a choice but to be his right now. But how long would that last?

He yanked hard on her hair. "Leaving me so soon?" His eyes snapped onto hers.

"No." Not a single sensation had gone unnoticed while pondering his words. Everything about this blended together. His words, her thoughts, his touch, and every thrust. Every sensitive scrape over her clit pushing her up.

"Now, Sophie. Come."

Her body obeyed, exploding. And so did he.

His teeth bared in a growl against her mouth while hot jets spurted inside her. The sensation of that alone made her orgasm sharper.

She collapsed into the mattress in a shivering mess.

"Fuck, princess. I meant to pull out."

"Pill. On it," Sophie muttered. She closed her eyes and gave herself a silent pat on the back for remembering to keep up with it through these hectic couple of days.

THE LAST COUPLE of hours had wrecked Dak. His lungs struggled and his heart pounded hard to keep him alive. He slipped from her body and released her hair. Sensation rushed back into his hand from the white-knuckled grip he'd had. He rolled to his side and let his fingers play while Sophie dozed in and out of consciousness. Over her breasts and nipples, over every inch of smooth skin. Then down to the wetness between her legs. Around her swollen clit. Moving her juices and reaching down to feel his own spilling from her.

He'd scared the shit out of himself. But his cock grew hard as he circled her entrance, coated with his seed. It was a fierce primitive urge that filled him to do it again. He was going to ruin her.

And life with him wasn't a life. Just as his heart had

claimed his princess, he had to let her go. But not yet. Not until she was safe. Dak wasn't gentleman enough not to fuck her senseless in the meantime.

Eyelids lifted, and she turned her head. "Dak?"

He nodded and continued with his light touch.

"What happens now?"

"As much as I want to do it again, we shower and go back downstairs." What he wanted was to wrap her hand around his cock, put her on her knees, and fuck her mouth. Another time. That would be too much too soon. Sophie wasn't ready for all of him.

Now that he'd had her, the need to keep her safe exploded ten fold. Dak needed to find out who the suits were.

"I might need help with that." Her cracking, sleepy tone tore away any suggestiveness. Her muscles quivered as she tried to move from the bed. Dak stood before she got both feet over the edge and lifted her into his arms.

"I have a better idea." He took her into the master bathroom and set her on the wide counter beside the single sink.

"Oh? And what's that?"

He turned to the bathtub he hadn't wanted, but was thankful for now. The tub nestled into the corner could easily fit two, but had never been used. Until now. Checking the temperature, he adjusted to increase the heat. "I don't have salts or bubbles."

"I don't need them. Uh, Dak? I'm okay with a shower."

He looked over his shoulder and studied her. Longing filled her eyes. She forced her gaze away from the bath. Muscles twitched around her lips.

"Really."

"No." He put the stopper in the drain and turned on her,

arms crossed over his chest. "You're having a bath and going to bed. I'm showering and going back downstairs."

"I don't want to be left out of this. I need to come downstairs, too."

"You will. But not right now."

Her shoulders slumped.

"Touch yourself, princess. We have a few minutes to kill. I want to watch." Dak planted his feet against the tile. No more touching for him.

"I haven't done that in... Dak, I can't do that with you watching."

"Finish that first part, Sophie. You haven't done that in..."

"Years. High school."

"I'll help. But you need to get started. Your bath won't take long."

Sophie placed her hands on her thighs and looked down.

"No. Look at me." He wanted to see those eyes gloss over. "Spread your knees and touch your clit. If it doesn't feel good, try something different."

A blush crept over her skin. Her middle finger stroked over her clit. Her breaths filled with shock the more she moved.

"Looks like you know what to do, princess. Better hurry. Your bath is almost ready."

Her finger moved harder and her head rolled to the side. "Please. Dak, I need you to finish this."

"No, you don't. You can do anything." He believed that. It made her that much more special. Anyone that belonged to him had to have steel running through her. Even if she only belonged to him for a short time. "Put your heels on the end of the counter and let me see it all. Come, Sophie," he snapped.

She lifted her feet, and he had a clear view of her swollen folds. Her finger turned furious as she tried to meet his demands. The climax burst free from her body and her lips. Her eyes watered.

Dak turned off the water and stepped toward her. "All for me, princess. You don't do that unless I'm here." He kissed her and pulled her off the counter.

Placing her in the water so she faced the glass door of the shower, he ran his hand over her eyes to close them and left her alone while he showered. But he never took his eyes from her, clearing the condensation from the door to keep a clear view of her. Lathering himself, he reached his cock, and gripped it tight.

"Open your eyes."

Slowly, her lids lifted.

"Watch."

She bit her lip and her eyes dropped to his cock. He stroked it hard from base to tip.

"You see what you do to me?" The glass steamed between them, but neither broke their gaze.

"Is it too much?"

"Too much? Fuck, princess. Yeah, it's too much, but I don't want any less."

She licked her lips, and he groaned.

"Careful. I already want to fuck your mouth."

She licked again through a grin. There was that steel spine. The temptation she threw at him. Dak moved his hand faster, imagining her tongue licking over the head of his cock. His lungs seized the instant his climax hit, and he emptied into the water.

Sophie closed her eyes again, but her breathing was no

longer even. Her breasts rose above the water. His cock didn't soften. He needed to get away from her before he restarted everything.

Out of the shower, he wrapped a towel around his hips and left the bathroom. Dressed, he stood in the doorway and watched her slowly run the bar of soap over her body, then she sunk under the water. A bubble reached the surface before she did.

"Done?"

"Yes." She stood in the water and he passed her a towel. Fuck, if she didn't get covered soon, he'd never get back downstairs. They didn't need him to do their job. He was their employer, not their babysitter.

Stepping from the tub, she wrapped herself up. She used the ends of the oversized towel to soak most of the water from her hair.

"How do you feel?" He'd never asked a woman that before, but with Sophie, it mattered.

"Sleepy. A little worried. Maybe confused."

He understood all of that, but that wasn't what he wanted from her. "Anything else?" Dak pulled her against him and lifted her with an arm under her ass. Walking backward, he took her to the bed.

"A lot of things I can't explain."

"Mmm." He could accept that for now. "Rest, Sophie. You won't like what happens if I come back up to check on you and you're not in this bed." He set her down and pulled the towel from her. Covering her up, he kissed her, devouring her taste, then stepped back. "Understand?"

"I understand." She pulled the covers over her and tucked them under her arms. "I don't agree. But I'm exhausted."

He should have known a threat would be useless against her. "Behave."

She smiled and closed her eyes, settling her cheek against the pillow. Dak shook his head and left her behind. In his apartment. In his bed.

This was a first, and Dak's world changed as he locked the door behind him.

7

———

Dak slammed the door to the stairwell leading to the main level, making heads turn. "What have we got?"

"Nothing on Morgan. They left his car at the airport. Roen started running some programs before he left. We're trying to identify the goons and what they were doing there."

"Best guess is they've been watching Morgan and planned to use whatever possible to their advantage. I'd say they were there looking for an opportunity. When they saw Sophie approach her parents, they found one." Hendrick tossed an apple in the air, catching it and taking a bite.

It made sense. If Morgan owed Dak, he'd watch everything the man did. He wouldn't be able to take a shit without Dak knowing. That included bringing in retired in-laws.

"What I need answered is if they know who we are."

They all shrugged.

"Helpful."

"We won't know that until they show up at our door."

Hendrick twirled a knife around his finger and took another bite of the apple.

"Then we need to knock on theirs first."

"Have we thought about just giving the money back and moving on?" Gear turned a chair around and sat, resting his arms on the back.

"Yes. But we aren't doing that." They didn't need that money and that money didn't need to be put back out there to cause any harm. Not when it was there for Sophie. For her to live well and safe. Well and safe when she was no longer with him.

Gear shrugged. "Just a thought. But now we have to ask." They all fell silent.

"Say it."

"What's going on with you and Sophie?"

"Not your business."

"It is. All of this is our business. We may work for you and King, but you made it clear when you and King created this business that we have minds of our own with every job. So, what's going on with you and Sophie and does it affect this job or future ones?" Gear tilted his head, the only hair he had on top of his head falling slightly to the side. Tattoos lined one side of his shaved head and down the other side of his neck. He never feared speaking his mind.

He sighed. "She's mine. For now. That's all I can say. And that she isn't paying us. You'll all get paid, but it isn't coming from her. Or the money sitting in her account."

"So will Sophie be joining Ember with training?" Hendrick tossed the core across the room to the garbage can and rubbed his hands together. Ember loved the crazy man unless he helped with her training.

Dak didn't answer. "Check in with Roen." He stormed from the room.

The only way King allowed himself to be with Ember was if she was as good as him. And King was the best. She trained hard and trained every day. With King, with Dak, with all of them. It seemed to become an unwritten rule that any woman taken in would do the same. Can defend themselves, keep themselves safe, and even take out the enemy if needed.

He wanted to own her and lock her away. He tried to imagine forcing her to fight, teaching her to kill. She couldn't be his princess, no matter how many times he said it.

In the front office, he called King.

"Don't bother." King and Ember walked in through the front door, King slipping his phone back in his pocket. Dak hung up.

"Everything go well?"

"It went great." Ember sat down with a bounce.

"Great?" King turned on his wife, glaring with a look Dak had seen too many times over the years. "We seem to have different definitions of great, little girl. You got fucking lucky."

Dak held in his wince. This lesson would be hard for Ember. He didn't need the details. Getting lucky meant she fucked up. Whether fate intervened, or she fixed it herself, it didn't matter. It wouldn't be an issue if any of the men working for them got lucky. But being King's woman meant nothing could ever go wrong.

Ember's face hardened and King turned away from his wife. Dak expected to find them in the gym soon.

"How's everything here?" King sat down in the opposite chair.

"Fucked. Her parents are in a safe house with Roen after Sophie's husband flew them in and they ambushed us at the airport. I assume whoever wants that money back. They took her husband after they failed to get Sophie."

"Where's Sophie?" Ember straightened.

"She's fine, sweetheart." Dak winked when Ember's lips pinched. She hated being called sweetheart. "She's upstairs."

"Upstairs where?" King cocked his head.

"My apartment."

"Ember, go find Hendrick. Tell him you want to play hide and seek." King kept his sharp eyes on Dak. He now understood what happened on their job. Hendrick would be the one to hide and Ember had to find him without being seen. And Hendrick would attack if he saw her. She had yet to seek without being found.

"Now?"

"Now, girl." King snapped his head around. Ember left, but not before matching her husband's fierce expression. King turned back to Dak. "In your apartment, huh? In your bed?" King was expecting Dak to answer in a specific way. The same way King had when Dak questioned his intentions with Ember.

"Yes." He made it blunt. "I can't say she's just a client. But she isn't sticking around once this is over."

"You know what I'm going to say to that."

The same thing Dak had said to him. Being with him was like a target on Sophie's back. Except they weren't in the same scenario. "This job didn't start with me. When Ember was left on your property, it was a trap for you."

"One sighting from the wrong person and it won't matter what this job is about. You might have been the shadow man in the past, but people in this underworld knew who you were and they definitely know who you are now. Part of *King's Mercenaries*. Your identity has answered some mysteries from our pasts. It would thrill many people to take a blow at you. Many who love to hurt women."

"Then she stays where she is until this is over, then she can disappear as she chooses."

"Or the *pretty piece of ass* doesn't decorate your bed and is sent to the safe house with her parents."

Dak held tight to the rage he expected to rise. King threw his own words and challenge back in his face, having insinuated Ember had been a pretty piece of ass affecting King's judgment.

"You get my point. All I'm saying is that she isn't temporary. Either claim her now or send her away. There's no in between."

"I already fucking know this." It's why he'd been telling himself to keep his hands off her. Not that it had been doing much good.

"Yet, she's in your bed."

"Fuck off, King." The obsession grew in his gut. He'd touched her, kissed her, pinned her against the wall at every opportunity and fucked her like he said he would.

"If you can't send her away now, then this isn't temporary."

Dak surged up, his fists on the desk. King matched his stance.

"I'm going to join a game of hide and seek and teach my wife not to make assumptions." King left before they came to blows. Neither would win.

Dak sat back down, vibrating. He leaned his head back and stared at the ceiling. He offered to send her with her parents, and she stayed. His control had been gone the moment she was in danger.

He was too rough and raw to have a woman. Temporary was all Dak would allow himself. Sophie would disappear when the time came. And until then, Dak would lock his princess in his tower to use when he pleased. In between slaying her enemies.

***

SOPHIE WOKE WITH A DEEP BREATH, waking her muscles as the air filled her body. She'd slept. Until morning, judging by the light shining through the windows. Part of her hadn't thought she would. Not that what she and Dak had done hadn't worn her out. But the adrenaline from the chase and gunshots continued to hover. A low, cold hum.

Her eyes searched the room. Dak's room. Dark grey fabrics, black furniture, and the same odd pop of blue that decorated the rest of his apartment, but in here, the pop of colour was softer despite being the same shade. She was comfortable.

That wouldn't do.

Sophie had to let all of this go at some point. What fool would run from an abusive husband into the world of mercenaries? What was the life of mercenaries like? While she had no problem with Karma taking care of things or someone getting what they deserved, she wasn't sure if she was ready to find out how Karma dealt her hand.

So then why the hell did she need to obey Dak and stay in bed until he came back? Throwing back the covers, Sophie swung her legs off the side. His dark eyes flashed in her vision, sending her right back under the covers. She shook her head at herself.

Folding the covers back again, Sophie made it all the way to standing and even a step away from the bed before his deep rumble echoed in her ears.

"Damn it." She flopped back onto the bed and tucked

the covers back under her arms. "He doesn't scare me." Sophie whispered into the quiet room to see how it sounded. "I am not scared of Dak." Not in the way she should be.

With a deep breath, she got out of bed and three steps toward the bathroom before she thought she heard something. Her gut reaction tossed her ass back into bed. Ears pounding, she struggled to listen. Nothing. She'd imagined Dak coming in. But that still left her with the need to use the bathroom. And that wasn't his call to make. If she had to go, there wasn't any demand he could give to stop her.

But the scare made her more cautious. This time, she didn't throw the sheets off. Sophie slid one foot out of the sheets and off the side of the bed. It was a stretch, but her toes touched the smooth wood of the floor.

Something creaked, and it wasn't her. Snapping her eyes to the door, she saw Dak staring at her foot. He wore the same clothes as yesterday, and she realized the other side of the bed was cold. Sophie tucked her foot back into the bed and gripped the sheets tighter under her arms. A single brow raised, followed by his gaze. Methodical steps brought him closer until he stopped next to her feet.

"Give me your foot, princess."

"What?"

"The foot that was out of the bed and on the floor where I specifically told it not to go. That foot. Give it to me." Dak held out his hand. Sophie's leg moved on its own from his demand. His voice. The darkness in him called to her.

She slid her foot out from under the sheets again. Dak gripped her ankle and lifted her leg. His fingers tightened. His almost bruising grip sent shivers through her.

Her? Scared? Of course not.

He turned sideways, his eyes following down the line of

her leg to meet hers. Then Dak opened his mouth and bit down on the fleshy part above her ankle. Slowly, he squeezed, increasing the pain in the bite.

Sophie whimpered. The muscles in both legs tightened, ready to kick him, but she didn't dare. His other hand traced up the inside of her leg. The contradiction between his bite and his touch clenched her core. Her body begged for him to stop and for him to do his worst.

He bit harder before releasing her. "Don't disobey me, Sophie."

"That isn't what I've signed up for." She'd already crossed a controlling man off her bucket list.

"I gave you the chance to leave, princess. This is what you get." He tucked her foot back under the blankets.

"I've changed my mind. I can't go through that again. I want out. I want the new identity and I'll disappear with my parents." Part of her hurt as she let those words loose. *I want out.* She didn't. It seemed to be an impossible decision for her. Sophie craved his touch, but she had to think of what was best for her future. She had the chance to be happy and free. Why wouldn't she take it?

She didn't want to take it because there was a difference between Dak and Alan.

His eyes narrowed. Shadows covered the tops of his cheeks. How did he do that? His lips firmed, and he took one large step toward the head of the bed. "No."

"No?"

"You heard me. It's too late. I've fucked you and claimed you for the time being. There's no changing your mind."

Something had to be wrong with her. Fire lit through her body. And not the fire of anger, but the burning heat of desire. Fucked and claimed. He made it sound so primal. So real. All she'd known in her life was fake. Nothing about the savage standing over her was fake.

He pulled the sheets away from her body. Cool air made her skin pebble, made her nipples tighten and reach upward. Dak circled a hand around her throat, then moved it down the centre of her body. "You don't want to change your mind." His thumb touched her clit, and she gasped.

His phone buzzed in his pocket. He circled the bundle of nerves while he answered and didn't stop until he let a curse past his lips. Dak settled his hand over her belly.

Sophie knew from the look in his eyes she wouldn't like what was happening. A gleam flashed in and out of the grim darkness that clung to him.

"I think your husband is about to die."

The savage in him was too real.

DAK FOUGHT the urge to rub his face as he listened to the message a second time. *He's dead in twenty-four hours unless you produce the wife and the money.* Sleeping in a chair in the computer office didn't give him enough rest to deal with this. Spending the last several hours in the gym and jacking off in the gym shower hadn't helped either.

"That takes care of one problem." Although Dak would have liked the pleasure of killing the bastard himself.

"What do you mean?" Sophie's breath hitched, and she turned toward him. Everyone filled the back office, waiting to find out what to do. As his hand had reached Sophie's sweet centre, Dak had received the call from Roen. He'd intercepted the message from his system and sent it. They all had geared up and were ready to move on his order, but no one looked like they expected to be put to work. They all knew Dak wouldn't lift a finger to help Morgan.

"Your husband is a problem. They're taking care of it for us." Which showed how much of a problem they were going to be about getting their money back. And their own pound of flesh from Sophie.

"You're going to let them kill him? I can just return the money." His morally grey princess wasn't too dark.

"They want you too." Without knowing who they were, his imagination ran wild with what they would do to her.

"It's just the money. If they get that, they'll forget about me." She didn't look like she agreed with her own statement, giving Dak some comfort in knowing she wouldn't throw herself at them with false hopes.

"No."

"They're going to kill him."

"They got to him before I did." He'd shrug if that fact didn't piss him off just a little.

"Before you did? You were going to kill him?" Sophie took a step back, and she struggled to breathe. The tension in the room changed. Fear from her put them all on alert.

Dak let the air out of his lungs, a heavy sound releasing from the back of his throat and out his nose. He invaded her space. The scent of her arousal still clung to her skin, and he wanted to devour her all over again. But her wide eyes looked up at him for answers.

He slid his hand under her shirt. She froze until he reached the healing bruise. Cupping his hand around it, he leaned in.

"I've only seen one, but there were many more. All of which are left to my imagination. But this one alone is enough for him to die."

"He deserves a lot. But murder?"

"Yes." The chorused answer came from everyone in the room. Dak recognized the deep growls that said if he didn't do something about the husband, they would have.

"You need to tell me if you can't handle this." If she couldn't accept that he killed, he needed to let her go. He looked down at her with a fierce calm, but his chest constricted with the thought of having to let her go. His fist clenched and his fingers tightened on her skin.

"If I can't?" Her voice trembled.

"Then I'm sending you away with your parents." And never see her again, because if he did, he'd never let her go. "This isn't negotiable, princess. This is what I do, who I am."

"Why do I need to be okay with it?"

Because you're mine. The words roared and shook in his head. But he couldn't say what wasn't true. Not completely.

"Boss? They're sending an exchange location." Cole spun around in the chair.

"Tell them no." Morgan was likely going to die by their hands soon enough, anyway. The only thing Dak could do was protect Sophie without letting on that she meant something to him.

Permanently his? No. Would he cover the world in darkness to protect her? Abso-fucking-lutely.

"Done." Cole slapped the enter key on the keyboard.

"They're going to... he's going to..." Sophie looked all around the room, meeting the eyes of each of Dak's men. Dak saw the fight she had with herself. Full panic wasn't there, but she fought with right and wrong. He watched the pulse at the base of her neck jump and slow.

"This is more merciful." Hendrick adjusted himself against the wall. "Dak's fucking you. I'm not, and I'm ready to go set your husband on fire. Not the good kind. The painful, slow, tortuous kind."

"I'd ensure there's a bloody mess." Gear crossed his arms and glared at Sophie. She shivered and worried her bottom lip between her teeth.

Dak took her chin and leaned against her, trapping his hand against her ribs. The bruise burned his palm. "Can you handle this, princess?" He didn't know how much he needed her to say yes until she did.

"Yes." But she still shook.

"We have a reply." Cole paused.

"Read it." Dak let go of Sophie despite the way her body trembled.

Cole's shoulders tensed as he read before meeting Dak's eyes. "Then we'll come get her."

8

Fear sliced through Sophie, but fear of what, she didn't understand. It was with Dak that she felt safe, but he was the one willing to allow someone to be killed. Hell, he'd do the killing. As would every other man in the room. And not just *would do,* but have done. Sophie didn't doubt that.

She'd known what kind of men surrounded her, but faced with the bold statements was another thing.

Her husband was going to die. Sorting through her feelings on that wasn't easy. After they killed him, they were coming for her. So much for getting her new identity and disappearing. She had her parents to think about, too. *King's Mercenaries* was the safest place to be.

But there had to be another way to deal with her husband. This was all on her. She should have come forth and pressed charges against him years ago.

"Sophie?" Dak's voice changed. He didn't say her name the same way he called her princess. It was the savage mercenary in front of her right now. It was that man that invaded her space. The darkness in his eyes still held the heat, but the darkness of his soul reflected outward. That would keep her safe. But would she be safe when this was over?

Her husband deserved a lot. She'd taken her own pound of flesh and wouldn't mind taking more, but if she allowed him to be killed because of her, what would that do to her?

"You can't let them do this. And none of you can kill him, either." She didn't sign up for murder. Every set of eyes in the room had a unique reaction. Cole's widened with surprise. Hendrick's laughed. Gear's held doubt. King's filled with a dangerous anger. But it was Dak's gaze that narrowed to a sharp point that pricked.

"What reason do you have for him not to die, princess?" This time, she didn't like the way he called her princess.

"This is my fault. I stole the money."

"Your husband's clock has been ticking ever since he got involved with these people." King pushed off the wall.

"How can you be sure without knowing who they are?"

"Because they came for you and your parents at the airport. Because they took your husband. And because they've made the threats. People dealing with the amount of money you now have in your account don't fuck around."

Dak hadn't spoken again, but he closed the distance between them. The intensity coming from him burned her.

"Sophie." Hendrick still had laughter floating in his eyes, but he sent her a serious expression. "His days have always been numbered. You could hate me, but I'd kill him for what he's done to you. And every single man like him."

"None of you are angels." The hypocrisy of deadly assassins casting judgment wasn't lost on her. Sophie regretted the words as all the lips turned up into smirks. Including Dak's.

"Trust me, princess. That's a good thing." Dak set his hands on her hips. "I could save him from them if that's what you need, but it will only be so that I can kill him myself."

"So no matter what, it's my fault he's going to die." She could have handled all of this so differently. All she'd had to do was be honest with her parents from the beginning and press charges. She never would have walked into *King's Mercenaries.* Been touched by Dak.

"His fault. He beat you. That's the only reason he's dying. If he hadn't and you loved him, I'd save him for you. Is there a part of you that still loves him?"

"Not since his fist first hit me." Sophie burned from the inside out at the memory. Hatred filled her. Fear too. Worry and disappointment. But the hate for him had been a living entity. Just not strong enough to overcome everything else.

"Then he's going to die. You need to deal with that. You need to deal with the fact that this won't be the last time something will test your morals."

"Test? I'm being tested?"

"Maybe." His thumbs put pressure over her hips. She shoved against his chest, but he didn't move.

"I have no choice in how to handle this?"

"No." Dak pressed himself against her and looked over his shoulder. "We need to find out who they are. Before they come for Sophie."

"It's just a threat. They only want the money." She tried again to force a logical statement to be true.

"It's personal now. They want you too. If not for their own revenge, but to send a message." Gear's jaw clenched, and his shoulders lifted. He looked ready for battle.

"We'll know which when we figure out who they are." Cole stood from the computers and swiped through his phone.

"Set a guard rotation and be prepared." Dak looked away

from them all and back at her, weighing her down. He didn't move while he waited for everyone to clear out, King trailing last and moving with what seemed like a warning for Dak. A warning he sent back.

The click of the door sounded heavy in the room now that they were alone.

"This should be my choice. I came to you. I wanted to hire you. I'm the client. I choose how this goes." No matter what they said, his death was her fault, leaving Sophie to wonder if she'd be able to live with herself.

"You aren't the client anymore." His head dipped.

"Then who is?"

"No one."

"But you're in charge?" She shook her head at him as she tried to get out of his hold.

"I gave you a choice when I took you up to my apartment, princess. You made it. I'm dark. I'm savage. I'm as close to evil as you can imagine. You're stuck with me for now. I'll let you go eventually, but it won't be soon."

"You can't do that."

"I already did."

Sophie's heart hammered. Her fight or flight instinct screamed through her blood. She was on the edge of a dangerous life. Somehow, both dangerous and safe. Dak was both things.

"Are you going to run from me? I can see it. You don't know what to do. Do I chase you and catch you?"

"This isn't fair. You aren't giving me any choices."

"I gave you a choice last night. You made it."

"I'm not sure if I can survive you." Sophie let her head fall forward, resting it against his chest.

"You will. I'll make sure of it." He released her hip long enough to run the back of his knuckles down her cheek.

Those fingers stroked down her neck and over her shoulder. Over her head and through her hair.

Sophie closed her eyes and only listened to her body. Not her head that screamed this was wrong. Her body pounded with a natural reaction to him. A push pull that made her weak.

Dak slid his knuckle under her chin and lifted her head off his chest. "On your knees, princess. Or run."

His words, his control, made her core clench. Sophie looked at the door. She'd never make it. But did she want to? A little. Would he chase her and bring her back to him?

"I won't give you a head start."

Sophie didn't want one. Not right now. A head start meant running out that door and past everyone else. None of them would let her run away either—not that they would know she was running because she wanted to get caught.

Placing her hands on Dak's chest, she slid them up and down.

"I'm scared of the choice I've made."

"Good girl." His praise might have been for her choice or because she feared it. But it didn't matter. That praise from him warmed her. Dak's heavy hand landed on the back of her neck and he pushed her down.

Her knees hit the floor and Sophie looked up at him while he undid his jeans. He towered over her with protective possession and strength. She hoped she could fight off his addictive taste when it was time for her to move on.

HAVING HER STAY WITH HIM, lower to her knees in front of him, with desire roiling through her uncertainty and fear, did something to the panic that had gripped his chest.

Sophie wasn't cut out for this life. When it came to the uglier side of his business, she couldn't handle it.

So Dak had to savour every minute with her.

He adjusted his hand into her hair. The control that gave him made his cock twitch.

"You ready for this, princess?" He'd wanted this from the moment he first tasted her.

Her tongue darted out along her top lip, leaving a shine behind. A growl erupted from his chest.

"Fuck, Sophie." Dak undid his fly and set himself free. Pulling on her hair, he tilted her head back. The movement made her gasp, setting an invitation on her tongue. He slid inside her mouth and she closed her lips around him, hollowing out her cheeks and he set the pace. Reaching the back of her throat and out to the tip.

Sophie placed her hands on the backs of his thighs and gripped, trying to pull him closer. She held his gaze until he pushed in too far and her eyes closed tight. When she opened them again, a glossy sheen covered them, brightening the blue.

"My princess." The words were free because they were true.

She pulled in a sharp breath through her nose.

"Tell me it isn't true." Denial became difficult for him, and he believed it was the same for her.

Sophie ran her tongue in circles on the underside of his cock. His chest rumbled with warm satisfaction.

"That's right, princess." He lost it. Harsh thrusts took him down her throat. Her nails dug into him through his pants. Fucking heaven. And Dak knew he'd never reach the divine palace, but Sophie's body was the next best thing.

She relaxed beneath him, allowing him to do as he pleased, trust shining up at him. His spine heated and his balls tightened. He wanted his seed to spill down her throat, wanted to mark her in every way. When he was about to explode, he pulled free.

"Please," she begged. The sound of her husky whine almost did him in. "Dak, please. Don't stop."

"I'm not done." He never would be. Dak lifted her from the floor and set his hands on her jeans. Once he had them to the floor, he forced them off her ankles. Running his hands up her legs, he stood with the motion. Moving inward, he set his fingers in her folds. "Fucking your mouth left you soaked."

Sophie nodded.

"I'll do it again as soon as I sink into your heat. I'm coming down your throat, princess."

She whimpered, clinging to his shoulders. There were chairs, desks, and a floor to take her against, but Dak chose the wall. With two hands under her ass, he lifted and took the four steps toward the wall behind her.

"My favourite place to have you." He slid into her in one easy thrust. "You need to come fast, Sophie. Use your fingers."

"No, please. I just want you."

"Now." He'd take his pleasure, then release in her mouth, but he craved her body squeezing his.

Dak adjusted his hold when she let one hand slide from his shoulder and down her front to reach her clit between them. The moment she made contact, she rubbed furiously.

"Good girl."

She sighed at his words. Dak realized she needed that praise. She needed that kind of care from the people around her. He wanted to give it to her every day.

Her heat contracted around him and he went harder, faster, until her head slammed back against the wall and she cried out. She was still coming down from her climax when he pulled from her and let her slide to the floor. "Keep being a good girl and open up. Taste both of us, princess."

Looking spent and sleepy, Sophie opened, setting her tongue out for him to slide along.

He growled and held both sides of her face while he moved in and out, trying to make it last. But his cock wouldn't cooperate. It only took a few thrusts until the first spurts of his seed spilled. He set himself at the back of her throat and let go. Dak refused to close out his vision of her working hard to swallow him down. Long after she was gone, that sight would forever be a part of him. No woman would ever be enough for him after Sophie.

Those were some serious thoughts entering his mind. If he felt this strongly, why the hell would he let her go? Let her live her own life and find some other man that would get to fuck her mouth and enjoy that look in her eyes? He'd kill every single one of them.

Fuck. Dak had to do something. Put distance between them or make it clear she was never leaving his side.

***

Sophie wanted to be his. The attention, the care, the passion, all things she'd never experienced. Each time she let go with him, she reached a point of no return. She could look back and see where she should have gone, what she should have done. But now she feared this was her life. A life with morals greyer than grey.

Dak helped her dress before sitting in a chair with her straddling his lap. He kept a firm grip on her hips.

"I've killed before and I'll kill again. Run from me if you have to, but I can't promise I won't come after you."

"Why?"

"Why what?"

"Why have you killed?" But did the why really matter?

"When their disgusting being doesn't belong on this earth and my ending their life will save at least one other." Passion filled his deep voice.

"Would someone say the same about you?" From a different perspective, Dak, King, and their crew were the disgusting beings.

"Yes. I haven't always done jobs that were for the good of the people. That's still the case sometimes. But I always did my best to limit causalities or clean up my mess. I learned the hard way the consequences of others." Pain lanced through his tone.

"What happened?"

"My mother." Those two words were a heartbroken whisper. "I don't exist."

"I don't understand."

"My mother lived on the streets when she got pregnant. Getting pregnant didn't change that for her. She never went to a hospital, clinic, or doctor. Never found a shelter. Even when she went into labour. I was born on the streets and that's where she raised me."

Sophie's first reaction was to rail at how horrible a mother she was, but she still heard the heartbreak in his voice, so she stayed silent.

"No birth certificate, no last name. But she taught me. Reading, writing, math. Everything that other kids learned in school and more." Dak's pupils dilated as he relived the past and his gaze settled on something distant rather than her. Sophie was glad she hadn't disparaged his mother.

"What was her last name?"

"I don't actually know. She never told me and I was too young to think to ask."

"What happened to her?" And what would you be like if she hadn't stayed on the streets with an infant?

"She was the one person that would have been saved if someone else had died." His pain fed the savage in him.

"Did you kill him?"

"Yes. With King's help. It was how we met." Dak blinked, the past vanishing in his eyes. He looked back at her and she saw that it wasn't the right time to ask for more.

"What do we do now? Do we wait for Alan's head to show up on the doorstep?" The joke left a sour taste on her tongue, but what else was she supposed to do? Here she was, so she needed to build a callus over these things.

"We wait for them to make a move. They may follow through, or they may try to use him again to get to you." His fingers dug harder into her hips.

"Why can't I give them the money?" They may still try to come for her, but the money would distract them long enough for her to get away. Away from everyone and everything here.

"I don't want that money on the streets. And you need it."

"I don't." She didn't want a cushion to fall back on. Sophie wanted to hold her shoulders high and work on making the right decisions. Having money to bail herself out when she fucked up wouldn't teach her anything.

"Don't use it or donate it. But that money isn't going back into that world."

"Your world," she whispered.

"Yes. Do you want to live in this world, princess?" Dak used his hand to smooth down her hair. Her scalp tingled with pleasure.

Why was he asking her that? "I don't know."

He nodded and pulled her closer to kiss her. A soft kiss with a harsh nip, as if to warn her, but all it did was entice.

Sophie climbed off of him and waited for him to stand. Dak took her from the back office and back out front, but Hendrick blocked their way. "New client walked in. Keep her out of sight."

"What's the job?"

"Don't know yet. Cole is asking questions and Gear is listening in. King went to find Ember."

They waited in the break room. Hendrick sent a smirk her way.

"So, what did you two discuss back there?" Hendrick rocked back on his heels.

"If you're trying to cause shit, stop. If you have something to say, say it." Dak stepped in front of Sophie, facing off with his employee.

"Causing shit." The crazy showed on his face as he laughed. He didn't seem at all affected by Dak's authoritative side.

Sophie sat at the table. The two men turned silent and grim as they waited by the door. Was this how it was when every potential client walked in the door? Sophie had walked in only to see Dak and he hadn't tensed at her presence.

Cole came back. "He's looking for private investigation services on his wife. He thinks she's cheating or worse. I gave him the cost and all the information and said we'd get back to him."

Dak's eyes narrowed on Sophie before turning to Cole. "We already have a list of jobs waiting. Add him to the bottom of the list. Take a look at the kidnapping we have waiting. Get the background information, but don't go too far. We might as well get started while we wait."

"You got it, boss." Cole returned to the front and everyone followed. He sat at the desk and made a call from the landline. King appeared from the elevator with a short, dark-haired woman in front of him.

"Hi." She smiled brightly.

"Sophie, this is King's wife, Ember." Dak placed a hand on Sophie's back. The touch kept her in place.

"It's nice to meet you." The wife of the king of mercenaries. Intimidation crept up, as if speaking to a queen, but Ember looked nothing like royalty. Gorgeous, yes. And about the same age as her. But not a queen. Not in the slick, black yoga pants and crop top, showing off the rest of her toned body. King stood behind her, dressed for a similar occasion.

"I'm so happy to meet you, too. I hope your stay here isn't so isolated and lonely."

"I can't say it is, but I haven't been here very long." To be honest with herself, there had been parts that were a bit of both, but Dak had fixed those problems.

"It doesn't take long to feel that way." Both her brows raised high as her husband pushed her along past them all.

"How sore are you?" Dak slid a hand over her middle.

"I'm not." Her set back from her escape only lasted the first day. She felt more like herself since arriving here and getting proper rest. She supposed she had Dak to thank for that.

"How much self-defense do you have?"

"Is there a number I need to give you?" She blinked up at him, but his frown suggested he didn't care for her sense of humour. "None."

"That needs to change." He looked her up and down, then turned her so they followed King and Ember.

"Finally. Another woman." Ember let her head fall backward to look at the ceiling.

"Another woman for what?" Sophie tried to catch Ember's eye, but she was still being ushered forward. Dak looked determined. Hendrick grinned, rubbing his hands together, and Gear's lips flattened. As they all fell into step behind them, Sophie would bet that self-defense wasn't the right term for what they were about to do.

9

————

Dak ushered Sophie into the middle of the floor mat. Everyone circled around her with anticipatory grins, but Dak tuned them all out. He hadn't intended to make this a show. Each of them had something to offer when training, so he wouldn't turn them away. And Sophie needed to see how hard they all pushed Ember if she were to stay with him.

She spun around, her shoulders sinking as she set eyes on everyone. That had to be the first thing to change.

"You look scared, princess."

"Let's go with intimidated." She moved herself so she faced him.

"That isn't good either. Intimidation leads to fear. Do I scare you?" This wasn't the first time Dak had asked. It didn't matter which answer she gave him, it bothered him. She should fear him. But he didn't want her to.

"No."

"What about Hendrick?" The crazy one of the bunch made most people flinch.

Sophie frowned and Hendrick chuckled. "No."

"Cole?"

"No." Her answer was instantaneous for him. The man had a kind face that fooled many. Cole was as deadly as the rest of them when needed.

"Gear?"

"I don't know."

"Look at him."

Sophie turned. Gear let his true self show, darkening his face and straightening his shoulders. The man kept the sides of his head shaved, showing off his tattoos. "I think so."

"And King?"

"Yes," she whispered, hiding her eyes from all of them.

"Princess, you should be terrified of every person in this room."

"Except me," Ember called from beside King.

"Except Ember," Dak confirmed. "But you've made some enemies and you need to learn how to get away from people like us."

"You expect me to get away from all of you right now?" She took a step back, but it did her no good with a mercenary at every angle.

"Not yet." If she was around that long to learn it all.

Her eyes snapped up to his, bright and searching, when he said yet. Yet, in this case meant longer than the time to deal with the threat against her. Dak wanted her to learn it all. Ember herself still had a lot more training to go, but they were all confident enough she could dish out some serious damage and get away from an attacker. His chest constricted with what could happen to Sophie without him around. And if she stayed with him, she'd have more than some mysterious organization after her for her money.

"We'll start with the basics. Where on the body will a strike cause the most damage?"

She tilted her head and looked down at his groin. The others laughed. Even Gear cracked a grin.

"Where else?"

"The nose, the solar plexus." Her brows dropped as she tried to think, looking him over as she did it. "The feet?"

"Most anyone you come across will have their feet protected. Can't crush toes through boots like these."

"The throat." Her eyes gleamed. "And the eyes."

"Those will work if you can get to them fast and hard. Good."

Her shoulders rose with a spec of confidence. It wouldn't last long, but she'd need it.

Dak started walking toward her.

"What are you doing?" She took steps back to match his, swinging her head over her shoulders to the others.

"I want to see what your instincts tell you to do first. And you're not off to a good start." He nodded to her feet.

Panicked breaths heaved from her lungs, but she planted her feet and faced off with him.

"Good girl." Dak closed the distance, swiping his arm around to the back of her head to grab her hair. He pulled to bring her head back and get her into position before she reacted. Rolling his arm, he spun her so her back landed against his chest. By gripping her hair, he didn't cut off her air or circulation in her neck.

"That hurts." She whimpered and Dak almost let her go.

"It's supposed to. Pain makes people pause. It's how you lost your easy window to get away from me."

"You moved too fast."

"I always will. Now, what are you going to do? The longer you take, the harder I'll pull." Dak twitched his wrist.

"He's left..." King's hand cut off Ember's frustrated cheer.

Dak glared at Ember. "No help from you yet, sweetheart."

She snarled behind King's hand. Her husband bent his head to whisper in her ear, making her settle against him.

"Your time is running out, Sophie." Hendrick growled from behind them.

Dak felt her muscles tense before she made her move. Swinging her fist up, and brought it down toward his groin. Dak blocked her.

"Make that move quicker next time and they *might* not see it coming." Dak lessened his hold, but kept her in place. "Next move."

She tried to swing a foot behind him, but the result was twisting her hair further in his grip.

"I'm too big for that to work from this hold."

"The eyes, then." Sophie gave up trying.

"You can't aim from where you are."

"Then what do I do?" She slumped against him. Dak hadn't been expecting it and needed to adjust his arm. Sophie seemed to realize what she'd done. Her entire body relaxed. She moved quicker with sudden excitement. He didn't get his arm around her shoulders in time, but he kept a tight grip on her hair. She struggled and twisted herself around to face him.

"That's it, princess." His own excitement grew. Pride, too. "What are you going to do now?"

Her hands reached up and grabbed his hand, holding her hair. He straightened his arm to keep her out of his reach and grinned at her frustrated growl. She was getting mad. Good.

One hand left his and swung with a fist toward his elbow. He could have stopped her with his free hand, but he let her figure this out first. His elbow bent with her blow, and she pushed her weight forward.

She surprised him with her next move, lifting her foot and kicking him in the knee. His grip loosened, and she did it again. Dak moved enough to avoid damage, but let her go as if the blow had landed. She stumbled, straightened, and backed away from him. Straight into Hendrick.

Sweat coated Sophie and her chest burned. They didn't give her a break for an hour. Sympathy shone on Ember's face as one man let her go and another came at her. They were all conscious of her torso, never grabbing her around her middle or putting her to the ground.

As Dak let her go for the fourth time, she prepared for the next attack, firming her feet and readying her arms. She looked around, but none of them moved from the side of the mat. Sophie didn't trust them. Waiting, she circled, giving each of them her best glare. Still, no one moved.

"All done, princess." Dak's voice sounded raw, as if all of this had bothered him. But it was his idea to bring her down here. She could have said no. They may not have listened. If they had, Sophie wouldn't have learned what she did. She was no match for any of them, but if she'd known even a little of what they'd just taught her, Alan never would have done the damage he had.

She still didn't relax, not until she took one more look at each of them.

"You're up, little girl." King gripped the back of his wife's neck and moved her to the middle of the mat. Sophie stepped out of the way and stood next to Dak. He wrapped his arm around her, setting his hand over her ribs.

"You okay?" The rawness still scratched at his throat.

"Yes."

"We'll push you harder every time we bring you down here." It wasn't a question, but he seemed like he was looking for an answer. She didn't have one. Bringing her down here meant this was where she was staying. For a long time. Sophie didn't know what the next few hours would bring, let alone months or years.

"Okay."

"Ember has been doing this for just under a year. Watch."

Watch, so you can see what you'll have to go through. They attacked the tiny, black-haired woman faster and harder than they had her, some two at a time. Bending to lift her, she folded over to match their stance to keep them from getting a grip. If any of them got a hold of her hair, it wasn't for long. The other woman landed on her ass several times, but she shifted to avoid anyone reaching for her and got to her feet.

Sophie started watching the men. Despite how much harder they attacked Ember, they didn't huff or puff or struggle to grab her. But Ember worked hard to keep herself away from each of them.

"Attack me, Ember." King's voice silenced the others. Sophie leaned harder on Dak.

"What?"

"You want to keep coming on jobs. You need an offense and not only defense. It's time."

That was the first time Sophie saw the confidence wane from the other woman. He'd said *keep coming on jobs.* Did Ember work as a mercenary alongside them? Is that what they would expect Sophie to do?

"Dak?" Sophie put her chin over her shoulder and whispered. "Why are you teaching me this?"

He let his head drop so his breath brushed her lips. The sounds of Ember and King sparring drowned out in the background while the air she breathed came from Dak. He didn't answer right away. The man who never faltered stuttered with open lips before he answered her.

"So you can take care of yourself." It was the first time Sophie heard an untruth in his voice. And she didn't like it.

What was the untruth? The thought of having Ember's confidence to handle her own situations called to her. That trait shined bright in the other woman, despite having a very alpha mercenary for a husband. She was just as badass. Sophie didn't see a problem with learning those same skills herself. Except she wanted to know why Dak brought her down here. Teaching these skills wouldn't be part of their unspoken, unwritten, undefined contract of protection.

She opened her mouth to challenge him, but Dak covered it with his hand. Calluses scratched at her cheeks and lips. Turning her head back to King and Ember, he nipped her ear. "Watch, princess."

He kept his hand there for a while longer until Sophie's attention was entrenched in the other couple. After every series of moves, King paused, waiting for Ember to come at him again. With each set, her uncertainty lessened, but she wasn't getting far.

An internal battle cry shone in Ember's eyes and she charged at King, aiming high. The mercenary shook his head, but Ember faked her move and slid low. She moved to the side and skidded across the floor, grabbing an ankle on her way. His foot moved with her and he lost his balance. She swung her foot around and kicked King in the back of the knee. The massive man went down and the tiny woman wasted no time in getting on top of him and pulled his arm back into a hold.

Cheers erupted from around the circle, and Sophie smiled. But Ember's focus remained until she took several deep breaths, then got off him and stepped away.

King stood. "Good girl." He stalked toward his wife and took her mouth in a bruising kiss.

Sophie felt the warmth from across the room. Dak slid his hand over her shoulder and up to cover her throat. He said nothing, but the pulse of his possession was clear in his grip. But that possession wasn't permanent. Sophie laid her hand over his, trying to imprint it into her memory to use when she needed to feel safe.

As things wound down in the gym, and wound up for King and Ember, they made their way back up to the office. Sophie's focus had left the impending death of her husband. Dak was proud of her. He wished he had the right to keep that pride, wished him being proud of her meant something to her.

When she'd asked why he took her down to the gym, his lungs seized. The why was because she was his and he wouldn't have her unprotected. *His. His* would carry the skills to live in this world. To stand by his side and to protect herself and those around her. To change the target on her back to a fierce warning for all who'd think to use her against him.

That's why he took her down to the gym. To give her something. And to test her. Dak scrutinized every move she made and considered what she would be like going through the same regimen as Ember.

Sophie would shine. She did shine.

Cole made it to the front office first and was listening to the messages. He slid his thumb over his cell phone at the same time with a frown. Dak peered over his shoulder. He'd opened the office security feed that they each had access to. The guy on the video tried the door, then pulled out his phone while still staring at the handle.

"He left his information and is looking to hire us to track down a thief." Cole's eyes shot up in mock horror at the word thief. "He said nothing else."

Dak pulled out his own phone and studied the guy who'd left the message. "Call him back and get the details. I want to keep the manpower here, but let's see what the job is first." Whoever was after Sophie was a step ahead and had the manpower. But this dance between them could go on for a while. Or could end in the next hour.

Cole sat down at the desk and used the office phone to call him back. Dak only half listened while he kept watch on Sophie. She hung back toward the door, and had clasped her hands in front of her, making herself appear small and unnoticeable in the room. He wondered if she was doing it on purpose or if it had become an unconscious habit from living with her husband.

"What's wrong?" He stood in front of her and lifted her chin. What was it about this moment that gave her the need to hide in plain sight?

"Nothing." She whispered in a sweet tone. Another unobtrusive habit.

"Truth." Dak stretched the word with warning, with a demand. Her inhale was sharp and short.

"You..." she started.

"Someone stole money from his account." Cole interrupted. "He thinks it was one of his employees. He wants to hire us to track the money and deal with the employee accordingly." Cole's tone made it clear that dealing with the employee had nothing to do with handing him a pink slip. "Should be a quick job. At least the first half."

"See if Roen can squeeze it in from where he is." They still had four of them here, if any shit happened regarding Sophie. "If it gets complicated, then cut ties. And find out why the hell he came to the security side of the business rather than the mercenary channels." They kept the face of this business legitimate, which meant they only took legitimate legal jobs from the front office.

"Got it."

"Channels?" Sophie muttered under her breath, but in a quiet pause between conversation, they all heard it.

"Yes, channels." Dak nodded.

"My friend told me about those and that I might need to contact you that way."

The thought of her in *Lowell's Bar* or one of the other businesses used for contact blackened his vision. He'd trust Jacob Lowell to make sure nothing happened to innocents in his establishment—hell, his wife was the resident entertainment and the sweetest being alive—but even he couldn't have his eyes on everything in every instance.

"The bouncer wouldn't let me in. Even after I said the magic *open abracadabra*." She lowered her voice, twitched her nose, and waved her hand in front of her face.

"How did you learn about that?" That information wasn't easy to find and someone like Sophie should never come within a hundred feet of it.

"A friend told me." She lifted her chin and challenged the anger buried deep in him.

"A friend?" Dak wanted to meet this *friend*.

"Sort of."

"Sort of?"

She glared. "Stop doing that."

"Finish your story, princess."

"Months ago, I ran into an old classmate. It took me by surprise because we didn't graduate here. I don't run into people I know often. He'd changed. A lot. Not a good guy anymore, but he was still nice to me, and we talked. He bought me a drink, and he guessed what my marriage was like." She shrugged. "But once my reaction confirmed it, he told me about *King's Mercenaries* and how to contact you."

"What's your friend's name?"

"You seem upset." Sophie took a step back, clasping her hands again and hunching her shoulders.

"His name, Sophie." He growled. Guilt struck when she flinched, but that flinch only lasted a second before she narrowed her eyes. She had her problems, thanks to her husband, but she had so much strength buried and growing stronger.

"Griffith." She ground out the name between her teeth.

Dak gave Gear a look that the other man had no problem translating. *Find out everything you can about him.* Gear nodded and left.

"Dak? What are you going to do?"

"Nothing. I only want information." For now. If this friend knew what Sophie's husband was like, then he might know who the man was involved with.

10

Dak had taken Sophie back up to his apartment and locked her in. That was two hours ago. He'd done a good job of distracting her since the call about Alan. But left to stew on her own dragged everything up again. And now she was worried about Griffith. Maybe she didn't need to, but Dak's eyes said he'd hurt Griffith if he had to. Sophie didn't understand why.

She paced through Dak's apartment, afraid to touch anything. But as her anger grew, so did her curiosity. Tiptoeing as if he could hear her from downstairs, she moved through the kitchen, first searching through his cupboards. Perfectly organized dishes weren't what Sophie expected to find. Everything was arranged by colour and size. Wincing, she closed the door and moved into the living room. Open space and open shelves beside the television. Nothing to see here, except a portion of the wall that appeared bare.

Dak had said the two apartments had a connecting door. What did the passage look like? Was it simply a door?

Turning around to peer at the main entrance to the

apartment, she made her way to the wall. She smoothed her hand over the wainscoting. Everything blended. With a sigh, she backed away with her hands on her hips. She considered the layout of this apartment and the other and where she'd seen him disappear before. This had to be the spot.

Grunting, she let it go for now and searched his bedroom. His closet and drawers were as immaculate as his kitchen. Sophie wasn't a messy person, but she didn't come anywhere near Dak's level. Guilt settled as she let her fingers trail down his clothes in his closet. Expensive suits. Not-so-expensive suits. Uniforms of different kinds. All clothes to make him blend in somewhere. But none of them suited Dak. Not the Dak she'd gotten to know over the past few days. But this was all part of what he did.

She was about to step out when a door at the back caught her attention. She found the knob, but she also found the security pad prompting for the code to unlock. Sophie didn't bother with an attempt to unlock it. There was no way Dak wouldn't find out. But if he didn't want her to go snooping, then he shouldn't have left her alone.

With a firm nod to help herself feel better, Sophie went back to the bedroom and opened the drawers of the nightstand. Her lips fell apart, and she stepped back. Knives lined the inside in tidy rows. Different shapes and sizes. Some with wooden handles, some with metal. Ones like Hendrick had with metal circles on the ends. She ran her finger down the edge.

"Careful. They're sharp." Dak's rumble vibrated up her back, and she jumped back. Her finger caught on the edge. Gasping, she made a fist and held it against her chest. The cut stung, but she didn't want to bring attention to it in front of Dak.

He sauntered across the room and settled himself along

her back. Large hands pried her fist open and held her index finger.

"You've been busy up here." Dak pulled her finger over her shoulder and toward his mouth. His tongue darted out to lick along the cut before taking the whole tip of her finger in his mouth and sucking. Tingles sped through her hand and arm. Her core clenched.

"I'm sorry."

He pulled her finger from his mouth. "Don't be. Although, watching you tiptoe was cute."

"Cute?" He called her cute.

"Would you prefer to be something else?" Dak licked at her finger again, holding it back to inspect the cut.

"Well, yeah." Not that she didn't mind being cute, but that wasn't what she wanted the man holding her to think.

"What?" He nipped her neck and Sophie struggled not to melt against him.

"Not cute."

Dak reached around her and shut the nightstand drawer. "Don't touch the knives unless you know how to use them, princess."

"Will I learn how to use them?" She'd seen a couple knives attached to Ember's thighs. She was learning everything because she belonged to King. Dak's answer might help her figure out what was going through his mind.

"That depends." Here it was.

"On what?" With a breathless whisper, she turned around in his arms.

"On what happens next."

Sophie wanted to slam her head against his chest. What kind of an answer was that?

"And how long you'll be here."

She had her answer. "Of course." The time in the gym was nothing more than a little self defense like he'd said and something to pass the time.

"What did you discover on your search of my apartment?"

"You're organized."

"That's it?"

"I can't find the door that connects the apartments, and you have a locked door in the back of your closet. You already know I've seen the knives." He soured her mood, and her tone clipped.

"The locked door has weapons. And I'll show you the hidden door."

"Dak." She didn't want him to show her things. Showing her things meant she'd stay. That couldn't be the right decision for her after all she'd been through, and he didn't seem like he wanted her here forever. "I think it's time we found another way to deal with this. I'd like my fake identity now and for you to put me in a safe house. One away from my parents so they don't get caught in any cross hairs."

"We've already addressed this, princess. You aren't leaving."

"Then when am I leaving?" Sophie pushed against his chest and he let her go. "Why are we attracted to each other and following through when you're just going to send me away when you're finished? Not when *I'm* finished. But only when *you're* finished."

His jaw clenched, and he backed away from her. Three steps back and two forward. His hard presence pushed against her. "Sophie." Harsh rocks ground through his voice.

"You don't have an answer for me?" Her breathing picked up, her chest heaving. But she narrowed her eyes at him, studying him. His glare darkened and his nostrils flared.

He reached for her and she stepped back. His growl wrapped around her throat.

If he touched her, she'd cave. So easily did his touch and voice stroke her core, but the sensation was moving to other places. It wasn't a purely physical attraction anymore. Not for her, and she didn't want to chance the pain of continuing things with him.

"Don't move away from me, princess." The threat sent chills over her skin. Her heel lifted, but she stomped it back down on the floor.

"I need an answer, Dak. Please." She didn't want to be mad at him. He'd done things for her she hadn't thought possible. The way he made her feel was a strong electric burn. But she needed more than that.

"I don't have one." He ground the words through his teeth. "You aren't going anywhere right now, but to that bed." His usually silent steps carried sound as he charged toward her. Sophie lost every argument as his hands wrapped around her waist and he threw her on the bed.

———

DAK HELD SO MUCH in his chest it hurt. The anger, the fear of losing her. The growling erupted in spurts and if he didn't give himself relief, the final eruption would echo through the entire building. He'd told himself she needed to go. She'd given him an out, an opportunity to send her away and be done with her. Dealing with the people after her and her husband would be a lot more efficient without her here.

Dak should have answered her. He should have sent her away. But he wasn't capable.

His palms burned when he wrapped them around her waist. The savage beast within him had taken over. Reaching into the one drawer of the nightstand Sophie hadn't opened, Dak pulled out the rope he kept there. It wasn't rope he used for sex. It was there for the same reasons the knives were and the other weapons in his closet. The fabric was rough even against his callused fingers. It should never touch the skin of his princess. But he needed to secure her. The urge rushed strong through his blood.

Secure.

Safe.

Mine.

"Dak? What are you doing?" Her breath caught and her gorgeous eyes widened on the rope.

"You aren't leaving, princess. I won't hurt you. I'm going to show you why you can't leave." He reached for one wrist, then the other, placing them together above her head. Winding the rope, he secured them together and pulled them up to the headboard.

Sophie pulled against them, trying to bring them back down. Satisfaction filled him to see her secured to his bed.

"You look good there. But you could look better." Dak opened the drawer of knives and pulled one out, letting the metal cling against the others to see her reaction.

A touch of fear. Good. She needed to keep that. But there was trust shining in her eyes. Anticipation quickened her breath.

"Don't move, Sophie." He dropped his voice to a harsh warning.

"I won't." Her whisper shot straight to his cock. With her secured to the bed, the anxiety inside him had settled and he wanted to take his time.

She'd been right. Whatever this was between them was

only on his terms, not hers. How badly was he going to hurt her? Because he was about to make it impossible for her to consider leaving him again.

Lifting the hem of her shirt, Dak slid the knife underneath. He tilted his head to watch the back of the knife scrape against her stomach. Her belly indented with the contact.

Pushing up, he sliced through her shirt, up and between her breasts. Sophie lifted her chin as he reached the neckline. A quick swipe opened the front of her bra and cut both straps, and the straps of her tank top.

Dak pulled the fabric free and ran the back edge of the knife down between her breasts. Fucking perfect.

He did the same to her jeans, slicing his way through the denim to bare her. The panties she wore were damp between her legs. He ran a finger down the wetness. "Good girl. You want this."

"So much. But I'm scared."

"I know." He cut through the cotton. A squeal escaped from her throat.

"Can I move now?"

Dak wasn't ready to let the knife go despite that she had no clothes left to cut away. "No." He caressed the top of her thigh with the tip.

Sophie stopped breathing. He held it there until she couldn't hold her breath any longer, then gently slid it up her thigh with the beat of the breath—the contact only enough to tickle. He turned the blade so that the back edge rested against her skin. Dak made three parallel red marks along her thigh.

"Dak?"

"I won't hurt you, princess. But you already know that,

don't you?" Dak pinned his gaze to hers until she answered him.

"I don't."

He froze, lifting the knife away from her. Dak wouldn't continue if she believed he intended harm.

"Physically, no. But I don't know that you won't hurt me emotionally. I've tried to leave."

"I want to make the same promise. I can't. But you aren't leaving until I say so." For that alone, Dak didn't deserve to keep her.

"Then make me feel good, please." She locked her eyes on his, pleading with him to give her whatever he would.

"Always, princess." He moved the knife back to her skin and made a mark with the back of the blade for every gasp that escaped her lips. Once the shine between her legs caught the light, he stopped and tossed the knife to the floor.

Dak touched her clit and her thighs trembled. The buildup shook through her body in spurts. And his cock made its own desires known, pushing against his jeans. Sliding his finger down, he pushed it inside her. Hot, wet, tight, and ready. Despite only taking her hours earlier.

He added a second finger. Then a third. Sophie arched her back as he filled her. The pressure was unbearable. Dak undid his jeans as he pumped his hand. Not wanting to stop touching her, he only freed his cock and stroked himself to the same rhythm.

"Come." *And only for me, never again for another.* Dak wanted those words to escape, but that wasn't fair. Not that he ever dealt with fair. She deserved happiness and a good life. He could force the promise from her, that she'd never again let another man see the pleasure of her release, damning her to eternal sexual frustration because he wouldn't be there to give it to her. He wouldn't.

"Dak." She cried out his name, and the sound was like a warm touch down his spine. A satisfying hum that meant something more. But he wasn't ready for what it meant.

Her core clenched around his fingers, trying to push them out, but he kept pumping to milk the orgasm for all he could get from her. Sophie's whimpers as her climax eased made him feel ten feet tall. He had to release her to get rid of his own clothes. Tossing his shirt to the floor and kicking his jeans away, Dak lowered to his knees between her legs. He lifted the knife from the floor and sliced through the rope, freeing her hands from the headboard.

Blue eyes searched his face. "I'll never be the same now that I've met you."

Those words both cut him and overjoyed him. Dak closed his eyes and thrust deep.

***

THERE WAS NO MORE fighting it. What would be, would be. She'd either be alone, destroyed, and in pain. Or living whatever life would be with Dak. Sophie had no control over what happened next. Dak made that clear. If she was strong enough to pick herself up after Alan, she would pick herself up after Dak. But Sophie would never trust another man after this.

Dak filled her again and again. She clutched at his back, the rope dangling from her wrists, and wrapped her legs around his hips, trying to hold him to her. Neither of them had any more words for each other.

An odd mix of fear and comfort entered her when he first pulled the knife from the drawer. That feeling would live in her heart forever. Dak was not a safe man, but he was for her.

She tilted her hips up, letting him hit her clit. He rested on one elbow and let that hand knead her breast. Sophie let go of her struggle. Let go of her plans to run away. She ran, but she just didn't have to run as far or as hard as she thought. Callused fingers moved up her side until they wrapped around her throat. Tilting her chin, she gave him full access. It was already too late for her.

"Good girl, princess." He nipped her ear.

Sophie met him thrust for thrust. As sharp as the knives, her climax rose and sliced through her at the same time Dak exploded. He roared into her neck and she struggled to breathe as wave after wave of ecstatic sensations poured through her.

"Don't ask to leave again." It wasn't a plea. It wasn't a request. It was an authentic threat. One that Sophie would heed.

"I..." She didn't know what to say to him, but she didn't have time to let her heart do the talking for her. Dak's phone trilled from his jeans, cutting her off.

He heaved as he pulled himself free from her. She gasped, left bereft on the bed, until she caught his eyes. They didn't leave her like his body. Heat coaxed over her skin. Dak still didn't look away as he dug for his phone and answered.

Thunderous anger tightened his face and leaked into his eyes.

"Call back in five minutes." He hung up. "Get dressed."

"Dressed in what? Someone cut up my clothes."

Dak dressed himself with the clothes he'd discarded on the floor and reached into the second drawer of his dresser. He tossed her a pair of jeans and a soft, loose sweater.

"Whose are these?"

"Yours." He frowned.

Sophie eyed the clothes. They weren't hers. Not clothes that she'd brought with her, anyway. They must have been the ones Hendrick brought her that first morning. No tags hung from the garments, but they had that distinct fresh smell that only came from a retail store. When had he moved them over from the other apartment? She held the clothes against her chest and moved toward the bathroom.

"Sixty seconds, Sophie." That phone call had changed things. Dak had been so cavalier about all of this, but that call seemed to make things urgent for him. Her heart beat hard and slow.

She rushed to do her business and clean herself up until Dak knocked on the door.

"Now."

Sophie pulled the jeans on, wincing with the denim against her sensitive core. He didn't give her any underwear or a bra. She was pulling the sweater over her head when the door opened. He tossed a pair of sandals in front of her and she slipped them on.

Dak urged her in front of him and kept her pace up any time she lagged. He practically punched the buttons on the elevator. When they reached the main office, Dak bellowed. "Gear, get to the computers and get Roen on the phone."

"Already here." Gear called back, and everyone headed in that direction.

"Call coming in any minute. I need as much information as possible."

"Got it." Dak's phone drowned Gear's answer out. He put it on speaker.

"What the hell makes you think you're calling the shots

and can hang up on me?" A disguised voice echoed over the line.

"You have nothing I want." Dak had pulled back his calm. That calm sounded more deadly than any rage.

"I'm not trying to deal with you. Put her on the phone."

Sophie stepped back. Other than Ember, she was the only other *her* in the room, and if they were looking for Ember, Sophie doubted they'd be calling Dak or that Dak would have rushed her downstairs.

"She's here. Talk." Dak looked at Sophie.

"I want to talk to her alone."

"You talk to her now or not at all." He pulled a piece of paper toward him and wrote on it, pointing for Sophie to read. *Tell him you're here.*

"I'm here." Her voice cracked, and she tried to clear it.

"Pick up the phone and take it off speaker," the garbled voice demanded.

Dak held out his arm to stop her from moving as if he thought she would listen. "She isn't touching the phone. You have ten seconds to talk to her or I'm hanging up."

The sound over the line muffled, as if being moved. And then the voice that came through was clear and too familiar.

"Sophie, baby." Alan. She hated his voice. But this time, it sounded whiny and sniveling. Sophie should feel bad that she took some joy in that, but she didn't.

"I'm here." She stayed back from the phone as the machine had morphed into her husband's face.

"They're going to kill me." His words were choppy. "You need to give them the money back."

"I don't know who they are."

"They'll tell you what to do. Please. Give it back. Please." To hear Alan beg twisted her stomach. He deserved this, but did he deserve to die? Didn't he deserve the chance to change? Did his family deserve to lose a son and brother? That wasn't up to Sophie to decide, but she couldn't cause his death.

"Whose is it?" If she could get some information for Dak to use, she would.

"I can't say. Sophie, they have a gun to my head. They said they'll shoot me now over the phone if you don't agree to give it back." Tears and ugly sniffles muffled his words, but Sophie heard it and envisioned it.

She looked at Dak for an answer. They'd been over this. He wouldn't let her give the money back. But would he spare her husband for her own conscience? Her eyes filled with frustrated tears.

"Sophie no longer has control over that money." He held a finger over his mouth and shook his head. That wasn't true, but the people on the other end didn't need to know that. "It isn't her you need to deal with. And I don't see any reason to spare your life."

"What have you done to my wife?" Alan's anger was weak through fear.

Dak didn't answer, but glared at the phone. More muffles indicated the change of speakers.

"You're lying."

"I never lie." Dak winced as he said it. He did lie, but he didn't like it.

"This man is going to die. And that's on you."

"That man was going to die one way or another. You planned to kill him anyway and if you didn't, I know several others that would. Your threat has no weight with me."

His true voice broke through the disguised sound like a glitching video game as he roared into the speaker. A gunshot sounded before the line went dead.

Sophie's breath stopped, and she grasped around her for

something to hold her up. Hendrick stepped forward and held onto her elbow. She locked eyes with Dak.

His resolute darkness held no sympathy for what had just happened. It was almost as if he challenged her. *This is what this life is like, princess. Can you handle it?*

Dak had to harden his heart. The torment on Sophie's face hurt him as much as that bullet would have. She didn't belong in this life. He watched her to make sure she didn't fall apart. Hendrick held her elbow, but she still held her own weight. Losing her husband didn't bring her to her knees. That steel Dak admired so much held her up, filled her eyes behind the tears and fears.

Come on, princess. Show me what you're made of. Because deep down, he couldn't let her go. The episode upstairs showed him that. This was on his terms.

"They were going to kill him no matter what." Hendrick spoke low near her shoulder.

Her lips trembled and her nostrils flared. With an audible swallow, she lifted her chin.

That's it, princess. You belong with me.

"Nothing I did would have mattered." No more question. Acceptance filled each breath as they evened out. The change in her captured him.

"No." Dak didn't need to remind her he would have killed him.

"But this isn't over, is it?"

Dak shook his head. The husband hadn't been a problem to begin with. But the money. Money controls and changes situations in a way that's unpredictable.

He looked at Gear, who was on the line with Roen, and just finished typing furiously. Cole could pass for Roen in a pinch, but Gear looked frazzled, which was hard to do with that man. Computers weren't his thing, but he was next in line with Cole working the kidnapping. "They're in the north part of the city. That's all we got."

Roen's voice came over the line. "They've got some serious blockers up. But with that much security, I'd say it's their primary location. Knowing this much will help with everything else I've got. I'll find them." Roen hung up before Dak answered.

He hoped they found them before they made their next move.

"Where are King and Ember?"

"They stayed up front." Hendrick cocked his head to the door. "Someone walked in as you bellowed."

Dak frowned. Business was good—on both sides of it— but people walking in the front was rare. Ember came back.

"King is still up front. The guy hasn't left yet. I love watching tiny men shake at the sight of one of you guys. But he's determined." Ember shrugged.

"What's the job?" Dak waited for something ridiculous.

"Company theft. They need the proof. King told him he'd have to wait, the men needed for that are already occupied, but he won't leave."

"Pull him up on surveillance, Gear." Dak turned to the monitors and waited while Gear pushed the few keys needed. The man struggled to breathe and hold himself up as King glared down at him. "Run his face."

Gear's eyes widened, but he grabbed the still image and put it into the program Roen had. Dak called King and watched the other man answer his phone on the video.

"The only reason you're waiting is because he isn't leaving on his own?" Dak believed King had the same suspicions as him.

"Yes."

"Get rid of him. I don't have time for this petty shit." Dak had a sense crawling over his skin that he never ignored.

King looked up at the camera and raised a brow.

"Get rid of him, anyway."

King hung up and tucked his phone back in his pocket before he wrapped his hand around the man's throat. His eyes bugged out, and he gripped King's wrist. King backed him to the door and shoved him through. He landed on his ass and scrambled away. With the door locked, King made his way to the computer room.

"You sure there isn't a connection?"

"No. But it doesn't make sense if it is." Someone was trying to distract them.

"They called you. They know who you are and where Sophie is." Gear pointed at Dak's phone he still held in his hand. He hadn't let that piece of information piss him off yet. "We've been at a disadvantage from the beginning."

"Not for long. If they know who I am, then I know them." But there were too many people in this city who dealt with that kind of money.

"You don't know any of your husband's interests?" King looked at Sophie. Dak was starting to hate the word husband.

"No. I tuned out everything he did or said years ago, after the first hit. And when we first started dating, his interests were everywhere. We travelled, went to concerts, races, casinos, bars, friends, camping, fishing." A wistful twist pulled at her lips.

Dak wanted to wipe those memories away and replace them with ones of him. But he didn't go to concerts, bars, fishing. He didn't have friends other than King.

"I only memorized when he came and went. I didn't need to memorize it after a while. I felt him." The curl of Sophie's nose made Dak want to bring the bastard back to life and kill him again.

"Call if his face shows up anywhere." Dak pointed to the running program on the screen, then cupped Sophie's chin and tilted it up to look at him. "Upstairs, princess." He let her go, and she turned to walk in front of him. But he didn't follow.

She looked over her shoulder.

"Alone."

Narrowed eyes were sharp against him and her next step stomped hard against the floor. He thought she would argue. She should have. Dak wanted her nose to nose with him. He'd always win, but he didn't want any defeat in her. Only the steel shining bright and drawing him closer. But at the moment, she seemed drained.

"Sophie." She stopped but didn't turn around. Dak had nothing to say to her that he already hadn't. And definitely nothing in front of everyone here. When he said no more, she started walking again. Pulling along a tether with her that held onto his strength.

SOPHIE STORMED AWAY toward the elevator, pressed the button, then left without getting on as the door closed. She wasn't going to be tossed in a room and only played with on his terms. Only allowed to be part of this on his terms.

Alan was dead. Whether that was because of her, she couldn't be sure. Maybe she could have prevented it, but did she want to? And that sent bright glowing guilt rushing through her. What kind of person was she becoming? What had Ember been like before she met King?

Had this life changed her?

Sophie poked her head in every door she passed, but found herself in the basement gym. It was void of people, as they were all still in the computer room.

She moved around the room in a circle, looking at each piece of equipment. At the back of the room was a wooden chest. It had a place for a lock, but no lock. Opening it, several layered trays opened up with the lid. On each, she saw a similarly arranged array of knives and other weapons. This time, she looked over her shoulder before running her fingers over the handles of the knives.

A crossroads was right in front of her. One she never intended to be at. Both paths had shallow views of what came next. But Dak held her here, not letting her go and refusing to keep her.

Soft footsteps echoed into the gym, and Sophie shut the chest.

"It's me." Ember called out. Sophie turned and smiled at the other woman, but the smile didn't sit right. Ember's lips lifted sideways with sympathy, giving Sophie permission to drop the politeness.

She sighed.

"I figured you weren't the type to listen and march yourself upstairs. How are you doing?" Ember sat on the closed chest.

"I don't know."

"You're trying to figure out if you're okay with your husband's death. Questioning what kind of person you are." Ember's face said she'd gone through the same examination of herself.

"The first part, yes, but now I'm wondering about the second part." If she was okay with Alan's death, what kind of person did that make her? If she stayed around here long enough, would she get used to it?

"If you're wondering, you won't get used to it. You're okay with it or you're not. Sorry if that's too blunt." She winced.

"Don't apologize. I'd rather honesty above all else." She'd had a fake marriage to a fake man.

"It's difficult to be part of this."

"What did you... How did you meet..." Sophie had a hard time wording the question, *What kind of person did you used to be?*

Ember's face softened, understanding dawning. "What's my story?"

"Yes." Sophie sat down on the chest next to the other woman.

"It's complicated, but I was kidnapped and left on King's property. He kept taking me home, only for me to show up again the next morning. Turns out it was a trap for him. He'd retired from this life. But we fell for each other. I didn't want to be useless, and he refuses to let me be anything less than him. It's why I'm training."

"You go on jobs with him?"

"Some. The ones I want to and he lets me. I don't think I could ever be part of assassinations."

Griffith hadn't been exaggerating about the abilities of *King's Mercenaries*. She let the information rotate in her head while she changed the subject between them. "What did you do before you met King?"

"Before someone dumped me at his door?" A dark brow quirked, old bitterness lurking. "I was in school. A professor and my ex were involved in the trap for King. I couldn't go back and feel safe after that. I can't look at people the same since. It destroyed my trust. But these guys, I trust explicitly."

"I get that."

"They're too blunt not to trust."

Sophie nodded her agreement.

"I haven't been around long in the grand scheme of things, but I've never seen Dak act like this." Ember softened her voice as if she expected Dak to appear around the corner from the mere mention of his name.

"Act like what?" Sophie frowned.

"Obsessed. He's never obsessed over anything." She paused and turned to face Sophie. "But he is with you."

"It's temporary. He won't let me leave. I've asked several times to go to a safe house, to disappear on my own, but he refused. All in the same breath where he said I'll leave when he says I can."

"I think it's safe to say welcome to this world. Unless you don't have the stomach for it. I'm not sure what Dak will do in that case."

"If I stay, what do I need to have the stomach for?"

Ember's lips twisted. "The world of mafias, crime kingpins, underground wars, torture, the deaths of bad people, mercenaries who are just as evil but somehow still on the right side of it all."

Sophie started shaking her head involuntarily. Ember laid her hand on Sophie's shoulder.

"If you need to talk some more or need help with anything, just ask. It takes time to accept it all. If you choose to stay."

"He hasn't been giving me a choice." She tried to take herself out of the equation to get some distance.

"But did you really fight him that hard?"

Ember was right. She didn't fight him on it. When he refused, she begged him to make her feel good. "No."

"If it makes you feel better, I don't regret my decision to marry King. Even after two attempts to kidnap me to use against him. They didn't get very far."

"It must have been scary, though." Would people want the same of her for being with Dak?

"Terrifying. But I knew I'd have a target on my back." Ember pinched her lips, the words *as will you* trapped behind them.

Sophie nodded her understanding of the unsaid. Ember hopped off the chest, her legs short enough they'd been dangling above the floor.

"Feel free to use the equipment and if you're looking for a sparring partner, I'd love one. Even if you don't stay, I'd love to keep in touch." Ember squeezed Sophie's wrist. "I imagine he'll head upstairs to look for you soon, but you do you, lady. Even I tried to run from King."

"Are you suggesting I run?"

"Only if you need to. But I doubt you'll make it."

Sophie's lips cracked into a grin. "That isn't really helpful."

Ember laughed. "I know."

The two women laughed low together over nothing that made sense. But the idea simmered in Sophie's mind even after Ember left. If she wanted to get distance to sort through her thoughts and he wouldn't let her leave, running might be her only option. Or to make him think that she'd run.

DAK KEPT himself frozen in place. If he moved, if he spoke, if he looked at anyone, he'd lose it. Silence reigned around the room, closing him in a circle. Each of them recognized the tension running through him. They must or they would be working. But they all stood as still as him, waiting for the explosion. He'd kept the rage contained until Sophie left.

These people knew who he was, had his personal cell number, and knew Sophie was still here. And Sophie landed on their to-do list, not just the money. Which meant the name King didn't terrify them. They weren't terrified of the dangerous shadow that worked alongside King for decades.

One step ahead of them and Dak was stuck here with no way to move forward.

His chest heaved. Sophie ran through his blood. The need to keep her safe became his number one priority. Another thing to piss him off. She didn't deserve this, didn't deserve to have to deal with him for the rest of her life. And Dak had more than one priority. The safety of his tenants, the business he ran with King.

They needed to move. And now.

Dak didn't enjoy being on this side of a war. He wanted the shadows where he saw and heard everything. Where he always had the advantage.

"King." His voice sounded like a monster from hell. "Call Jacob and explain the situation. See if he has any idea how to find out the identity of these guys."

"On it."

"Hendrick, call Roen." Even though Roen worked as hard and as fast as he always did. He needed to take control of something.

"Sure." Hendrick agreed, but didn't move. Dak doubted the other man would even bother making the call.

A roar echoed between his ears and hummed through his blood. Dak had buried this kind of rage a long time ago when he'd lived on the streets.

"Sophie has to go." Shock of each of them snapped in the room. "Tell Cole to wrap up what he can and get the fuck back here. We're turning this around."

"How?" King asked, suspicion dropping his tone.

"Take Sophie out of this and do it the old school way. Not like a roadside security business." Dak needed to go back into the shadows to deal with this. But not with Sophie beside him or waiting for him.

"I'll set up a safehouse for her and send Ember with her," suggested King, but Dak heard the disapproval in his voice.

"Something else you want to say?" Dak turned on his friend and partner.

"Don't need to. You already know it all."

Yeah, he did. He was too emotional. King knew the damage Dak's current state could cause. He'd been a witness to it before. The day his mother died. The day they met.

But Dak desired causing that kind of damage. These people needed a reminder of who the fuck they were dealing with. He'd take them out and anyone else that thought they'd like to stand up to *King's Mercenaries*. The name still put fear into most, but if they didn't give the community something to fear, that would fade. Dak wouldn't give it a chance.

The savage had bent the bars of its cage.

"Let's move." Dak left the others to work. He took the elevator up to his apartment to find Sophie and tell her she was getting her wish. He was letting her go. It pissed him off even more to let her go. Pain sliced through him, his chest, his gut.

He took a deep breath inside his apartment, preparing himself to push her away. But the stillness engulfed him. Dak frowned and searched his apartment. She wasn't here.

Taking the hidden door, he went into her apartment to find the same thing. Where the fuck was she? He pulled up his phone and the security footage to find out if she even came up here when he told her to, not panicking as he had last time and called Roen. Nothing. Nothing in the elevator. And she hadn't locked herself in the stairwell again. He should have known from the glare in her eyes that she wouldn't have obeyed him.

Scrolling through the footage, he followed her from the moment he told her to leave. She walked to the elevator and turned. Searching every room she passed until she found herself in the gym. He switched the footage with each room she passed. In the gym, she slowed her progress and looked around. Thoughts crossed her soft features.

Ember walked in and the two women sat on the chest full of weapons together and talked.

Ember was doing fine living this life. She had been even less suited to this before meeting King than Sophie. But Ember had a better taste of King's capabilities. Dak hadn't shown Sophie the same.

Soon, Ember left the screen and Sophie roamed the gym. Dak looked at the timestamp of the footage. Ten minutes ago, and Sophie didn't look like she was in a hurry. He turned off his phone and made his way down to the gym, passing King and Hendrick still standing inside the computer room.

Entering the gym, he felt her. He smelled her. But he didn't see her. A grin split his lips. His mood lifted as he set himself back against the wall. He cut the lights and her intake of breath hushed through the darkness. Guess he got to have his own game of hide and seek before he sent her away. He'd find her, catch her, scare her, but he wouldn't touch her in the way he craved again.

He moved to the left, tracking where he'd heard her breathe. The air shifted, and he paused, tracking her movement. She was better than he'd expected. He wondered if this wasn't the first time she'd played hide and seek. To get away from her husband's wrath. And he wondered what she suffered when he found her.

Dak shook his head, shook the rage-inducing thoughts from his mind. He refocused on Sophie. She was further away from him than he expected. But he couldn't let that change his mind. He followed her rather than moving around to cut her off to give her a sense of victory.

Sophie backtracked, coming closer to him herself. Dak frowned. She moved again, but deeper into the gym, then all movement stopped. No breathing, no rustle of the air. Utter calm filled the space, but she was still here. He felt her.

Fuck, she impressed him. More strength than even she knew embodied her. His princess. Dak took the chance and moved. And so did she, but he missed her direction while concentrating on keeping himself silent. He wanted to grin and growl at the same time. And he was going to let this woman go?

He kept his patience this time, but she outdid him. He started to move and froze to catch her movement. A small scuff of fabric came from the back of the gym again.

Silence.

The next time he moved, she didn't.

"Princess." He called, his voice still sounding like evil

from hell. He wanted to get a reaction out of her. How did she track him?

A breath. But she'd moved again. Closer to the door.

"Don't run from me, Sophie. I'll catch you." He moved with his words, but changed his position closer to the door once he finished talking.

Dak listened, closing his eyes to use his senses. Nothing. He stalked to the last position he'd tracked her. She wasn't there.

"Sophie." He growled, so the sound came back eerie in the darkened room. "Fuck." Dak threw on the lights and did one last look through the gym before accepting that he'd been beaten. He left the gym and followed the path he thought she'd most likely take.

12

Sophie didn't let herself breathe properly. Thrills and fears rushed through her. She made it out of the gym. All Dak had to do was look at his cameras and find her, but she continued to skulk through the main floor of the building. He'd been the one to shut off the lights and turn this into a game. All she'd wanted was some privacy. Sophie had to hope he kept playing the game and didn't cheat.

Voices came from the computer room. King and Hendrick. She took three steps closer to the door, and they paused and so did she, forcing herself to stay still and calm with her eyes closed. Focused. They'd felt her presence as Dak had.

The rumble of their voices continued, and Sophie listened.

"You've known Dak the longest." Hendrick's voice lost all crazy and laughter.

"I've only ever seen him this emotional once. It wasn't pretty. And we were kids." Sophie suppressed a shiver from the image King invoked.

"Nothing he does ever is, but it's calculated."

"This still is, but he's compromised."

"He won't be once he gets rid of Sophie."

Gets rid of her? Rid of her how? She kept herself focused, so she didn't react to what they'd said.

King took a few minutes before he answered. Sophie thought he must have heard her until he spoke again. "He should have gotten rid of her the day she walked in here. It's too late now."

A whip of a breath escaped her chest, and she moved past the doorway before they came out and saw her. She had precious seconds before Dak emerged from the gym and found her skulking out in the open.

"Shit." King's curse echoed out from the computer room.

Sophie kept moving, but she abandoned her hiding. With three of them on her tail now, she had no chance to stay out of sight.

"Sophie." Dak's growl slashed out at her spine. He was close, but still in the back room when she entered the main lobby.

"She got past the door without us seeing her." Hendrick sounded awed.

Sophie saw the front door. It was within reach. And she was almost within reach of Dak, whose footsteps made deliberate rhythms to scare her. She couldn't sit around and wait for him to make up his mind about her. According to King, he was dangerous to be around in this state and she was the cause. A danger to him and a danger to everyone here.

The door beckoned her closer and Dak's voice pulled her back. He couldn't solve his problem. She'd do it for him.

Sophie dashed for the door.

"Sophie." Dak's growl breathed down her neck. She screeched and yanked on the door. It was locked. Dak stood on the other side of the room, his eyes boring into her while she reached for the lock, but she didn't dare look back. He didn't stay still long when the lock gave way without a struggle. "Sophie, don't!"

His hand brushed across her back as she darted out into the busy street. Her momentum took her past the sidewalk and into traffic. Dak followed, yelling after her, but she kept going, hoping traffic would stop for her and not Dak. Tires screeched, and she swerved with only one eye open.

Across the street, Sophie ducked into one alley and took off running until she came around the building and up another, back onto the street.

She never looked back, just kept weaving around buildings, cars, people, in and out of stores and restaurants to lose him. Tucking herself into the seat of an outdoor bistro, she sat and picked up the waiting menu. She didn't breathe, didn't turn around. Just closed her eyes and listened. Waited.

A waitress came over. "Hey, sweetie. What can I get ya?" The fifties-something woman cocked her hip and smiled.

Sophie snapped her eyes open and choked on air. Clearing her chest, she looked up the woman who lost her smile.

"I'm sorry. I didn't mean to scare you. Are you okay?"

Just order lunch and blend in, Sophie. But as she came up with her new plan, she realized running hadn't been her plan at all. The adrenaline of the chase and hearing King say she shouldn't be there led her way out like bread crumbs. She had nothing with her. No money, no clothes. Hell, she wasn't even wearing underwear or a bra.

"I'm okay, thank you. Just a water would be good. I'm waiting for someone." Sophie pulled a smile up from somewhere for the kind woman and went back to reading the menu.

What the hell was she supposed to do now? She'd left everything up in the apartment.

"I'm impressed, princess." His voice was next to her ear. She closed her eyes, defeat settling hard and feeding on all the adrenaline from her system.

"Let me go, Dak." She sounded stronger than she felt, confident in her decision to leave him. Staying with him would only cause more trouble. Would lead to more danger for both of them. Her own two feet could support her and that's what she'd wanted.

"No." He took her elbow and pulled her up, but his grip didn't hurt. Bringing her close to his chest, he bent his head. "But you are leaving."

"You just said you wouldn't let me go."

"Not on your own. I was going to send you to a safehouse with Ember."

A sleek SUV pulled up in front of the restaurant. Gear stepped out of the driver's side and walked around to the back. Crossing his arms, he leaned against the back door.

"You're going with Gear."

So she couldn't escape again. "And then what? Then will you let me go when this is all over? When will you finally get rid of me?" She kept her voice low, her tone even, so they didn't draw attention from the handful of other customers sitting outside.

"Everything okay, sweetie?" The waitress came back and set her water down on the table.

Nothing she said to this other woman would stop Dak and Gear from taking her away. "It is. Thank you."

"You guys ready to order?" She eyed Dak and the hand

he had on Sophie's elbow that didn't seem as threatening as it had felt.

"Another time." Dak answered for her. He reached down for the water and passed it to Sophie. "Drink."

The scratch in her throat from her run made itself known. She tipped the glass back and gulped down half the water before passing it back to Dak. The waitress hovered long enough to take the glass. She left with a frown.

"How far did I get?" She wanted to know if escape had even been possible.

"Further than I expected." She'd surprised him. That alone was something to be proud of.

"How far?"

"Two blocks before I caught on to your pattern." He sighed before answering. He didn't like admitting that, but she shook her head and leaned her forehead against his chest.

"Did I even have a chance?" Sophie didn't see her own pattern.

"Maybe. With practice." Another statement that made her think he wanted to keep her as he was sending her away. All on his terms.

Gear grew impatient and took over, stepping over the two-foot tall fence that sectioned off the outdoor dining area from the sidewalk and grabbed Sophie's other elbow to pull her away from Dak. But Dak stopped their progress with a fierce grip on her chin.

"Don't run again, princess."

She lifted her chin and glared. "Then you should have let me go when I asked the first time." She wouldn't make him any promises or cooperate any longer. His rules didn't apply to someone he wouldn't keep.

DAK WATCHED Gear drive away with Sophie in the back seat. He never expected her to run. Or to get as far as she did. Fucking impressive. But she would have crashed and burned on her own. Maybe the people searching for her wouldn't have found out she was gone from his grasp, but eventually, they would have caught up to her. She had no resources with her to fall back on.

But what made her run when she did?

He stalked back to his building, meeting King on the street.

"She's gone?"

"Yes." And a storm raged inside his gut. It was the right decision. He'd deal with the threat to her and then he could have a clear head. He'd fuck her brains, and his, out one last time and send her on her way. No one knew what she meant to him. There was no need for anyone to see a target on her back.

"Dak," King started.

"Don't." He didn't want to hear how he should keep her the way King kept Ember.

"She got past you. Past myself and Hendrick."

"I know," Dak growled.

"Then what are you doing with her?" King followed him back inside. Hendrick waited there, his phone to his ear.

"Yeah, I'll tell him." Hendrick hung up.

"Tell me what?"

"Cole said he'll be back tonight. He has everything we need for the kidnapping whenever we're done with this job."

Dak wanted him back now, and he wanted Gear in on this too. But he didn't trust Ember not to help Sophie escape on her own. And with the way she sneaked past all of them, she could do the same to Ember.

"You going to answer my question?" King stepped in front of him.

"You think Ember deserves someone like you?"

"Fuck no. But it's me she has. That why you're only telling yourself you're fucking Sophie and will send her on her way when this is all over?"

"I don't fucking know anymore!" Dak's uncharacteristic explosion made Hendrick's eyes widen. He closed his eyes and breathed deep. "This is why I'm letting her go. She's ruined me."

King laughed, not a pleasant laugh. A bitter, hysterical chuckle. "You broke each other. Now you need to fix it before either of you gets killed."

Dak heaved. He needed to kill. He needed to maim. He needed the shadows to calm his soul and put him back in control of everything around him.

"Gear up, Hendrick. And tell Cole to hurry. If he doesn't have it finished in two hours, tell him to call it." King whipped out orders without looking away from Dak. "Lock up. We're out of here."

Hendrick whistled to himself while he moved to the back rooms. King gave Dak one last look and walked back to the front door to lock up.

This business had grown beyond what they started as mere kids. Street thugs that perfected their skills and grew into the most feared men. The air chilled around him. Dak had come so far from what he considered home. For the better, but for the first time, he felt out of his element. Having Sophie brought him out of the comforting shadows.

A crash through the door interrupted the snicking of the

lock, throwing King against the back wall. Dak swung around to see half a dozen men charge inside.

Fuckers. They came at him and came fast. These weren't suits either. They were the upper level security thugs of one particular casino owner. He did more than own the casino. The amount of money sitting in Sophie's account made sense.

Guns appeared, pointing at both King and Dak. They'd locked the door behind them.

"Where is she?"

Dak grinned and tilted his head to look at the gun. "The last time I saw you, I held a knife to your junk until you pissed yourself."

Devon, the former street gun runner, snarled. His arm twitched as if coming to a conclusion. He moved his aim lower to Dak's groin.

"You used to be smart enough to avoid us. What happened?"

"You're not as scary as you think you are." He waved his free hand around the room. "You've gone good." The last dripped with contempt. "Helping people. Thinking you're better than the rest of us."

"Good?" Both Dak and King scoffed at the same time. They both let their evil shine. The monster and the savage that the world feared with every breath took over. Devon's eye twitched before he firmed his grip on his gun.

The six of them had circled Dak and King. Hendrick hadn't returned from the back yet. And none of them were smart enough to go looking through the other rooms.

Maybe Devon had a point. If they were all bold enough to charge in here in broad daylight, then he and King had lost some of their edge. That was going to change. Now.

A round about whistled tune echoed from the back as

the lights went out and flashed back on with bright beams from the corners. Dak and King attacked the men in front of them, and Hendrick charged up from the back with an insane cackle. The six men were still disoriented and shocked by the lights.

One of them shot out the lights in the corners, but not before Dak had disarmed Devon in front of him.

Hendrick had his hands full with two of them. Ember ran up from the back and jumped at the closest one to her, pulling a knife free from her thigh. King's rumble turned to a growl. And the man had the audacity to say Dak was emotional. They both were. They all were when it came to Ember getting hurt, and now that extended to Sophie. Whether she was here or not—his or not.

Ember cried out, following it with a snarl. The sound created an instant reaction from King. His focus didn't change. He punched hard at the guy in front of him before throwing him toward Devon. The two tumbled to the ground together, leaving them both for Dak to deal with.

But before he could dig in, King was beside him with two guns pressed to the heads of the two men on the floor. Dak looked behind him. Ember slumped against the wall, clutching her stomach, and Hendrick dragged away two unconscious thugs.

"You've made more than one enemy here today. Not just your boss. You." King's menace bled from each word. They came in here and hurt King's queen. Their lives were about to end.

Ember whimpered, but it sounded muffled. She was holding in her pain for King.

"Weak." Devon croaked as he kept his eye on King.

Dak laid his hand on King's arm. "Why does he want the woman and not just the money?"

"I'm not telling you shit."

King pressed the barrel harder against his skin. Dak looked around the room. Hendrick came back from securing the two unconscious ones. Two laid injured and bleeding on the floor. And Ember looked pale.

"We already have blood to clean up. Finish them now." Dak made the decision. Ember needed King. They didn't have time for an interrogation. Sophie was safe, and they were going after their boss, anyway.

"He always gets what's his." Devon squeaked out his last words before King pulled both triggers. He didn't waste a second watching the life drain from the two men before turning to his wife.

Blinking, Dak imagined Sophie lying on the floor, clutching her bleeding stomach. His vision turned black and he knew he was fucked.

SOPHIE WATCHED Gear's face turn murderous as he pressed his phone to his ear. She recognized the low, rough rumble, but couldn't make out the words.

"What happened?"

Gear kept driving through traffic with one hand on the wheel. His eyes glanced back in the rearview mirror. Sophie had to work hard not to wince. Something was wrong.

Whatever had happened, it was time for Sophie to make her own decision about Dak. Follow his edict and go with Gear, hide until this was over and then be on her own. The distance would douse Dak's obsession with her as much as it would hers. Or... Choose Dak. Take the risk that he'd crush her and get rid of her when he saw fit. But the choice would be hers. For once, she'd be doing what she wanted and dealing with her own consequences. She'd soak up every single thing Dak and the others taught her and despite being destroyed inside by Dak's eventual rejection, Sophie would come out stronger on the other end.

"Got it." Gear hung up the phone.

"What happened?"

He paused as if he didn't want to tell her, considered keeping her in the dark. "They attacked, looking for you. We know who they are now." His lips settled into a flat line.

"What else?" She felt the horrible news in the air. "Who's hurt?" She hoped it was only a matter of someone hurt and not killed. Hurt held hope.

"Mostly Wayne's guys." Gear pulled in a breath. "And Ember."

No. "We need to go back. How bad?"

"We're not going back. They're taking care of her." He drove through a string of green lights, racing toward the yellow up ahead. "You just ran. Why do you want to go back?"

"I hadn't planned on running. And I shouldn't have."

"No, you shouldn't have."

Sophie closed her eyes and asked a question that would hurt if it was true. And Gear was the one to give the honest answer. "Is this my fault? Because I ran?"

"They were going through that front door whether you ran or not. If you'd been there, they may have gotten you."

"But they might not have hurt Ember."

"Or they still would have. Or someone else. Regrets don't help you."

"I don't want to run anymore. Please. Take me back."

"Who were you running from?" They'd sped through the yellow and stopped at the next red. The busy street had long lights.

"Dak."

"Scared of him, are you?"

"No."

"Sorry, Sophie. We aren't going back."

Then it was up to her to find another way back. To make the best out of the life she'd put herself in. Going back to Dak meant accepting everything he was.

She watched as the cars sped up through the green in the other direction, as if they all sensed the coming change of the light and didn't have enough time in their day to spare a few more minutes. The only doors that would open with Gear allowing it were the front doors. She had precious seconds to time this right.

The lights in the other direction turned yellow. She braced herself. They turned red, and she bolted into the front seat.

"What the fuck are you doing?" Gear growled, his head moving back and forth from her to their light that turned green. His arm banded out across the seats, but Sophie kept struggling past. Cars behind them honked their horns. Short bleeps. Gear hit the gas, but Sophie got past his arm and reached for the door, flipping the lock before pulling on the handle. She didn't care that the car was moving, gaining speed, or that the cars behind them followed closely.

Opening the door, she held her breath.

"Fuck!" Gear slammed on the brakes. "Don't do it, Sophie." He reached for her, getting a grip on her shirt. She kicked back and lunged out of the car. Gear's curses carried out after her and the car horns blaring faded away as the drivers all saw the small woman leap from a vehicle in the middle of an intersection.

It hurt. Her arms and legs ached from the impact with

the pavement. But adrenaline rushed through her, so she ran.

Gear spun the car into the lane next to him and parked along the adjacent street. He was going to chase her on foot. That hadn't worked out so well for her last time.

Damn it.

She remembered what Dak had told her. They'd figured out her pattern. Her destination wasn't a secret to Gear. She'd told him she wanted to go. She just had to get there before he caught her. Or lose him and take a different route.

A strip mall lined the other side of the street. She'd lose him in there. Looking both ways across the street, she moved one foot off the sidewalk when an arm wrapped around her middle. She screamed and kicked.

"Damn it, Sophie. Don't fight me." He wrapped his other arm around her shoulders. He held her the same way he'd attacked her in the gym. Sophie threw her head back to hit his nose. "Nice to see you retained something from that session, but not enough to get away from me."

He turned her around and threw her over his shoulder so fast she was dizzy. People stared as he stalked through the crowd. Some had their phones in their hands, furiously tapping. A couple had them to their ears. He had a tight grip around her legs so she couldn't kick him, but nothing stopped her from beating on his back.

"You're causing a scene."

"Then let me go." Obvious solution if you asked her.

"Not happening."

Frustration boiled hard. She was helpless. Now she wanted to go back for another reason. Just to learn, so she never ended up in this position again.

A tear slipped, and Sophie snarled at it.

"Getting mad won't change anything." Gear reached the

car and reached in behind the back seats before letting her go.

Metal clicked around her ankles. Sophie went wild, pushing up to get leverage, but it was useless. He had control, and she panicked. He was stronger, bigger, and trained. Before she guessed his next move, she was laying down on her stomach on the back seat, her hands behind her back. More metal clicked around her wrists and pulled her feet back.

Sophie only had enough room to flop around, turning her face toward the front. Her hair criss-crossed over her eyes.

"You fucking bastard." Fuming anger heated her skin.

"I'm worse. Don't test me again." Despite the devil in his voice, he brushed her hair back from her face. Shutting her in, he climbed in the driver's side and pulled into traffic.

Her shoulders ached as they drove. Sophie closed her eyes. She'd failed twice. All her failures before had been disappointing, but none as much as this. This was embarrassing. Defeating. She no longer wanted to be this person.

"Shit." Gear's low growl had her snapping her eyes open.

"What?"

"We're being followed." Accusation clipped with each word. This time, it was her fault. No one was following or knew she wasn't at *King Security* until she ran from Gear.

"I'm sorry."

"Be sorry later. Too bad you can't hold on to anything. This is going to be a rough ride." Gear hit the gas hard enough to roll her into the back of the seat. Sophie held in her whimper. She caused this. She'd suffer in silence.

13

———

Hendrick left to light up the remaining guys with a torch to get them to talk. He had a special way with torture. Hot, efficient, brutal.

Dak helped King get Ember to the doctor. A quick exam confirmed the knife didn't hit anything vital. They all avoided the hospitals as much as possible, giving them the necessity to learn certain skills and to make friends with a handful of doctors over the years. They each had their own contacts.

King carried Ember down to the parking garage and sat with her in the back seat. Dak made a call on the way to King's home. The home he'd rebuilt after he came out of retirement and allowed his face to be connected to his name. On the edge of the city with immense security and privacy.

Dak pulled up at the same time as a small blue car. Thane West grew up on the streets alongside Dak and King, but turned his life in a different direction. Except the times he got a call from one of them. Which wasn't often.

Dak opened the back door for King. Holding Ember

tight against his chest, King climbed from the back.

"Stay strong, sweetheart." Dak winked instead of wincing at her pale complexion. Her nose curled at the hated endearment, but she kept her head against her husband.

Thane waited at King's door. "You let your wife get hurt?"

"Fuck off." The king of mercenaries growled and punched in the security code to unlock the door.

Dak would check in with them later. He climbed back behind the wheel and started the car. His hand paused above the gear shift when his phone rang. Gear's number flashed.

"What is it?"

"We're being followed. I'm having trouble shaking them."

"How the fuck did someone find you? They still thought she was at *King's Security* when you were on the road."

Gear only breathed into the speaker.

"What happened?"

"Sophie ran."

Dak closed his eyes to hold his patience. And his pride. It wouldn't have been easy to get away from Gear. "Fuck."

"Yup."

"You can't go to the safehouse. What's your location? I'm on my way."

Gear rattled off their location and where he planned to go from there. Dak wasn't even five minutes away. They hung up and Dak tore out of King's driveway. Single focus took him straight to the two black SUV's travelling identical routes.

He called Gear. "Lead them out of town. Down the old highway and turn right up one of the side roads. Stop after a few turns." Those old roads had little traffic, were crowded in by trees and windy.

"Got it."

The car between them, likely sensing the trap he was now in, tried to hit Gear's bumper. Gear corrected himself and sped up. He turned off and the car between them tried to keep going past. Dak wasn't having that.

Ramming the back corner, Dak turned the SUV ahead of him onto the old single lane side road. *You aren't getting away, you fucking assholes.* No one that threatened Sophie would get away from him. With him or not, he'd always make sure she was safe. He was a fucking mess.

Gear slammed on his brakes and stepped out of the car, gun raised and aimed at the SUV. Dak followed. Three guys wearing the same type of suits as the guys from the airport jumped from the vehicle and started shooting.

Dodging toward the ground, Dak and Gear aimed for their legs. Two of them screeched and their bullets hit the trees. The third took direct aim at Dak before jerking backward. Gear changed his aim from the third to the closest one to him on the ground. Dak towered over the last one struggling to grab his gun he'd dropped. The death of the other echoed back as Dak stepped on the guy's wrist and aimed his gun.

"You work for Wayne?"

The guy swallowed and nodded.

"Good." He shot and stalked toward Gear's car. He didn't see Sophie sitting up in the back seat. At least she was smart enough to keep her head down when bullets were flying.

Opening the back door, shock held him still. He didn't know who to be angry with. Sophie, Gear, or himself. Ankles and wrists cuffed together behind her, she struggled to turn her face around to see who'd opened the door.

Gear looked at him over the top of the car, unapologetic. Dak would have done the same, or worse, in his shoes.

"Learn your lesson, princess?"

She didn't answer him. No steel. No flame in her eyes before they shut to rest against the tops of her cheeks.

Gear rested his forearms against the car and waited, not moving to let her loose.

"Where were you running to this time, Sophie?"

When she still didn't answer or open her eyes, Gear answered for her. "Back to you."

Him? After she'd run *from* him?

"I want to help Ember."

He had to hold in his laugh at her childish denial. He didn't doubt what she'd said was true, but that truth hid the rest of her intentions. For the first time in a long time, Dak didn't know what to do.

Pulling on her knees, he lifted her from the back seat. He held her against him with an arm under her ass.

"Go help Hendrick."

Gear reached into his pocket and pulled out the keys to the cuffs and tossed them over the top of the vehicle. Dak caught them and he carried Sophie to his SUV. Her sharp intake of breath was loud in his ear as they passed the dead bodies.

He settled her in the back seat the same way Gear had. After a lingering look down her body, he shut her in and got behind the wheel. He drove, taking turns he didn't pay attention to. The hum of the car and ping of the gravel beneath the tires helped him think.

Half an hour passed before he stopped the car. Sophie hadn't said a word, and neither had he. Slamming the door, he paced back and forth.

She was his from the moment she walked in and always

would be whether or not she was under his hand or on her own. Sophie belonged to him. Someone would find his weakness and if she wasn't next to him, he'd never know she was in danger and he wouldn't be able to teach her. Dak now understood the misery King had gone through when he'd almost lost Ember.

Reaching into the back seat, he unlocked the cuffs. Clenched teeth held back her whimpers as she moved her shoulders back into place. Dak helped her from the car and stroked her shoulders.

They were safe and he let the feel of her under his palms calm him. He tried to remember all the advice he gave King. Either claim her or whatever was between them would get someone killed. Fully within the fold or gone from it.

"There's no in between, Sophie. You either never want to see me again or you're mine forever."

Her eyes widened up at him.

"Which is it?"

"ARE YOU KIDDING ME?" Sophie tried to push him away from her, but her arms were still too weak. The muscles gave way with the pressure. Dak countered her move and pressed his body along hers. She had to tilt her head back to meet his gaze.

"I'm not. Which is it, Sophie?"

"What? No more, *you don't go anywhere until I'm finished*?" Sophie dropped her voice, mocking his demands. "Now I have a choice? You won't bulldoze this one, too?"

"No. It's all or nothing."

"It wasn't all or nothing a few hours ago. It wasn't all or nothing when I asked you to send me to a safehouse days ago. It wasn't all or nothing when you fucked me and made sure I understood it was all your choice." Sophie squirmed her way out from between him and the SUV, surprised he let her go. She wasn't under any illusions that if he didn't allow her to move from where he'd trapped her, she wouldn't.

"You had a choice that first night. You let me own your body." His arm in front of her stomach stopped her progress away from him.

"Things changed." He made her feel too much. She discovered more than a new world.

Dak pushed her face up with his knuckle under her chin. Glazed, dark eyes bore into her. "Yeah, you got scared."

"Didn't you? Why did you send me away?" The assumption was a leap. This man feared nothing. But confidence let a smug smile slip. According to Ember, he didn't act the way he did with her.

"Why did you run?" He tried to grip her chin harder, but she lifted her head and pushed past him. She screeched a frustrated garble and threw her arms into the air. They were getting nowhere.

Sophie hadn't intended to run. She'd only wanted a little distance. Some peace to sort through her thoughts. So why did she run? Because overhearing King and Hendrick, she believed he was done with her and it was safer if she wasn't around. She'd been right. The moment he caught her, he sent her away.

"Why did you run from me, princess?" His voice dropped, sexy and crooning, begging for an answer.

"You were finished with me. Why shouldn't I leave? At least on my own, I'd finally be my own person." Sophie let her honesty out, hoping it would inspire his.

"Why did you think I was finished with you?" His voice,

like his eyes, covered her body. Familiar flames ignited along her skin.

"You were getting rid of me."

He was quick to mask the surprise on his face, but Sophie was watching him as closely as he watched her.

"I overheard King and Hendrick." She answered before he could ask. "Your turn. Why did you send me away?"

Harsh steps hit the gravel. Sophie refused to back down. "Someone threatened what was mine." Dak ran a finger down her cheek, along her jaw. The trail heated down her neck and across her chest. "I want you safe while I go after the bastards instead of waiting for them to make their move."

"All or nothing? And if I choose nothing?"

"Then I will never see you again."

He expected her to believe that when he'd made declarations of possession so strong they made her heart thump harder?

"If you choose all, you're mine. There's no going back. You'll train like Ember every day and you'll be under me with my cock buried in your body every night."

"No." She shook her head even as her core throbbed from his promise.

"No?" His jaw clenched. "No to all, or no to nothing?"

"No to both."

"Not one of your choices, princess."

"Then it isn't my choice." Sophie stepped away from him. It would be up to him to do as he wished then.

"What do you want?" Flared nostrils pulled in a hard breath.

"I want to be my own person." She felt more like herself and like a whole new person all at once since she ran from

Alan. Dak did that for her. But he held too much power. "And I want to train."

"You are your own person. I'd never bend that steel in you." Awe slipped through his tone. He admired her, settling hope and warmth in her chest.

"I don't think I can survive you, Dak. You're too intense. But I want what you and all of *King's Mercenaries* can teach me."

He reached for her, air sawing in and out of his lungs. Sophie moved to the side, away from him and the SUV.

"You can't touch me."

"Why is that, princess?" Oh, he knew.

"I'll change my mind, but it won't be fair." Her mind would cloud and she'd choose something she's unsure of.

"I don't play fair."

"I know." She waited. Would he play fair this once to get what he wanted?

"Get in the car, pr... Sophie." It wasn't the first time he'd used her name instead of princess, but it didn't hold the same sensual heat and possession. It was cold and sharp. Painful.

"Where are we going?" She wouldn't move until he told her.

"You're getting what you want." His face had closed down as he opened the driver's door and got in. He didn't start the engine until Sophie walked around to the other side and got in the passenger seat. Not the back seat.

Tension filled the drive and every ounce of it radiated from Dak. This was for the best. Sophie just had to repeat that to herself over and over until she believed it. Until she came out on the other side stronger than ever before.

Veering off on the outskirts, he turned up a long, secluded driveway.

"Where are we going?" Sophie scanned everything in front of them.

"King's. Checking on Ember." His short answers carried a heavy frustration. But that was something he'd have to deal with. And so would she, when he took it out on her.

"Oh. Good." Her fingers shook before she closed them into a fist and hid her hand between her leg and the door. With the reminder of Ember getting hurt and the threat of Dak not playing fair, Sophie's confidence hadn't lasted.

Dak parked and waited while Sophie climbed from the car, taking in the cabin-looking home. Dak caught up to her and punched in the security code to unlock the door and held the door open for her. She stepped through. The house had the same dark feel as Dak's apartment, but with a woodsy, comforting atmosphere. Until the man who owned it stepped out of the hall at the back side of the house.

"What's she doing back here?"

"Nice to see you again, too." Sophie muttered under her breath.

"New deal." Dak didn't elaborate. "How's Ember?"

"Resting. She'll be fine." King's eyes crinkled. The man was worried about his wife. They'd all made their true selves known to her, so Sophie had a hard time wondering how King wasn't tearing through the people responsible for hurting his wife. Worry may be clear in his features, but so was his rage.

"Can I see her?" Sophie looked King in the eye. King glared, letting the force of his power down on her. She wondered if he blamed her for Ember getting hurt. Sophie reminded herself of what Gear said. They would have gotten in there and attacked, no matter what.

King nodded, leading her down the hall and opened a

door for her. Sophie stepped in and King let the door shut, closing her in the dim bedroom.

"Sophie?" Ember's voice was a whisper from the bed.

"Hey. How are you?" Sophie made her way across the room and settled herself on the foot of the bed. Far enough away she wouldn't hurt the other woman.

"Better now. The doctor gave me the good stuff." Her smile was loopy.

"What happened? Where are you hurt?"

"They didn't tell you? Flesh wound." Ember deepened her voice and tightened her chin with a cock to her head, mocking a macho man. Sophie let herself giggle. Ember did too, but winced and got herself under control. "Knife." She laid her hand over the left side of her stomach. "Nothing vital. I'll be fine."

Sophie hoped she held in her reaction, her fear. This was what she signed up for, wasn't it?

"Hurt like a son of a bitch."

"I'm sorry."

"What for?" Ember tilted her chin down to look straight at Sophie.

"Maybe it all would have happened differently if I hadn't run." Gear was right. It would have been different, but that didn't mean someone wouldn't have gotten hurt because of her. It was her they wanted.

Ember grinned. "You did what you needed to do. I don't blame you."

"I ran from Gear, too." Embarrassment filled her again. She'd failed and set a tail on them.

"You got away from Gear?" Her glazed eyes widened.

"For a little bit."

"Damn. Way to go, girl. So, you're back with Dak now?"

"Not exactly. I'm not with him." And how long would

that last? Sophie wasn't sure how strong she could be when he stopped playing fair. "But I want to train."

"He agreed to that?"

"Yes. Not willingly."

"In a few weeks, I'll be back there beside you. Give them all hell for me in the meantime." Ember's eyes drifted closed. She fought them open, but Sophie stayed silent to let her body do what it needed to.

The door opened, startling Ember awake. King and Dak came in.

"Good painkillers, sweetheart?" Dak stopped beside the bed, keeping his distance from Sophie.

Ember nodded softly.

"Time to sleep, little girl." King rested his hand on his wife's head.

"I don't want to." Ember sighed and tilted her head toward King.

"Too bad."

"We'll go." Dak met her direct gaze for the first time since he agreed to bring her back. Dak leaned down to speak low in her ear. "Ready to change your mind?"

"No." Her voice trembled, and she made no effort to hide her reaction.

"You're scared." No question.

"Of course I am." It would be foolish not to be. But she trusted him enough to let him see her fear. And teach her how to hide it in front of others.

DAK PREPARED himself to live in agony as they drove back into the city. Maybe her choice was for the best. He'd be putting himself through everything King was going through right now. Dak didn't understand how the other man wasn't tearing down the entire organization with his bare hands. Sophie hadn't gotten hurt, only threatened, and Dak was ready to rip out their throats. But she wasn't his to protect anymore. He suppressed his growl.

Sophie never stopped surprising him. She owned her fear and still walked with him back into *King Security*. No one was in the main lobby scrubbing away the last half of the blood.

Dak watched Sophie. She paled at the sight, but kept walking past. Her breathing turned shallow. It wasn't his job to worry about how she felt. She'd asked him to train her. He wouldn't coddle anyone else at the sight of blood.

He stepped past her and led her to the elevators. She took deep breaths in through her nose once the solid doors slid closed. He wanted to hold her. Stroke her back until the urge to vomit passed. Her expression was one he recognized well. Parted lips to breathe, eyes that wouldn't close or remain open. But still, he kept his hands to himself. For now.

To train her, he'd have to touch her and he couldn't wait to get his hands on her.

Opening the door to the spare apartment, he held it, but didn't enter the space. Sophie walked past him.

"Use the hidden door to go into my apartment and get anything of yours that is in there. Move everything back into here. This place is yours until you decide otherwise." Until she decided to stay with him. He'd get his *all*. If he was patient enough.

"Then what do I do?"

"You wait. Get some rest. You're going to need it."

"We're back to this?"

"No. I have to help with torturing and clean up. You're

waiting here because you can't handle that yet. You'll train. I mean it when I say you're going to need your rest." Dak wouldn't hide anything from her anymore. He shut the door, closing himself off from her.

In the lobby, he picked up where the others had left off with cleaning. They needed the evidence gone sooner rather than later. The torture was ongoing or already over. He'd find out what he needed soon enough.

Thirty minutes passed with Dak letting his mind sit blank with the mundane task. Hendrick walked in, wiping his hands on a towel that he tossed over his shoulder when he finished.

"Get all the information?"

"Oh yeah. And I had a little fun." Hendrick popped his neck from side to side. Picking up another mop, Hendrick joined Dak. "Gear is sitting with them now."

"And?" Dak wanted Wayne's location so he could get rid of him.

"Wayne has been working hard to build his little empire. Stays in his own lane. But has plenty of men to do his dirty work for him. Then he has ones that owe him a debt work it off. That was what Morgan was doing with all that money."

Dak had figured as much.

"Lots of guys like the ones that showed up at the airport and like the thugs that stormed in here. He's not looking for revenge with Sophie over stealing his money."

Dak paused and turned on Hendrick. "Why the hell does he want her?"

Hendrick paused in his mopping to meet Dak's gaze. "She was part of Morgan's payment. For Wayne himself." An animalistic rage thrummed in his wild eyes.

"Where. Is. He?" Dak ground each word out through furious fire. His anger hurt as it released from his pores.

"Not here. He moves from vacation house to vacation house and only shows up if needed. Like when dealing with Morgan and calling you. He disappeared right after that."

"Get R…"

"Already called Roen. He's on it." Hendrick continued to clean.

"He needs to work faster."

"He's already the fastest there is."

"I know." Dak took out his anger on the blood staining his business, his home.

"Where's Sophie?"

"Upstairs." Locked away. The safest she'd been since coming to him for help.

"Good for you."

"It's not like that." The rest of them had to know that she didn't intend to stay.

"Oh?" Hendrick tilted his head, turning his attention to Dak instead of what he was doing to the floor.

"She's only here to train." It grated to say that, to admit she wasn't his. Yet.

"So she's fair game?" Interest echoed in the crazy man's murmur.

Dak had Hendrick against the wall in the flash of a bullet. "Keep your cock and mouth to yourself."

He expected the grin, but knowing he'd fallen into Hendrick's trap didn't help Dak's mood.

"You fucker."

"Just keeping it real, boss." Hendrick shoved Dak off him. "So we train her the same way we train Ember?"

"Yes." And it would hurt to watch and hurt him to do, but in the end Sophie would become deadly. Whether that was how she used her new skills didn't matter. She would be safe.

14

———

Sophie had let herself into Dak's apartment to get her change of clothes she'd left there. What little she ran with hadn't left her apartment. She didn't linger, knowing Dak could see whatever she did in there.

Nerves tingled through her system. She'd struck a deal with a savage. He wasn't sending her away, and they weren't together. He wouldn't lay a hand on her. Sophie didn't doubt for a second that he would stop playing fair the moment it suited him.

She lay on top of the covers in bed taking deep, steady, calming breaths, trying to take his demands to heart. That she'd need rest before he came for her again. At least she had control now.

She scoffed at the thought. Only a fool would think Dak didn't have control.

Only time would tell what came of her life after this, but no matter what, Sophie would step into it prepared.

Something tapped against wood. Sophie lifted her head off the pillow. She frowned and stopped breathing as if that would help her hear better. Another steady tap, harder this time. Someone knocked on her door.

Shock kept her on the bed longer than it should have. Why wouldn't Dak just let himself in? The knocking increased as she made her way to the door. Sophie tried to tell herself that it wasn't disappointment creeping down her spine at the sight of Gear on the other side of the door and not Dak. But she admitted a bit of fear since running from Gear.

Pulling her shoulders back, she opened the door. He thrust a bag at her without a word and only a glare. Sophie looked in the bag. Clothes.

"Something more appropriate for training." Gear, with an anticipatory glint in his eye, was more terrifying than the day Dak took her to the gym and asked if she feared each of them. He stepped through the door, forcing her to move back. "Get changed. We start now."

Sophie didn't bother answering him. She'd asked for this. Slipping back into the bedroom, she changed into one of the four outfits from the bag. All spandex shorts or capris and sports bras. She clasped her hand around her exposed middle. One piece swimsuits and full length shirts were her wardrobe of choice. And that had nothing to do with having an abusive husband.

"Sophie," Gear snapped from outside her bedroom door.

"Tying my shoes." With a sigh, she slipped on the sneakers. Gear opened the bedroom door, taking all of her in with a long look. "One more thing." She looked through the bag of clothes from Hendrick that first morning. A soft, plain T-shirt sat on top of the pile. Perfect. She slipped that over her head and turned to face Gear. "I'm ready."

He waved his arm out of the bedroom and she moved

ahead of him and out of her apartment with her head held high.

Misery lay ahead, but she'd be better off for it in the end.

They took the elevator down to the main level. The smell of cleaner filled the space, strong enough to make her eyes water. An obvious sign, but she assumed this wasn't their first rodeo and they knew what they were doing.

Dim light covered the gym, but enough that she saw all the equipment. And the wide empty sparring mat in the centre.

"Do you workout regularly?" Gear stopped beside her as she continued to take in the gym with new eyes. New expectations.

"No. I couldn't."

"Right. Then that's where we'll have to start." Gear had her warm up on the treadmill, keeping control of her speed. He swatted her hand away every time she tried to adjust it herself. Twenty minutes passed before he made her get off and stretch before going back on and making her run hard.

Her chest hurt from heaving, but Gear gave her no mercy. When he allowed her some relief, he threw a bottle of water at her. She fumbled to catch it, rolling it in the air before it hit the floor. Her face heated, and she closed her eyes, giving herself a moment. And that was when she felt him.

Someone else was in the room. Watching her. Dak. That dark heat was unmistakable. Sophie snapped her eyes open and turned her head, pinning her gaze to a specific corner of shadows. When he didn't make himself known, she turned back to Gear standing next to the weights.

He was patient when teaching her the proper way to use them and what muscles each exercise worked. Dak's presence weighed on her. She wished it would make her work harder, but her nerves still vibrated from shock.

By the time they finished with the weights, Sophie trembled with weak muscles. But Gear still led her to the mat. They'd been down here for over an hour and it seemed they weren't even half done.

Gear started with a list of all the things she'd done wrong the last time. And not just with words, but with examples that landed her hard on her ass with each lesson.

"And last." Gear crowded her space. The scent of their sweat mixed and twisted with the leather of the equipment. "When you ran from me. You're so focused on everyone who's in this room right now, you need that focus when outside of this room." He'd seen her watching the shadows. "I was barely out of reach as soon as I gave chase. You stopped to cross the road."

As if Sophie needed something else to make her feel like a bigger failure.

"You didn't know I was that close, did you?" His tone demanded an answer, and she had no reason or pride left not to.

"No."

"I hear you're good at sneaking past people. Use that."

Sophie waited for his next move, but it never came.

"Go home. Go shower. We're done." He left her personal space, moving to the side rather than leaving the gym.

She had to force her stare to the door rather than back to the shadows, as if she could see Dak and what he was thinking.

Mistake or not, Sophie committed herself to her decision. She belonged here. For now.

A week. A fucking week of not touching or speaking to Sophie. But he watched. And a fucking week of never catching up with Wayne. They found him, but never had enough time to get to him before he moved. He only had so many vacation homes. He'd come back for Sophie. Roen was watching for any patterns in his movement. And they'd recruited spies inside his casinos. They'd get him soon. Patience.

Cole had returned after the attack He'd joined in Sophie's training. She'd discovered only a taste of how deadly the cheery boy scout looker could be.

She'd sparred with Hendrick's crazy, faced Gear's wrath, felt shock from Cole's discipline, and even kept her chin high when squaring off with King.

And every time, she found him in the shadows. She never saw him, but knew he was there. Dak watched her fail day after day—watched her motivation drain with each session.

Dak slid himself into the corner of the gym once again. Sophie worked with Hendrick and Cole on the centre mat. Words stopped. They no longer taught and corrected. They took turns attacking and landing her on the mat in a hold. It was up to her to take what she'd learned from the week to get herself out of it.

Almost an hour passed with no results. Sophie was dejected. Something was missing inside her. Dak could bring it out, but he didn't want to. She needed it without him.

Hendrick and Cole sensed it, too.

"You aren't cut out for this." Cole growled as he swept her feet out from under her. Sophie hit the mat hard. Her eyes squeezed tight as she dragged a harsh breath into her lungs.

Come on, princess. Take the bait.

"I thought you were going to be more of a challenge." Hendrick's disappointment held clear disgust.

"Sorry to disappoint you both." Sophie took her time getting up from the floor, her gaze on the mat. Hendrick shook his head, unseeing to her, and flipped her on her back, pinning her in place with a leg around her throat and her arm hyper-extended between his legs.

"Get out of it." Hendrick ground the command through his teeth.

Tears crowded the corners of Sophie's eyes. Dak hated Hendrick in that moment with all of his being, but he stayed hidden.

"I can't." She gasped.

Cole crouched on her other side. "Then what do you think is going to happen to you?"

"I don't need to think. You've all made it clear in exacting detail the possibilities." Sophie snarled through her tears. They'd been brutally honest in the horrors she'd face if ever caught. The images haunted Dak every night as he went to bed in the apartment next to hers.

At an impasse, Hendrick lifted his leg off her neck. And she surprised them all. Rearing up, Sophie slammed her forehead into Cole's nose, then rolled toward her extended arm. Her fist slammed into Hendrick's thigh to loosen his hold, and she quickly reached for a second punch to his groin. She wiggled her way out from under his other leg, but Cole was ready when she got to her feet.

Sophie didn't wait for him to attack this time. Ducking around him, she kicked him in the back of the knee. She should have landed another blow to each of them, but she swiped at her eyes and backed away toward the door.

"Fuck you, both." Then she turned to the shadows. "And

fuck you." They'd pushed her too far. But Hendrick and Cole wore matching grins as she ran from the gym.

"Finally." Cole crowed and pushed himself up. "I didn't think she'd ever break."

"She could have snapped without going for the balls." Hendrick groaned, but still held a proud smile.

Dak didn't agree. Her dejected fear hadn't been the goal. Piss her off and make her realize her worth had been the outcome Dak wanted. He stepped from the shadows.

"You don't look happy." Cole nudged his shoulder. "She did good."

Dak didn't answer.

"She's not coming back stronger." Hendrick filled in the blanks. "I'm not sure we can train her the same way we would anyone else. Or the way we did Ember."

The two women hadn't had the same experiences from life. They didn't view this in the same light. Ember didn't trust anyone anymore. Sophie only wanted to defend herself. Against most people, she could. But not against the people who were after her.

"Give her a break for a few days. It's my turn."

A WEEK PASSED of getting ready for the gym every day with no one showing up to get her. A couple times she made her way downstairs and found no one waiting for her. They'd given up on her and could she blame them? Sophie didn't expect extreme results in such a short time, but some improvement, some skill and understanding would have been nice. Something to give herself motivation and a reason to continue.

Yet she still dressed for the gym and waited. If they came for her, she would be ready. Replaying her last words and actions in the gym didn't give her any hope. What she didn't understand was if they weren't going to train her, why was she still here?

Lifting her chin and her heavy shoulders, Sophie dressed into the clean gym clothes, once again covering herself with a T-shirt. They'd tried to tell her to get rid of it those first few days, explaining the baggy fabric only gave her a disadvantage.

Ready to go, she sat on her bed.

She hadn't seen Dak since he brought her back. But his presence weighed on her every day. He kept himself out of sight, but his gaze had been unmistakable. It only made her humiliation of failing worse. He likely watched to give himself a reason to send her away again. They hadn't expanded on their deal. She didn't know what would happen if she failed in her training.

Her head hung to her knees. But a hard knock on the door made her jump up. One controlled breath later, she made her way to open the door. Gear stood on the other side.

"Be in the gym in five minutes." He turned away and left. Sophie shut the door and pinched the inside corners of her eyes to hold back that single tear of relief. It was too soon to be happy about it. Somewhere deep inside her, she still wanted this. She still wanted to be strong enough to survive, strong enough to defend herself, no matter what.

Do better was her only option.

She tied up her sneakers and made her way down to the

gym. The building was eerily quiet. No one in the front lobby or the back rooms.

The gym was dimmer than usual, but the figure in the shadows wasn't hiding this time. A black T-shirt hugged every ridge over Dak's torso. Cargo pants hung on his hips, not at all able to hide his long, muscular legs. The man was death with blond hair.

Sophie's stomach dropped. A hollow thunk echoed through her body. Her skin tingled at the sight of him. She still wanted him, craved him and his touch. But this was the end of the line. The brief excitement thinking that she could still do this, vanished.

Lifting her chin, she prepared herself for whatever he had to say. What she wasn't sure she could handle was begging for another chance. There were other ways to learn to defend herself. If he sent her away, she'd start martial arts. It would miss a certain element she'd get from the mercenaries, but some day Sophie would more than hold her own. Even against someone like Dak. The element of surprise would forever be her friend.

"Warm up and stretch." His deep voice cut through the eerie silence. It was like a shock and a balm to her system. Like jumping into a lake in the evening. The surface of the water cold against her skin, but the bottom near the sand was warm as she waded further in.

Moving became difficult. It took her a few minutes to process the fact Dak wasn't sending her away, but was the one to train with her.

"Now, Sophie." He crossed his arms over his chest, patience leaching from his stance. Her feet put her in motion. One step, two steps. Left, right. It was all she allowed herself to focus on, so she didn't think about how she'd react once Dak touched her. Because he would. He'd have to.

Dak worked the weights while she worked on the bicycle. Harsh breathing sawed through his nose. In, out. Another two-step focus train to keep her thoughts from wandering. But the problem was, this one made her sweat in a way she only did in her dreams now.

Sophie may have chosen nothing from him, but it didn't stop her from wanting him. She just didn't trust herself not to fall into his darkness and build a home for herself.

"Time's up." Dak let down the weights and stood. Sophie slowed the machine and came to a stop before getting off and sipping at some water.

He waited for her in the centre of the mats while she stretched. Nerves made it hard to swallow, but she pushed herself forward. He hadn't sent her away yet. This may be her ultimate test, her chance to prove what she was capable of.

"Lose the shirt."

"No." She didn't need to hide her body from him, but she wanted to.

"Fine." He attacked faster than any of the others, spinning her and gripping her shirt mid-circle. Pulling upward, he had it past her head and her wrists wrapped tightly in the fabric in front of her. "First way to avoid that is to not wear baggy clothes. Second is to prevent someone from getting it past your shoulders. I'll show you that after. Right now, you need to get your hands free."

Her brows furrowed. He was teaching her. The others had done similar but broke nothing down into steps or options. They taught a specific move or one way to get out of a hold, then expected her to remember it and repeat it.

"Twist your wrists. Clothing isn't often strong enough to hold someone for long if they're quick."

Sophie twisted her wrists so her hands faced the opposite direction. The fabric stretched to give her room to move. Dak didn't attack. He gave her the time she needed to get out of it.

"Good." He pulled off his shirt and slipped it over her head. Her mouth went dry as she took in a sight only her memory had given her. And her memory had missed a few delicious details. "This time, don't let me get it past your shoulders." His tone held a warning, and she snapped her eyes back up to his.

Using a move for a different attack from Hendrick, Sophie made fists and crossed her arms in an x downward over one of Dak's. He still spun her and made her dizzy, but he couldn't pull the shirt up.

He hummed with approval as his head passed close to her ear. She did something right.

Dak spun her away from him and let her go. Catching her balance, she landed facing him and ready for another attack. The others never gave her a break. Sophie didn't expect Dak to be any different.

His lips twitched, and he nodded. "Do it again."

Dak made the same attack several more times, but never quite the same way. She had to focus on predicting which way he'd come at her next. But with every pass, his chest rubbed against her. His hands brushed her hips, her arms, her neck. It was as much torture as she'd imagined, and yet he never gave her time to soak in the touch she missed so much.

With the fifth round, she missed his arm, and he got the shirt up past her shoulders. Panicking, Sophie dropped and rolled backward. The shirt hung from his hands and off her.

Leaping to her feet, Sophie sucked in her breath at the melting, black ice in his eyes.

Pride. "Good girl, princess."

Those words had driven her to touch herself, staring at the vanity while in the shower. She shivered.

Dak passed her the shirt. "Don't get out of it this time."

She slipped it on. Dak didn't come at her fast. He ambled the few feet between them. His fingers grazed her torso while he lifted the shirt. Eyes bored into hers before the fabric hid her view. Running his palms up her arms, he wrapped the shirt around her wrists, tightening it more than he had before. The heat blazing through her veins was why she didn't want his touch. It hurt and felt amazing. His touch always made her choice for her, rather than her deciding the next step on her new path.

"Get out of it." He stepped back and crossed his arms. Waiting. Watching. Sophie struggled, attempting the same thing she had before. It worked, but it was harder and took her longer.

Dak grabbed the shirt from the floor and her wrists. He wrapped them. "Again."

Three more times, and each one more difficult than the last. But with each, the space between them warmed, until he tossed the shirt to the side and wrapped his hand around her throat. She froze and his breath heated her cheek as he spoke.

"Next lesson. Don't let the enemy get this close to you."

15

─────────

D ak wouldn't have gotten this close if she didn't still feel something for him. None of the others got close enough to her to cut off her air.

Squeezing to emphasize the threat was harder than he expected. Make himself out to be the enemy without making her hate him. Her blue orbs widened as she realized what she'd done.

He took a different approach. He stayed the way he was and waited for her to figure out what to do. And they'd repeat the exercise until it became easy and automatic. With time, every move she made to defend herself would become second nature.

Her pulse raced beneath his fingers. Struggling to keep her alive and fighting the attraction filling her. The matching reaction to his body.

"Come on, Sophie. You can do this."

"How can you say that?" His grip wasn't tight enough to strain her voice, only enough to show her the danger. "You watched me. You saw what I can and can't do." Her hands grasped the back of his.

"Yes, I did watch you. But you didn't see what you can do." Dak rested his free hand on her hip. "I did. So did the others."

"Right. That's why they tore me apart the last time I was in here."

"They were trying to piss you off."

"It worked."

"Yes, but it also took you to your lowest point." That hadn't been what she'd needed. "So I'm doing something different. I'm waiting. What are you going to do, pr... Sophie?" He'd let princess slip already, and he saw what it did to her. The flare of heat under her skin had made his cock throb. She'd be his princess again. But for now, he had to give her what she needed to be on her own. Not because she'd ever be on her own again, but only carry the knowledge that she didn't need him like he needed her.

"Dak?" Neither of them knew what she was asking for. Tension grew. Heat sizzled. She needed to make a move fast before he caved to his own desires and broke his end of the bargain.

"Do it."

She let go of his wrist and her hands came together, one clasping a fist in front of her face. One swift motion brought them up and then down in the crook of his elbow. The small increase in her strength was noticeable, bending his arm more than he expected. While keeping the pressure on his arm, the other reared back and aimed for his throat.

Dak moved out of the way, letting her go. *That's my girl.* Dak kept the words to himself. He charged at her again. She struggled, but he still got a hold of her throat. She stilled, and so did he. With a nod from him, she repeated the move, faster this time. He wasn't as quick to get out of the way from the strike for his throat.

Faster and faster, he kept coming at her until she moved as fast as him, striking him in the throat.

"Good." He growled his praise and shook off the pain. "Next."

Sophie was already tired, but she stood ready. Dak repeated the process for every hold he put her in, giving her time to figure it out and then repeat it until she got it. And with every brush of their bodies, desire erupted through him as harsh as the most dangerous rage.

Damn, he was proud of her. She'd learned more than she realized working with the others, using moves they'd all taught her and surprising him with variations of her own.

"Do you see what you can do now?" They stood apart from each other, catching their breath.

"You let me do all that. You waited for me to figure it out."

"Yes. And I can see I have to prove it to you. This time I'm not waiting." Dak dropped his chin and attacked. Not in the same order as the lessons. Sophie panicked and stepped back. He tsked and came at her harder. "What happens to your body when I touch you, Sophie?" Dak grabbed her and slammed her back against his chest. He stroked his hand down over her breasts. He reached the waist of her pants before she came out of the spell his touch put her under and snapped back at him.

"The same thing that happens to yours." She slammed her head back against his chin and brought her elbow to his ribs at the same time.

That's it. Come at me, princess. Dak didn't wait to attack again and with every attack, he let a hand touch her with passion. Her ass, her bare skin, his thumb circling her pulse at her throat. And with each one, she came at him harder and broke from every hold until he trapped her with one he hadn't worked on that day.

She wasn't quick enough. Dak had her pinned beneath him on the mat. Her hands were under his and above her head. His legs pinned her feet down. And his hips thrust once against hers.

Sophie gasped and Dak stopped himself from drinking it in.

"Now, do you believe me?"

"Maybe."

Stubborn woman. "I'll give you to the count of twenty to figure a way out of this one before I kiss you."

"You can't."

"I can. And I will. You'll keep training until there is a day you don't need me or anyone else. You won't stay with me because you need me. You'll stay because of what happens when I do this." He moved his body against hers. His hands tightened. Her breasts pressed harder against his chest.

"I want to live alone for once."

"You don't know what you want. You only think you want that." What a high-handed asshole to make that assumption for her. But he believed he was right.

Sophie snarled.

"I'm counting, princess." He didn't care that he let the name slip.

She went wild beneath him, getting nowhere except to rub herself against him more, increasing both of their torture.

"Fifteen."

Frozen, her eyes darted everywhere, searching for an idea.

"Ten."

She bent her knees, trying to pull her legs free. Dak pressed more of his weight on her.

"Five."

Lifting her head, she reached for his, but she didn't have enough room to give a hard hit.

"Two."

"Dak? I won't survive."

"One." His tone softened. "You will. I won't allow anything else." He took her mouth. Opening her to him and plunging deep with all the pent up tension from the past two weeks. Her taste filled him. Soothing him in a way nothing else ever had. The savage in his heart melted with a grin stuck on his face.

When she surrendered beneath him, he released her hands and ran his down her sides.

"It's all, princess. I get all of you." He slipped his hand under the waist of her pants. "And you get all of me." Something he gave no one.

THE PROMISES that poured from Dak did something to Sophie's heart. As did his hands. What was she so afraid of? What is it about a life with Dak that made her want to run? The lack of independence? That was an excuse. He gave her a place to stay and did what she asked. Until she'd snapped and given up on herself. Then he stepped in and wouldn't allow her to.

His veins were filled with a savage life and he poured it into her with every kiss. With every stroke of his tongue. But if this was going to be her life, she needed to make one thing clear.

Pushing against his chest, he gave her only an inch to say what she needed.

"You won't control me."

"Not in the way you're implying. I'd never dream of it. To keep you safe, yes." The harsh lines around his eyes lifted. "To force your body into pleasure all for me, definitely."

Sophie shivered. His rough fingers thrummed her clit, and he slid his other hand beneath her head to grip the back of her neck.

"Know your worth, princess. Anything I consider mine is priceless." He nipped her bottom lip. He rubbed up and down her clit, occasionally reaching lower toward her entrance, making Sophie gasp. Frozen with harsh breaths, waiting for more. But clothing still separated them.

"I don't know if I'm cut out to be yours. I'm trying." And that was the underlying reason she wanted to train. To be worthy of Dak. Worthy of this life. But the past couple of weeks had shown her she'd bitten off more than she could chew.

"You are." He pressed her to the mat with his hips. "When I first pinned you to the wall and lifted your shirt. Anyone who could walk around with that bruise, anyone who could run the way you did, was made for me. I won't let you fail, princess. Never." *I won't let you fail.* The vow from his lips was fierce. The force of him was too strong for Sophie to fight.

"Okay."

Dak paused, searching her face. A sinful grin appeared. And she realized she still could have stopped all of this if that had been what she'd wanted. He wasn't playing fair anymore, but he wouldn't have forced her to be his.

He lifted off her and pulled her up. Pulling at the sports

bra, he growled while trying to lift it over her breasts. "Fucking tight clothes."

"Too loose. Too tight. There's no pleasing you." Sophie teased while running her fingers over his abdomen. She traced each ridge and had the urge to lean forward to lick them to see if they all tasted the same. Now that she accepted this new fate, Sophie was ready to jump into the fire and get burned.

"Careful, princess." His warning was playful, despite the growl that still rumbled in his chest.

"Or what?" The challenge slipped. But she didn't want to take it back. He promised she was cut out to be his. But now she needed to prove it to herself.

"There are plenty of ways to torture someone." He got her bra off over her head and peeled her pants down her legs. Before standing straight again, he wrapped an arm around her thighs and lifted. Her breasts were level with his mouth. Pulling a nipple into his mouth, he suckled strong enough to steal her breath while he walked to one of the weight benches.

Releasing her, she slid to the floor. Dak gripped her chin and lifted her face to his. The moment between them stretched. Her tongue darted out to lick her lips, enticing a hum from his throat. Bending his head, he trapped her tongue between his teeth with the harsh beginnings of a devastating kiss. His tongue touched hers before running the same path over her lips. Firm pressure molded her against him. So much was unsaid in that touch.

Dak lifted his head with one last look before spinning her around. A large hand between her shoulders pushed her down. Her hips bent at the leg bar. She gripped the bench as only her toes touched the ground.

Probing fingers played and stretched while the

fabric of his pants rustled behind her. Sophie whimpered, knowing what was coming next. Dak settled his hands on her ass and opened her to him. She closed her eyes and waited. The seconds stretched into minutes.

After a few quick, short thrusts, Dak filled her. Sophie cried out. The sensation a sweet, painful bliss. He pressed her against the bar, holding her in place.

Sophie let herself focus on every drag of him in and out of her. Her body tightened with anticipation, knowing what he could do to her.

"Fucking perfect, princess." He sounded possessed. One hand released her hip and reached around to pinch her clit. "Don't come yet."

What? How the fuck did he expect her to do that?

His deep chuckle vibrated through her as he worked her clit in the way guaranteed to make her come.

Sophie tried holding it back. Pleasure throbbed, tapping the peak. Suddenly cold and empty, Sophie had to catch her breath. Dak had torn himself from her. Her core clenched, begging. But she refused to verbalize her need.

Gasping, she waited.

His hand on her hip was her only warning as he took her again and reached for her clit. The peak grew, expanded closer to her reach.

"Don't."

Sophie tried. But again, he played her to his own tune, forcing the orgasm forward. And again, he tore away from her at the first clench of her core.

"Poor princess."

This time, she let the whimper free.

"I told you there were plenty of ways to torture someone. Let's do it again." He reached for her clit before thrusting into her. This time, he moved slow. Harsh and measured. Sharp sensations clawed toward her climax.

"Please." She begged. She finally begged.

"No." Dak pulled away.

"Please. I'm yours. I'm here. I'll take it all."

"Such sweet words." He petted her. Over her ass, between her legs. He eased the ache, but never took it away. "This time, you can come."

Dak pushed his way into her body. With the right angle and the right stroke on her clit, Dak brought her to her climax. The pleasure was heavy and filled with promise. Promises from him and promises for the future.

"Come, princess."

Her body exploded. Fireworks shot through her veins with every contraction of her core. Dak roared behind her and slammed himself to the hilt. Warmth seeped inside her.

"Forever mine."

Sophie closed her eyes on the twin tears falling. Forever was a long time. And forever was what she craved.

***

DAK CARRIED A LIMP SOPHIE UPSTAIRS, leaving their clothes discarded on the gym mats. She rested against his chest, unaware of the raised brows they received as they passed the others. Their nudity didn't bother Dak. He thought hers might the way she'd tried to cover under large shirts since she started training in the gym. But he wasn't about to tell her the others were there.

He took her to the shower, washing her while he fucked her again. He covered her top half with suds as she pressed her hands to the tile. With her ass out, Dak filled her. He paused long enough to clean himself and their lower halves before claiming her again until her walls clamped tight around his cock.

"A week was too long." Dak dipped his mouth behind her ear.

"But you never left me." She tilted her head to give him more access. Turning off the water, he pulled her from the shower and dried them off.

"It wouldn't have mattered where you went. I never would have left you."

"You were going to send me away and go after them yourself. You would have had to leave me."

"I will always know where you are and you'll never be unprotected." His rage and fear had been what sent her away. Not because he needed or wanted distance. It wouldn't have been long before Dak tore the city apart and ran back to her.

Three words tattooed themselves across his chest. She was his and always would be. He had no reason not to say them. Except he'd never said them. Never felt them. The love for a mother didn't equate to this kind of love.

Instead, he carried her to the bed and proceeded to do his worst and bring her to the most excruciating pleasure possible. With his tongue on her already sensitive clit, Dak brought her to the brink before moving up her body so the two of them finished together.

He drank in her cries and fed her his growls. Nothing could take her away from him. Not Wayne, not the world. Not even her. And never him.

It seemed like hours had passed as he held her against him and she slept with her head on his shoulder.

It was time to ensure her safety. Watching her train had been a distraction while he waited for an opportunity to go after Wayne.

When Dak tried to slip out from under her, she woke.

"Dak?"

"Yeah, princess. I'm here."

"Where are you going?"

"I'm done waiting. It's time to finish this."

Sophie sat up in bed, holding the sheet over her breasts. Dak glared at the fabric.

"Drop it."

"Why?"

"You don't hide from me."

She let go of the sheet, and it rippled down to pool at her waist.

"Mmm." Dak hummed as he reached for his phone he'd set on the dresser. It started ringing with the exact number he was about to call. He answered.

"He's back in the country and on his way to the city." Roen rushed the words through the phone. "He's searching for her parents."

"How do you know that?" But Dak could guess. He had digital alerts everywhere, let alone they each had spies and connections of their own.

"I have my ways. We're on the move so he can't find them and use them."

"Good." At least Dak didn't have to worry about them.

"He's coming after Sophie again. I can't tell you how." Frustration snarled in Roen's voice. The man had tried.

"We won't be here." Dak hadn't planned on sticking around much longer. He was going after Wayne.

"You've got at least a day or two before he reaches the city." More time than he'd thought.

"Thanks. Keep in touch."

"Will do." Roen hung up.

"What's going on?" Sophie was out of bed now. Standing

with glowing and flushed skin, begging him to lick her from head to toe.

"He's back, and he's coming for you. But this time, no one will be here."

"Then let's do this."

"You're doing good, princess. But you aren't ready for this."

"Please don't just hide me away." Sophie moved to his dresser and pulled out one of his shirts. It hung far past her knees. Her hair was mostly dry and in disarray. The sight entranced him, keeping what she'd said from registering.

Until she huffed and crossed her arms. "Dak."

"You aren't ready." He couldn't wait until she was, knowing it would be an amazing sight to behold.

"Then make me ready."

"Not possible. We're dealing with this now."

"Right this moment?" Sophie glared and Dak glared back, savouring her sass.

"We have a day. Maybe two." He needed months at least to have her ready to face anything.

"I want to be involved."

"Do you?" Training her didn't mean she'd become a mercenary and do the same things as Ember.

Sophie tilted her chin up and squared her shoulders. Her body was asking for an invasion. So he gave it to her.

Dak stopped, so they almost touched. He left enough room for his hand to roam from her collarbone and down her body to her hip. "Is that what you want, princess? You want to be a mercenary?"

"I didn't say that. This is because of me. It's my fault. I..."

"It's not." Dak cut her off and pulled her against him. "It's the fault of the abusive bastard that made you part of his deal."

"What? He did... Part of his... What are you talking about?" Sophie tried to pull away from him. He hadn't told her. Getting beaten by the guy was bad enough. She didn't need a reason to feel worthless.

"It doesn't matter." But even as he said it, he knew keeping information from people was the quickest way to get someone killed. "They're after you because you're part of the deal to pay back his debts."

"Me."

"None of this is your fault."

"You aren't leaving me behind." Her fingers pressed into his skin as if trying to make fists. A bright flush filled her face. Anger seeped through her every breath.

"I'm not giving them an opportunity to get to you."

"Would you stay behind and let King and the others handle someone that was after you?"

"You aren't ready, princess. End of discussion."

"Says you." She left his arms, but Dak was quick to grip her chin.

"When you can best me, then you're ready. You are priceless. Irreplaceable. Even you will face my wrath if you put yourself in danger before you can handle it."

He held her long enough to satisfy himself that she would do as he told her. If she could slay, he'd hand her the knife and stand back with pride to watch the show. But until then, he would slay for her. With her safe in a tower. Or bunker. Wherever he could lock her down while he went hunting.

16

His fingers left an imprint on her chin. Sophie made a fist to keep herself from rubbing her face. In no way was she ready to face anyone. But she refused to be kept out of this.

Following him from his apartment, they met everyone downstairs in the computer room. It surprised her to see even King there, waiting and ready. Hard eyes and creases lined the faces in the room. They were ready to do business.

"Where is he now?" Dak charged in.

Cole sat in front of the monitors. "He's landed and has a convoy escorting him away from the airport."

"He has more than one convoy on the move." King slipped his phone in his pocket. "A contingency of armed guards left the casino five minutes ago. And they aren't heading toward the airport."

"We have incoming. How long until they get here?" Dak left the office, expecting everyone to follow. Sophie had to jog to stay behind Dak and in front of the others.

"Ten minutes. Maybe." Cole answered as he had his

phone to his ear. "Roen is tracking Wayne while we deal with this."

"We need a plan to end this." Dak punched in a series of five numbers to unlock one room she had yet to see. Inside, they all spread out and started taking knives, guns, and more off the walls. Fucking with these guys ensured someone had a death wish.

"He has enough people to take over the casino for him if we take him out." Gear's bored attention didn't leave the knives he strapped to his thighs and hips.

"I'm not trying to take out the organization." Dak paused, his eyes landing on her. *Priceless. Irreplaceable.* The weight of those words pressed down on her. She'd felt it upstairs, but one look shot it at her, hitting her chest with the weight of a gold brick. This was all about protecting her. Not the world. Not the others this man terrorized. Only her.

Sophie eyed the walls and drawers. What did she need? She'd never used a weapon of any sort in her entire life.

"No." Dak cut off her view of assorted weapons. "You're going upstairs."

"No, I'm not." Sophie hoped they didn't see the quaking in her knees. The quirk of the brows said otherwise.

"Have you forgotten what I told you upstairs? Even you won't be safe from my wrath." Battle ready, Dak was more intimidating than he'd been the day she walked in here.

"I'll face your wrath if it means I'm not hidden away." He wouldn't harm her. And she realized that hurt and harm were two different things.

"Being down here only gives them what they want." Her. Because she was part of payment from a dead guy.

"How do they know she's here?" Gear leaned against the wall, ready for battle. "The last they knew we'd taken her away. Why are they attacking us here?"

Dak turned toward Gear. "The only way is if they saw me drive up with her after we killed the tail."

"He's had eyes on us from the beginning." King growled. "Fucking fools. Attacking in public. Not once. But twice."

"Get upstairs, Sophie." Dak took her elbow and turned her around. "We don't have time to get you out of here."

"No. Give me something to do." She wanted a purpose.

"Upstairs. Now." His grip changed to the back of her neck and he bent his head. The savage escaped in his whisper along her cheek.

Fighting him was a waste of time. And getting in the way could get someone hurt. With a locked jaw, she stepped away from him and made her way to the elevator.

Their deep murmurs followed behind her.

"Cole, get in a car and speed off as they arrive. Make them think we're moving her. Keep the tail for a little while." King slashed orders as easily as Dak did. One of them was dangerous, but the two of them, as a team, were horrifying to the wrong people. They were *King's Mercenaries*, after all.

She let the elevator finish the ride to the top floor. The doors opened, and time froze. She left, and she'd stay out of the way. But she wouldn't hide and be useless. Pushing the button for the main level, the doors closed and Sophie took long breaths.

Silence greeted her when she arrived. Dashing out the door, she winced as the elevator dinged. Signaling its arrival. But no one came running, and no one called out to her. No large, callused hands wrapped themselves around her arm or waist.

But murmurs floated from the front lobby.

Sophie punched in the security code she'd seen Dak use and slipped back into the room of weapons. A roll of tape sat on one shelf. Tearing off a piece, she taped the latch open on the inside of the door and let it shut. No one on the other side should be able to tell that it wasn't locked.

She searched the rest of the shelves and cabinets. She chose the smallest and most lightweight knives. If she knew how to use a gun, that would have been her first choice. The weapon that would keep her far away from an attacker. But since she didn't intend to join the fray at the front, she chose what she thought she could handle.

Slipping into a hiding spot near the door. She waited and listened, ready in case they needed her. Not to jump in and fight. Not to defend or attack.

Idiotic. But it was better than hiding away upstairs, unaware of anything happening down here.

Silence was deafening until it wasn't. Sharp snaps came from both the back and the front of the building. A quiet pause. Thunks, grunts, and moans of pain broke the hum clutching the air. Hendrick's laugh echoed from the back. The crazy sound sending chills down her spine.

Gunshots popped off with monotonous consistency. Sophie instinctively ducked, holding her hands over her head while she crouched on the floor. She didn't make a sound, but her heart hammered in her ears. Focusing, she tuned out the sound, letting the others back in. No one came toward these rooms. But she made out the tones of the different men. Soon she heard the harsh rasp of Dak. The chuckle of Hendrick. King's growl. And pain laced each one.

She tried to stay still, tried to stay silent. She couldn't help. Couldn't do anything but listen to sounds that made little sense to her.

A feral roar broke through it all. Seconds later, the door to the weapons room opened and Sophie stared at thick boots from her hiding spot.

DAK WATCHED the guy open the door that was supposed to be locked. The last thing any of them needed were more weapons. Hendrick was injured. But they only had a few left to take out.

If they kept getting attacked here, Dak would have to think of a different way to run the business. They didn't want or need the attention. Let alone the amount of innocent people they'd put in danger by staying.

But now, Dak had one in particular he wanted to kill. Then he'd figure out how he'd opened the door to the weapons room.

"Jackpot." He crowed and stepped further into the room. His feet fumbled hard. "What the fuck?" He fell to the floor.

Dak frowned. He tripped?

"I was wrong. You're the jackpot, bitch."

Ice spread and cracked in Dak's veins. His muscles screamed with pain and his chest constricted.

Sophie!

Footsteps inside the room forced Dak into motion. He didn't hear a sound from Sophie, only a snarl.

"You fucking cut me."

Good girl, but once I kill this guy, you're in a whole other mess of trouble, princess.

Dak filled the doorway. It would be agonizing to clean blood off of all the weapons in here. A wall, a floor, some furniture. But he didn't look forward to the tedious task of cleaning hundreds of knives, guns covered in blood spray, and replacing gear that wasn't possible to clean.

The guy blanched. Panicking, he lunged for Sophie. *Bad idea, fucker.* Dak beat him to it, stepping in front of Sophie and landing a solid hit with the butt of his gun on the guy's shoulder.

He groaned. "Just hand over the bitch. And we can all go our separate ways. We will conclude all business with you."

"No." Dak pulled on years of experience to keep his face neutral, not showing anyone how much he cared for Sophie.

"We will get her."

"You won't." Dak made the attack quick and ruthless. With little struggle, he moved behind him and gripped his chin and head. He met Sophie's gaze over the guy's shoulder. Holding her shining blue eyes, Dak snapped his neck. When he released the body, it tumbled to the floor.

Sounds of the fight still going on paused the words he wanted to say to her. One look at the door and he figured out how the guy had gotten in. Tape covered the inside latch. Ripping it off, he glared at Sophie.

"Don't fucking move."

Her fear and pale face of shock couldn't distract him. He slammed the door and left to help finish up. He tore through them all with a vengeance.

This world needed a message. Don't fuck with them in their place of business. This wouldn't happen again. Dead bodies spoke volumes.

Dak moved in behind the guy fighting with King. With similar quick motions as the guy about to attack Sophie, he snapped his neck and didn't spare a glance as he moved to the next one fighting with Gear in the back.

Hendrick bled profusely from his leg, but continued to fight. An injured beast capable of killing with a flick of his wrist. His knife flew and pinned the guy to the wall through his neck.

Shock paused the other two remaining, giving Dak and

Gear the opportunity to snap their necks before they saw it coming.

"Get Thane here. I have someone else to deal with."

Gear cocked his head.

"Sophie's in the weapons room."

"Brat." Hendrick's lips twisted with pain, making his grin gnarled. Dak didn't find the same amusement.

Letting himself into the weapons room, he found Sophie shivering. A knife in each hand up and pointing toward the door. He stepped toward her and she lifted the knives, unseeing of who approached. Or she was now terrified of him. Weeks too late.

"Sophie. Princess."

She blinked, but shook away his calm and thrust the knives upward again. Fuck. He'd traumatized her. Watching her lover kill in front of her seemed to be the last straw. She'd survived abuse, being shot at, listening to someone kill her husband, pushed to her limits with training by mercenaries.

"Shh." He started a humming in his chest to break through to her. "It's me, princess." He wouldn't tell her she was safe. She wasn't. Not from him and not from those after her.

Her eyes found his, and she lowered her arms.

"That's it, Sophie. Drop the knives."

"Dak." The knives clanged against the floor. She took a step toward him, relief releasing her taut body. But recognition hit and she backed to the wall.

"Come here." He filled his voice with an enticing threat. He wanted to hold her before strangling her.

She shook her head.

Instead of ordering her again, he went to her. He crushed her against him. After a beat, Sophie wrapped her arms around his middle. Dak took in her every curve with his hands. She was okay. She was unharmed. Safe. It took several minutes for his heart to beat normally again.

When it did, he tangled a hand in her hair and pulled her away from him.

"Why the fuck aren't you upstairs?" He kept one hand on her waist, his touch softer than what he had in her hair.

"I didn't want to hide away and be useless." She pulled in a breath and leaned into his hold.

"What was your plan? Were you going to jump out of the room and surprise one of them?" The image alone froze his blood again. She wasn't ready for this. What the hell was he thinking, agreeing to bring her back here and train her while there was still someone after her?

"No." She gripped his arms and her eyes pleaded with him to believe her. "I wanted to be close. Not pacing and wondering what was happening."

"Close? Almost getting caught and watching me kill traumatized you. These guys aren't fucking around."

"I know."

"Do you?"

"Yes." She tried to lunge for him, but he held her back.

He calmed long enough to assess if she was okay or if taking his next step would push her back in shock. With a kiss on her forehead, he asked. "Are you okay, princess?"

"Yes." For the breath they stood still, no anger pulsed. But he promised her his wrath.

"Good." Dak pulled away and pushed her in front of him to leave the room. "We've all made it clear what these guys will do to you if they get you. And this isn't about vengeance. You're a debt payment. That opens up a whole other set of possibilities of things they will do."

He led her toward the front where King still heaved,

moving the dead bodies around on the floor. He huffed when he spotted Sophie.

Dak took her to the back and prepared to catch her when her eyes settled on Hendrick lying on a table. Sophie leaned against him. Gear stood over Hendrick, holding his shirt tightly to his leg.

"That could be you, princess. And worse."

"It should be." Her whisper caught the attention of all three of them.

"What did you just say?" Dak turned her around, making sure he could see the words as much as hear them.

"You didn't ask for this. I haven't hired you to do this. But I walked in here and laid it all at your feet. First Ember gets hurt and now Hendrick. Who's next?"

"You're confusing us with good people, Sophie." Hendrick croaked through a grin. Dak didn't like the paleness seeping through his cheeks. He shared a grim look with Gear.

He didn't have time to teach Sophie a lesson or work through what she'd said.

"You've been good to me."

"I'll remember you said that the next time you punch me in the balls." Hendrick turned his head away and closed his eyes.

"You want to be in the middle of this, princess? Fine. But I'll deal with you later. For now. Stay with Hendrick." Dak released his hold.

Gear motioned her over. "The doctor will be here soon. Until then, don't let off any pressure." He placed her hands under his and didn't move away until she seemed steady.

Dak sighed as she shook and paled. But this was what she'd asked for, and he had a message to deliver and an assassination to plan.

THE FEEL of the blood under her palms and seeping between her fingers turned Sophie's stomach. But she held it back. This was all because of her. She needed to help.

"Push a little harder. You can't hurt me." Hendrick lolled his head toward her. His eyes had no shield from his pain. They pierced her as he continued to stare.

Sophie leaned harder on his leg, using some of her own weight rather than only the strength of her arms. Hendrick winced, and she started to back off.

"No. You're doing good, Sophie." Hendrick reached out and set his hand on her wrist.

"I'm sorry."

He scoffed. "I don't want your apologies. This isn't your fault."

"I.."

"Shut up, Sophie." Hendrick sighed with his words. "Where else would you have gone?"

She didn't bother repeating her original plan. They thought it wouldn't have worked. Not then. Her parents would have been in danger. But now? Her parents were safe.

She may not be ready to face villains with knives and guns, but she'd learned one thing about herself. She could hide.

"Damn it, Hendrick." A male voice cursed as he stormed in from the back. He had shaggy hair, light scruff, and was as large and muscular as the mercenaries that surrounded Sophie for weeks. But this man wore scrubs and carried a bag. "Don't let off that pressure until I say so." He pointed at her as if he'd known her just as long as the others. Like she belonged here.

"I won't." Cause more damage? Fuck that.

The doctor disappeared for only a minute and came back, digging in his bag for fresh gauze. "Okay, we're going to switch places. You're going to go wash as best you can, then come back and help me." He nodded for her as if he requested her help rather than demanded it.

And Sophie nodded along anyway, trapped in the command he held on the situation.

"Now." He slid into her place, pushing the soaked shirt away. Sophie moved with him, making the task seamless. She froze as the doctor moved the fabric out of the way, taking a quick look before pressing the gauze in its place. Blood pooled around inner tissue. "Go." The doctor snapped, putting her into motion.

As she left, their voices carried toward her.

"She yours?"

"Dak's." Hendrick answered with a chuckle.

"Never thought I'd see that. Besides, someone would have to be as crazy as you to handle your bullshit. Fuck, this is deep." The doctor growled.

Sophie used the sink in the break room, scrubbing until her hands and arms heated. More voices hummed from the computer room. Cole explained his race through traffic and how he lost the three vehicles that chased him.

"They weren't easy to lose. They believed I had Sophie with me. One started shooting, but someone pulled him back inside. They want her alive."

"Been a while since we've planned an old-fashioned assassination." The darkness in his voice was familiar. Something about that was comforting. "These bodies will serve as a message and a warning. Not only for Wayne and his business. But I want this message to go public."

Dak had a bigger plan in play. Sophie inched her way

back toward Hendrick, but she wanted to hear what they were going to do next.

"We can't have another attack here. And we're going to make sure everyone knows this place is off limits. Wayne is an arrogant idiot."

"But people will follow his actions and think here is an easy target." Gear growled.

"Get these bodies ready. And I want a bead on Wayne for tomorrow night. He dies."

Sophie made her way back to Hendrick and the doctor. Who else would get hurt during that assassination? All because they wanted her. Alive. She supposed a dead body didn't pay a debt well. Unless that body was a threat. She'd rather be a threat than an asset. As an asset, she put others in danger.

"Thank God they didn't hit anything vital. But he's bleeding too much." The doctor looked back and forth between Hendrick's leg and her.

"God ain't watching out for that crazy bastard." Cole walked through the room, lifting one of the dead bodies that were still sprawled on the floor.

Sophie tuned everything out except for the doctor's orders. She retrieved whatever he needed from his bag. When he asked her to help hold the wound closed for him to stitch, she paused.

"Now you're squeamish?" The doctor didn't sound rude, only curious.

"She's been squeamish the whole time." Hendrick's voice was almost gone, indicating the pain stretched further. Mix that with the drugs the doctor gave him, and he was ready to pass out. "She's been hiding it well."

Of course, Hendrick noticed.

"Keep hiding it." The doctor smiled at her, encouraging her to stay strong.

With a fast, shaky nod, Sophie stepped forward.

"That's it. Thank you." He started stitching the long wound.

Sophie forced her eyes to stay on the wound, time passing in odd waves with every stitch.

"You can let go now."

"Do you need anything else?" As she checked back into her surroundings, nausea swelled.

"Yes. For you to sit down over there." The doctor used his head to point to a chair on the other side of the room. Sophie looked around. They'd cleared out all the bodies and what bit of furniture had been in this room was back in place. She hadn't felt or seen anyone else come in here.

"Now, girl." The doctor firmed his tone, a different accent sneaking through as he called her *girl*.

"Do as he says, princess." Dak's frame stepped into the doorway, blocking the light from the hallway leading up toward the front.

Sophie walked to the chair and steadied herself on a table to sit without falling to the floor. Dak didn't leave to continue concocting his pans. He invaded her space and crouched in front of her. Those dark eyes that both terrified her and comforted her searched her face and down her neck. Strong fingers wrapped around her wrist, moving until they pressed against her pulse.

"Hendrick is all done. He'll be fine, but he has to stay off his leg. And he needs to sleep off the drugs I've given him. Gear and Cole are getting ready to move him."

Despite that he would be fine, guilt still filled Sophie. He was lucky. And so was Ember. Any of them could get hurt because of her. Deep flesh wounds were bad enough, but that was just luck. Either of them could have died. Sophie should have let Dak put her in a safe house.

You're not ready. The voice of every one of them echoed that statement together in her head. She had two choices. Give over to Dak completely, let him handle it all. Or lure them away so no one else got hurt. Neither sounded like a good option to her.

Good guys or not, Sophie cared enough for these mercenaries. She had what she needed. Wayne was watching. It was time to give everyone here a choice if they wanted to be involved in her problems.

17

———

Sophie's complexion terrified Dak. He kept his fingers over her pulse at her wrist. Thane joined them, crouching down and frowning at Sophie.

"Her pulse is erratic." Slow and weak when he'd first come over, but now raced.

"A bit of shock." Thane nodded as he felt her pulse on her neck. "Get her upstairs. Showered and give her some tea. Something hot. She'll be fine."

He'd make sure of it. But Dak saw something else in her eyes. He didn't think it was only shock that affected her. Guilt. Fear. And a spark. A small glint of her steel.

Something told him he needed to keep an eye on her.

"I'll be back tomorrow to check on Hendrick." Thane patted Sophie's knee. "You did good helping me, girl." He stood and nodded to Dak before leaving.

"Let's go, princess." They wouldn't set their plan in motion for another day, two at the most. He had time to take care of Sophie. And then teach her a fucking lesson.

She didn't fight him as he pulled her up and lifted her into his arms.

"You took years off my life."

"I don't suppose you have many to spare." Her lips moved against his chest.

"Glad to see your mind is still working. So there must be another reason you disobeyed me." Dak bent his head to nuzzle her neck. Pulling in her scent, he nipped the soft skin until she whimpered.

"Everything is working just fine." The sound of the elevator doors covered her breathless answer. In the apartment, he deposited her on the bathroom counter.

"What am I going to do with you, princess?"

"Is that rhetorical, or do I get a vote?" There she was. Steely sass. But the effects of the day and what she'd been through hadn't gone away. They'd drained her. Tired and hollow, she held most of her weight on the heels of her palms resting on the counter. Her body tilted to the side.

Priorities. Starting the shower, he put her on her feet and set her under the water. She closed her eyes and ducked her head. Dak stepped back and considered what to do with her. He couldn't let her get away with disobeying him.

The thought of losing her sent sharp shards of ice through him again, igniting his anger. If he stepped into the shower with her, he'd take things too far. Farther than she could handle in her current state.

He leaned against the bathroom door and waited. Lifting her head, she looked at him with shining eyes.

Dak nodded. He didn't trust himself with words. They'd be as harsh as his actions if he did.

She was safe. She was strong. He repeated to himself over and over while he watched her scrub the blood from her hands.

By the time she'd finished, he'd calmed enough to wrap her in a towel and dry her off.

"You're mad." Sophie took the towel from his hand and held it against her chest.

"Mad doesn't even come close." Dak stepped aside and pushed her in front of him toward the bedroom.

"Please understand, I had to. I can't stay in hiding." He understood she was struggling with the sudden change in her life and what she was about to become.

"And someday you won't. But until you would have been the one to end the guy who'd found you in that room earlier, you will be somewhere safe." He tore the towel from her body.

"I'm not trying to get hurt or get anyone else hurt. But this is all because of me."

"You forget I wouldn't let you leave. That I kept you here." Her head lifted, and she stared at him. She'd been blaming herself because of her presence. "You'll get there. Trust me."

Dak pulled a T-shirt from his dresser and slipped it over her head. He towel dried her hair until it no longer dripped and took her to the living room. "Sit." Pointing to the couch, he took the blanket off the back and tossed it on her.

"What are you doing?"

"Doctor's orders." In the kitchen, he made peppermint tea. He didn't drink the stuff. But the smell was calming.

"Tea." Sophie took the hot cup from his hands. "You're taking those orders seriously."

"Priceless and irreplaceable. You seem to have already forgotten that." Dak sat on the chair opposite her.

"I haven't forgotten what you said." She looked into her tea.

"Then we have a different problem."

"What's that?" She chewed on the inside of her cheek.

"You don't know your worth. You don't know what you

mean to me. Apparently I haven't made that abundantly clear."

"Priceless and irreplaceable are strong words." Sophie met his gaze.

"Not strong enough." He stood and crossed the few feet between them. Bracing himself on the arm and back of the couch, he leaned in until they were almost nose to nose. "Anyone who intends you harm isn't safe from me. That will never change. Whether or not you belong to me, princess."

"At what cost?" She met his declaration with a lift of her chin. "First Ember. Now Hendrick. Who's next?"

"This is what we do. If it isn't this bad guy, it's another. You waltzing in here and into my life didn't change that."

"Of course it did. I brought this specific one, this one that's bold enough to challenge you here. The one that will go away for a single price."

"You are not giving yourself up." Dak had to dig his fingers into the cushioning on the couch. If he moved, he'd grab her and shake her.

"Of course not. I don't want to. I just don't want anyone else to get hurt because of me. Both Ember and Hendrick will be fine, but that might not be the case next time. At least my parents are safe. I can never thank you enough for ensuring that."

Dak eased off, kneeling on the floor in front of her. "Would you do it again?"

"Do what?"

All of it. "Walk in that front door?"

"Don't make me answer that." Sophie tried to move further away, but she was already settled against the back of the couch.

"It's not such a tough question, princess."

"Is that what you think?" Her grip around her cup

turned her knuckles white. She had yet to drink enough to keep the hot liquid from sloshing over the top as she jerked with her anger. "Would I choose to bring trouble to your door and have people get hurt so I can be selfish with how I feel about you?"

That was precisely what he wanted to know.

Sophie closed her eyes, shutting him out. "Go away. Please."

Dak wanted to pin her to the floor and fuck her until she gave in to the same feelings he had for her. As it was, he couldn't tell if her heart was too damn big to be his. He hadn't thought that would be an issue.

Standing, he took one more look at her before turning his back.

"Fine, princess." Dak eyed the door. He didn't want to leave her, but they both needed to cool off. "Go to bed when you're finished with your tea."

He left to check on Hendrick. Sophie wasn't the only one who cared and worried about the crazy bastard.

She loved him and she'd choose him every time if it didn't put others in danger.

Was he right? If she wasn't here, would it just be someone else? But guilt wasn't always a reasonable emotion. She wasn't foolish enough to hand herself over. But she could help ease the pressure in her own way.

But as to not tip her hand, she did as she was told this time. Setting the cup in the sink, Sophie climbed into bed. Her body shut down as she shut her eyes. Nightmares invaded as faded shadows, never gripping her enough to wake her. Only remind her of the day.

Deep voices humming in the distance woke her. Darkness still shrouded the room. She hadn't slept long. Stretching under the sheets, she gave her body a moment to recover from the rest before creeping out from under the blankets.

She needed to know what their plans were to make sure hers didn't put them in danger. At the door to the bedroom, she opened it a crack to let the sound through and stood with her ear next to the opening.

Focused, she closed her eyes and worked on making out each word and who said what.

"He's called a damn summit?" King huffed.

"And we think it will be the best place to both send a message and take him out." Gear kept his voice low, and she had to strain to hear.

"I'd rather end this now, but the summit provides the best scenario." Dak's voice slithered down her spine. She couldn't forget how he'd looked at her earlier.

"Has anyone considered the summit might be a trap? *Here I am, come and get me.* He's already proved to be stupidly bold."

"We have feelers out about that now. I won't walk into a trap, but neither will I pass up the opportunity."

"All right. So what's the plan?" asked King.

"We'll occupy the summit seats before they get there. The message will be clear not to make the same mistakes Wayne has."

"We'll be outnumbered." Cole didn't sound worried.

"When has that ever been an issue?" Gear mumbled, sounding the farthest away.

"What are you going to do with Sophie?" She tried not to hear the disapproval in King's voice.

"Locking her down." Like hell he was.

"And what about when this is over?"

"She's mine." His tone answered more than his words. Searching the drawers, Sophie found a pair of jeans and pulled them on, wincing when she realized her rush to dress without underwear as a barrier between herself and the denim.

As she left the bedroom, the conversation stopped. She rolled their plan around in her head. It would happen with or without her. They had their own reasons for following through. "How can I help?"

Leaving wouldn't change anything. They were invested. As much as her feet itched to run, lead Wayne away from them and onto her, hide until he gave up, it would only make things worse for her with Dak. The restraint he'd held earlier shook his veins. He'd warned her of his wrath and hadn't followed through yet. Because of the state she'd been in. It was coming. And it would come harder if she ran.

That didn't keep the plan from forming, so she'd have it if she needed.

"You can't." Dak crossed the room, blocking her view of the others.

"She could work eyes and communication with Roen." Cole leaned sideways, his head visible beside Dak's shoulder.

"With Roen? Isn't he still with my parents?"

"Yeah. He's still working from there. You'll be somewhere safe but as eyes."

"No." Dak turned on Cole, who put his hand in the air and stepped back as if the ten plus feet between them wasn't enough.

"Why? Am I really safer here where they know where to find me?" Sophie stepped around him and settled herself against a free space at the counter. Cole snickered. King and

Gear glared at her. Dak kept his back to her longer than was comfortable.

"I didn't say you'd be staying here."

"Been there, done that. We've been over this. You brought me back."

Now he turned around.

Sophie shrugged.

"Find a safe vantage point for her."

Gear and Cole sent single nods toward Dak, but didn't jump to do his bidding. All eyes turned toward her, taking away the sprig of confidence she had when she set herself on the same level as the rest of them.

"It isn't only my trust you need to earn back, princess."

Sophie met the eyes of each of them, not allowing shame over her actions to creep through. But the glares were dark, even from Cole. Sophie imagined it would take a lot to get on Cole's bad side. Enough to earn the look he gave her.

"You disobey one of us in a situation like that, you disobey all of us." It was Cole that explained their censure toward her. "We all expected you to be up here. One of us could have put you in danger and not have known."

Fuck. He was right. But that didn't mean she was wrong. "Then do you all get a vote in what he decides?" Sophie pointed at Dak. "Cause I will forever have a choice for myself from here on out."

"You don't get it." Dak somehow stormed at her quietly until he landed in front of her. "I love you." The words exploded from his chest like the passionate growls he emitted when he was inside of her.

Sophie's breaths were short.

"You stubborn woman. I'm not taking away your choices. I don't want to."

"Then don't lock me away." The others still stared on, and her response to his declaration froze somewhere in her chest where she could hold it back. She hadn't loved for a long time. Had believed the ability had died. Yet here she was, beating harshly for this dangerous man. Hoping her life fit with him.

It wouldn't if she let him lock her away. Sophie stayed trapped in his gaze.

His hands started moving over her body. Up her sides and down her arms. His grip firmed until he gripped her hips and bent down. Before she guessed his next move, she was over his shoulder.

"Excuse us." Dak mumbled and stalked toward the bedroom.

She caught the approval in the gazes of the others. The air heated and she was about to come face to face with Dak's wrath.

DAK PULLED Sophie off his shoulder and let her slide down his body.

"Do you have anything you want to say to me?" He cupped the side of her neck. Her pulse jumped under his palm. Inhaling her scent like a drug pumping through his system.

Sophie's lips formed the beginning of the words Dak wanted to hear. But she stuttered. Her tongue darted out to lick across the bottom one. Her teeth latched onto that same lip. But her eyes spoke for her. Those blue orbs stared up at him, saying so many things. Love. Fear. Worry. Determination. Undeniable uncertainty.

"I've said you can come. But you will stay where I put

you. Am I clear?" He tightened his fingers around her throat.

"Yes. Thank you." Her bottom lip trembled. Dak couldn't hold back his grin. Anticipation of what he was about to do to her, feeding off her own nerves and desires.

"Don't thank me yet. You still aren't getting away with going back downstairs."

Sophie turned her head away from his hand and looked at the floor. "I am sorry. I don't want to give any of you a reason not to trust me. But I wasn't wrong either. It's not wrong to need to know what's going on."

"Curiosity kills. Or haven't you heard?"

Her lips pinched, and she looked up from under her lashes. If looks could maim.

"Strip, princess."

She stepped back and lifted her chin, but her hands moved to her shirt. His shirt. Every time he closed his eyes, he had visions of the trouble this woman would cause him. And yet, he licked his lips at the challenge.

"Don't lose that attitude, Sophie. You're going to need it to be with me."

"Don't I know it." She smirked, but her face changed to breathless as the shirt hit the floor. Pulling down her jeans, she stood naked.

"Fuck." A warm glow from the dimness of the bedroom covered smooth skin. The taste of her exploded on his tongue as if he'd just licked her. "You're fucking gorgeous, princess. But..." Dak firmed his jaw. "Lay on the bed. On your back."

Her next breath looked like it took effort. Trust had to go both ways. He crossed to the nightstand and pulled out the rope. The rough rope that he'd used before. Wary eyes settled on the coil, but she moved her hands above her head in preparation.

"No. Not like that." He took one wrist and tied it to one corner of the bed. Moving to the bottom, he did the same with that ankle. When he finished, he'd tied each limb to each corner of the bed. From the look on her face, she didn't like it.

Her brow furrowed, and anger twitched around her mouth.

"You aren't going to like this, Sophie."

He'd made it clear he wouldn't hurt her. She was too precious. There weren't many precious things left.

"I've been part of this world since I learned how to make my legs run faster than adults. When I say something isn't safe for someone, I mean it." Dak opened his closet. After the first night with her in his bed, he found the need to gather some much needed accessories. Pulling out the small pink tickler, he kept it hidden in his hand at his side. He'd thought he'd use this for pleasure rather than punishment. But this needed to be done.

Sophie's gaze landed on his hand and stayed there. He stopped at the end of the bed and waited. He wouldn't move until her eyes met his. As her breath quickened, she lifted her eyes.

"I'll never hold you back, so when I tell you to go upstairs, I have a damn good reason. Do you understand?"

"Do you understand why I had to come back down?"

"Trust me. This will be much more uncomfortable than having to wait up here with the unknown." Dak knelt on the bed and cupped the tickler over her clit. He turned it on high. Sophie's hips thrust up off the bed and Dak wrapped an arm across them to hold them down. Once her thighs quivered, he pulled back the round, pink toy.

"What the hell is that thing?" She panted, filling each word with an extra 'h' sound.

He held it up with a sinful smirk, showing off the flicking tongue-like appendage inside the pink knob.

Her eyes widened. An evil chuckle slipped from his chest as he pressed it against her again. This time she cried out and her whole body tensed, eagerly grasping for a climax.

Dak recognized the signs of her body and tore it away, leaving it on and holding it only inches from her.

"You aren't coming tonight, princess." Setting the tickler against her again, Dak repeated the process until she screamed. On. Off. Faster. Slower. The last time, he let her taste her orgasm. The initial spasm shook her legs. Dak ripped it away and brought his fingers down hard on her clit, the slap loud, matching her cries over her ruined orgasm.

He was unbearably hard. The tip throbbed and ached. He'd fuck her and he'd come, but she wouldn't. Dak only hoped this was strong enough of a lesson to ensure she didn't put herself in danger again.

Her eyes had snapped open and her head stopped thrashing. "What did you just do?"

"What?"

"I was... And then..." Frustration leached from her in a strangled cry. "You slapped..." She bit her lip.

Dak tilted his head to look at her cunt while he spoke. "I spanked your clit and ruined your orgasm. Is that what you're trying to say?"

"Y... y... yes."

"And I'm going to do it again." But not in the same way. Setting the tickler aside, he returned to the closet and pulled out the next item. Long, smooth, and curved, Dak inserted into her already dripping cunt. Turning it on high, he hit her G spot as Sophie pulled at all the ropes.

Watching closely until the quiver started, he turned off the vibrator, but left it inside her.

"Dak. Please."

"No." He growled, the rejection harsh. "I wonder how many you can take until it hurts."

Sophie whimpered, the sound sweet in his ears.

As with the tickler, he brought her to the edge and left her there each time. Until the last, when he let the beginnings take hold before he tore everything away from her and slapped her clit hard to ruin it all.

Her cries this time held an inkling of pain. Whether from the spanking or the edging, it didn't matter.

"Getting the point now, princess?"

He grinned at her incoherent answer.

"Still not done." Putting the toys away, he cleaned them and washed his hands.

"Dak?" Fluttering eyes found him as he returned and settled between her legs. With two fingers, he rubbed her clit to bring her back up before sliding them down to her entrance. But he had a purpose.

To drive her mad.

18

———

Her mind refused to work, and so did her body. Sophie struggled to focus on Dak. Her limbs felt numb, and it wasn't from the rope. Blood pumped hard, hammering at her sensitive flesh from the inside.

Something rough touched her clit again and sensations roared. No slow build up, no pleasurable rise. The climax shot straight to the edge with pain. But her body craved that pain because it meant there would be release soon. If Dak didn't take it away. If Dak didn't control her and her body.

His fingers scissored inside her. Thrashing her head back and forth, Sophie begged for the end, but she didn't think her sentiments made it through. The words sounded garbled in her own ears, and Dak didn't respond. Just drove her to the end and pulled away. She'd lost count ages ago.

Something thicker and harder prodded at her entrance. She lifted her head. Her vision was blurry, but she made out the edges of the naked man between her spread legs. Dak's eyes roamed her face over and over as he pushed inside her.

The glorious filling doubled the sensations and the pace

to reach her climax. Sophie stilled, hoping to catch it this time.

"Fuck." Dak growled and pulled from her. "You feel so good, princess, but it isn't taking much to set you off."

Again, she tried to answer him. "Please let me." Those three words didn't sound right in her own ears, but Dak seemed to understand.

"No. You are not coming tonight." He pushed into her again, only making it a few thrusts before her body grasped onto the promise of the friction.

With a growl, he pulled from her. Lifting her head, Sophie forced her eyes open and to stay on him. Dak wrapped his hand around his cock and stroked himself. Hard. He kept himself aimed at her cunt, where his fingers played once again.

"You going to disobey me again, Sophie?" He strained to speak and moved his hand faster. His fingers matched the pace.

She shook her head as her voice came out as little hiccups between panting.

"Next time, I'll do this while filling your ass. Am I clear?"

Her mind exploded with what he meant, the possibilities and more. He didn't say with what. Her core clenched.

"Fuck." Dak ripped his fingers away. "That wasn't supposed to make you excited."

Did it? But when she thought about it again, her legs quivered.

Dak slapped her clit, harder than any of the other times. With one hand, he used his finger to spread her lips. He came. Hard, hot spurts aimed directly over her centre.

Sophie cried out, knowing he finished and she wouldn't.

Staring between her legs, Dak stepped back.

"My princess." His voice echoed back and forth in her

head and when she could focus again, he was gone. But the shower ran in the distance.

He'd left her tied and aching on the bed. The ache was unbearable. Throbbing, sensitive, a dull edge of pain.

Rough fabric over her made her gasp and snapped her attention toward the bathroom. She hadn't heard the water stop. Dak wiped between her legs with a cloth. He tossed the cloth to the corner and untied one hand, then a foot. He moved to the other side of the bed.

"If you touch yourself or try to come in any way, I will tie you back up for the night and start again."

No. No. Fuck no. Sophie couldn't take any more. She curled up onto her side once all of her limbs were free. With her hands in fists, she tucked them under chin.

Dak crawled into the bed with her, his hand cupped her mound, but didn't move. Sophie held her breath, hoping for something. A small flicker. A press of his palm. But nothing came.

"Sleep." His command only frustrated her. He settled her head on his arm and curled it around her so he could run his fingers through her hair. The touch and light tingle pulling her into what felt like a trap. A trap that pulled her into restless darkness. Darkness of erotic pain and horrific nightmares. Both of which were her fault.

As each dream reached a frantic peak, a hand on her head brought both feet back to the ground and her heart slowed. And just like each edge Dak had brought her to, the process repeated until sunlight broke through the last dream.

Her core ached and sensations still ran rampant as she woke. A hard arm lay across her stomach.

"I've seen the worst of this side of life. I've been the worst. Created it. Nurtured it. Devoured it and destroyed it."

Dak's deep rumble was fuzzy with sleep, making him sound that much more dangerous. And sexy. "I'll trust you if you trust me."

Sophie let her head roll toward him. He didn't ask for anything unreasonable, or even difficult. It was only fair she conceded. Besides, the tortuous pleasure she'd experienced the night before and still lingered wasn't something to take lightly. Dak was lethal. In all things.

"Sophie?"

"If you'll trust me, I'll trust you." She gave his own words back to him like a vow.

Approval brightened in his eyes. "Good girl." He moved down her body. A trail of nips and licks followed his path. She froze, not willing to hold on to hope. Would he give her relief this time? And what would it feel like after so many denied and ruined? Sophie expected painful explosions that left her speechless.

Three swipes of his tongue and her body ignited. Like a curtain pulled, revealing a choreographed orchestra playing to an exact tune. Within seconds, the edge approached. As painful as she'd imagined, but oh so good.

He lifted away from her.

"Nooooo!" She screamed at him, her hands reaching out to pull him back. He laughed, a full and hearty bark. Cupping the backs of her knees, he spread her open and shoved himself inside.

Sophie clenched around him and lost her breath. His thumb touched her clit, and that was all she'd needed. She exploded. Hot and rushed, the drug filled her veins and excruciating pleasure throbbed in her core.

Dak kept pounding and his thumb continued to work, throwing her from one climax to the next. And with the third, he came with her.

Dak let go of her legs and set his weight on his elbows. One hand came up to cup her chin. Chills ran through Sophie. She felt the weight of his unsaid words as much as she felt the weight of his body.

"Tell me you love me, princess."

"What? You can't just demand that someone love you."

He grinned. "Of course I can, but I don't need to in this case. If you can't tell me you love me, then tell me you don't."

"I can't."

Dak crushed his mouth to hers and devoured her. And she let him. Sophie would never run from anyone or anything again.

"THERE'S an upscale restaurant three blocks from the casino. The owner is as unaffiliated with Wayne as possible. A bit of a rival and not interested. He cares about the image of his business. He maintains top security inside and out." Cole still tapped the location on the map with one finger. "I've been there several times. It's a quiet, dark, unobtrusive atmosphere. They also monitor the parking lot. I've got an in with one of the security guards. They won't bother a woman sitting in her car alone."

"Alone?" That bothered Dak the most. Leaving her alone somewhere.

"She has to be. We need everyone with Hendrick out of commission. Unless you two have changed your mind and she goes to King's and stays with Ember."

They'd already been over this. Multiple times. It's where Dak would like to put her, but in the end, these guys knew too much. And even King was stashing Ember somewhere else. "You'll need some weapons." Dak looked at Sophie, who stared wide-eyed as they planned the attack for that night. The bodies were ready to deliver. They were certain this wasn't a trap and was a true summit called by the arrogant bastard.

"What weapons?" She bit her lip, like a child with their first taste of independence. Nervous excitement gave her a little bounce.

"A small knife you can handle. Only enough to get out of someone's hold. It won't cut deep. And a small handgun."

"I've never shot a gun before."

"You will today." As soon as they were done here. "Your goal is to get away from an attacker and nothing else. Understood?"

"Yes." She nodded, and he saw the promise light her eyes.

"The first thing you do is drive away and back here."

"Understood." Sophie laid her hand on his chest, over his heart. She hadn't said she loved him. But in her touch, it was a palpable heat moving into him.

"You'll monitor the security feed and relay it back to us. Roen will do the same, but he's listening. You're watching." The thought of sending her to Roen to do this had crossed his mind, but Roen was locked down with her parents and wouldn't tell any of them where he was. This wasn't a job the other man needed help with, but having a second set of eyes would be good in case he had to get back on the run in the middle of it. A summit didn't mean they put everything on pause so they could chat.

Wayne had called together the leaders of crime syndicates, casino and bar owners that carried a specific clientele, loan sharks, and more. The only invitation for crime leaders missing was King's. But this was about coming after *King's*

Mercenaries. They provided the perfect opportunity to deliver a message to ensure not only Wayne wouldn't be a problem, but neither would any of the others. Not if they valued their lives or their businesses.

"You got what we need to get in the building?" Dak set both hands on the table and looked at Gear.

"I do." Gear pulled out four keycards with Wayne's casino logo printed on one side.

"That's all he has for security?" Cole's face twisted.

"No. Those are only for the doors. There's a code that needs to be entered within thirty seconds once the door opens or an alarm will sound. That code changes every thirty minutes." Gear passed out the cards as he talked.

"Roen already hacked the system and can get the code." King pocketed his card and stared at the casino blueprints. "Once the code is in, that's it. We don't need it again. Only the card for the rest of the doors. Every door into the building except the main entrance requires that code. He has no backup system."

"That we know of." Dak shared Cole's skepticism. But both King and Gear snapped their heads up.

"No backup system. His backup is in his numbers. He has guards on rotation everywhere. We need to blend in or avoid them. Taking them out too soon will draw unwanted attention." King scowled.

"They can't know we're there until they arrive for the summit." Dak had a specific vision of how he wanted this to go.

"Avoiding it is." Cole tilted his head at the blueprint.

Sophie stood beside Dak, but her gaze was everywhere. The maps, the blueprints, and listening to each of them speak.

"It's going to be up to you to help us watch for the

guards. Roen will too, but if he has to bug out, it's all on you. Can you handle that?" Dak worried they were putting too much on Sophie.

"I think so." She pulled her eyes away from the papers sprawled across the table and matched his gaze. "Yes. I can do it."

Dak nodded and looked at King. "When this is over, we're officially hiring." Parts of a job should never be dependent on Ember or Sophie. Or any other woman insane enough to align themselves with one of the deadly mercenaries here.

"I'll go get the uniforms." Gear pocketed his own keycard and left.

"Okay, princess. Time to learn how to shoot a gun."

Sophie swallowed, but straightened her shoulders. She didn't have anything to prove to him, but still she kept her chin high. Dak wished he had more time with her before jumping into the depths of the ugly side of the world.

Dressed in black leggings, a tight tank top, and a leather jacket of her own, Sophie stayed beside Dak as he and Cole took her to the restaurant. Cole bumped fists with a guy in a suit. His shoulders stretched the fabric tight. The man was wider than any of the mercenaries.

"This her?" He pointed at her with his chin.

"Yeah." Cole moved to stand beside his friend. Dak tensed beside her. "Sophie, this is Archer."

"Hi." *Don't look away. Keep your eyes on him. Be as bold as Dak.* The size of the stranger was what bothered her most. After spending time with Dak, no one seemed as scary. Still dangerous, but she knew there was worse out there. Like the man holding firm beside her. Not touching her, but not moving away from her. He'd told her he didn't want anyone to know how important she was to him. Not yet. But his presence alone made Archer speak a promise.

"She's safe here." Archer looked over her head and directed his promise to Dak. "I've secured one of the private dining rooms for her inside. It would be safer than the parking lot as you'd planned. But of course it's up to you. I'll keep an eye on her throughout my rounds no matter where she is."

Sophie searched Dak's face, and even she couldn't tell what he was thinking.

"Show us the room."

Archer inclined his head, and led them through the parking lot to the employee's entrance of the restaurant. Cole walked behind Archer. Sophie followed behind him and Dak took up the rear.

The back room had sharp fluorescent lights beating down. She had to blink to help her eyes adjust to the dimness when they stepped through into the restaurant. Red glowed from the shadows, from a waterfall in the centre, and from under the tables.

Archer took them around the edges of the room until he came to a line of double doors. Stopping at the second set, he swung one door inward and waved them all inside. A circle table sat in the centre of the square room with a single place set. It was decorated with black linen and a slim vase with two tall white flowers.

"If you're hungry, I can have food brought in for you, but you can also make whatever space you need to at the table and do what you need." Archer, although large, seemed kind and sincere in his willingness to help. Cole held no tension around him. She couldn't say the same for Dak. But she didn't think it mattered with whom or where they were leaving her, Dak wouldn't be comfortable.

"Thank you." But Sophie looked at Dak for the final decision.

He stalked around the room while Cole spoke quietly to Archer. After a few minutes, Cole nodded at Dak.

"You can stay in here. If you want."

Sophie had to admit, she'd feel better in here than exposed in a parking lot. But she supposed a car provided its own kind of security and escape. Taking in the room for herself, and sizing up Archer, who quirked an amused brow, Sophie chewed on the inside of her cheek.

Mentally, she checked the knives and the small gun hidden on her torso, their weight comforting. Her first lesson shooting a gun earlier had gone well, and ended with a fun challenge between her and Dak. Maybe he'd only done it to help ease her nerves, but it had worked and she'd enjoyed herself. It showed her another side of Dak. Life with him wouldn't always be serious.

"I'll stay in here."

"I'll leave you to it then. I pass this room every thirty minutes, and I'll poke my head in when I do." Archer knocked Cole's shoulder and gave a respectable nod to Dak before closing them in the room.

"If we're looking for guys to hire, Archer should be on the list." Cole cocked his head toward the door.

"We'll talk." Dak walked closer to Sophie, but still didn't touch her. She knew he feared cameras. "You're sure?"

"Yes." Sophie started clearing the table. As delicious as the smells wafting from the restaurant were, she wouldn't be able to keep anything down. Cole set the case down and unzipped it, producing the laptop and communication pieces she'd need.

"Set it up." Cole set the computer and equipment in front of her. They'd shown her how to do it all herself and made her repeat the process a couple of times. Sophie pulled the laptop closer and sat down. Within a few minutes she had everything booted, ready, and her earpiece in.

"Good." Dak took a step away from her. "We'll come get you when we're done. Be here." He'd reiterated his warning after he'd finished teaching her how to shoot. *Even you will face my wrath if you put yourself in harm's way.* His eyes had the same look in them now as they did then.

"I'll remember that." Sophie let her lips lift.

Dak glared. Cole had to pull him from the room.

With a shaky breath, Sophie settled in.

"You okay, princess." Dak's rough tone grumbled in her ear.

"I'm good." Sophie knew she was getting more out of Dak than he wanted to give. It didn't matter how much she begged, if he didn't want her here, believe in her enough to do this, share enough with her to allow her to try, she wouldn't. He could have still locked her away with force. She loved him for that. She loved him for many reasons. But that respect was invaluable.

Did she tell him that? No. Was she scared to admit that emotion again so soon? Yes. She hadn't spent enough time with Alan before falling at his feet. But one thing was different with Dak. Sophie didn't fall at his feet. They stood toe to toe.

"You in, Sophie?" Roen's voice came through the audio on the laptop.

"I'm in." Sophie pushed her focus to the task at hand. Tonight was the end of the worst chapter of her life.

19

———

A steamroller flattened Dak's insides. In his gut, he knew nowhere was safe for Sophie. Cole assured him he trusted Archer. It had taken over a year for Dak to earn his and Roen's trust. Trust from either of them didn't come easily.

He listened to her talk to Roen through his earpiece. Hushed tone and all business. After a couple hiccups, arranging the views on her screen, both of them gave the all clear to move ahead.

They split into pairs, each with a load of bodies. They had more than enough to fill the chairs in the conference at the top floor. Gear had already disposed of the extras.

King swiped his keycard and held the door with his toe while listening to Roen rattle off the latest security code. He tapped in the ten digit sequence and pushed the door wider. Dak pushed the trolley through with their load of bodies disguised as a furniture delivery.

"Two guards coming from the hall behind you." Sophie spoke evenly despite the slight rush to her words.

"The east corner, Sophie. Two guards coming from the

east corner," Roen corrected her. "You have about thirty seconds to get away from that door."

King stood beside Dak and helped push the trolley. The amount of bodies they had crammed in there made for a heavy delivery. They rounded a corner and waited.

"They're checking the door. One is taking the stairs." Sophie gave a clear play-by-play. Seconds passed. "The second is following." Another pause. "You're clear to get on the elevator." Sophie sighed through the comm.

King scanned his card to open the elevator. Putting his foot behind him, Dak pushed to get the trolley moving forward again.

"There are guards on the top floor. But you can't stay at the bottom level."

"No guards on the level below the top. Go there until the top is clear." Roen helped Sophie. "Need to look at the whole route, even when dealing with an elevator."

"Got it."

Dak pressed the button for the floor. By the time they reached it, Sophie and Roen gave the all clear.

"Anything going on we should know about, Roen?" Dak asked while they moved up the last floor.

"A couple arrivals, but they're in the casino. No chatter about Wayne, Sophie, or suspicions that something else is going on." Sophie couldn't hear the communications like Roen.

The elevator dinged.

"You're still clear. And the conference room is too." Clicking followed Sophie's voice. "Cole and Gear, be ready to move in."

With their delivery in the hall, King reached into the elevator to send it back down to the first floor.

"Go." Sophie and Roen spoke at the same time. Dak

scanned his card this time to open the conference room. They tucked themselves along the wall and waited for the other two to arrive before unloading the bodies. It would ruin the surprise if anyone walked in on them before they were finished setting up.

Tall leather chairs surrounded the long wooden table. Covered refreshments and liquor filled a table at the back of the room. They'd arrived between the caterers and the summit. Just as planned.

Dak closed his eyes and leaned his head against the wall behind him. His hands were at the ready at his sides. Listening to Sophie direct the other two was both calming and set his nerves on fire. She was doing great. Fear and pride warred within him over the right to decide her future within King's Mercenaries.

For the first time in a long time, Dak had a weakness. And a new strength.

Long, heavy breaths passed the time until the other two entered the room.

"More arrivals. Not everyone is spending their time in the casino. Fifteen minutes until the summit." Roen's tension filled his voice.

"What else?" Dak recognized the tension. There was more.

"Just chatter about King. About us. Apparently we've gone soft."

"Let them think that." Dak couldn't wait to see the looks on their faces when they walked in here. "Let's do this." He nodded to the others in the room. They dug into the reinforced furniture boxes and started heaving bodies out of them to position in the seats around the table.

The comms had gone quiet while they worked.

"Bar the doors. A few just got in the elevator." Roen's

voice came through instead of Sophie's.

Gear pulled out a chain from one of the boxes. That man thought of things even Dak never did. He ran the chain through the handles of the doors.

"Two more entered the elevator. Wayne was behind them, but three guards just pulled him away." Again, Roen spoke.

"What are they saying through the comms?"

"They aren't." His frustrated growl scratched through the speaker. "Half a dozen of the attendees are in the hall."

The door pulled and the chain rattled, covering up the grumbling coming from the hall. They waited. They couldn't come in until everyone had arrived. Especially Wayne.

But why was Roen relaying all the information and not a word from Sophie?

"Several more in the elevator."

"Sophie? Why aren't you talking?" Dak couldn't hold it in any longer.

There was no answer. The door rattled harder.

"Hold it in, Dak. I know where Sophie is." Roen's tone changed. An even roll that always came before bad news. "Everyone, make sure Dak puts on the act of his life. Sophie is coming in that door with the attendees for the summit. Last ones in. She's being held by one guard stalking closely behind Wayne."

King stepped partially in front of Dak, taking the lead like the king he was. Dak was the shadows and that's what he needed to remember. He couldn't give them any indication that they held the one person that could bring him to his knees.

"Time to open the door." Roen delivered what could be the final command of the night.

Gear removed the chain, wrapping it around his wrist and hand. He let it gently swing by his leg as they burst through the door. King stood at the head of the table. Dak stood behind his shoulder and at the corner of the table. Cole was at the other end and Gear was the closest to the door.

They filed into the room, pausing before the next pushed their way in.

"What's going on? Everyone take your seats. We need..." Wayne called through the open door and stalled once he stepped inside.

"My apologies. All the seats are taken." King threw an arm wide toward the table. Cole spun the chair closest to him that knocked the one next to it creating a domino effect, revealing the bodies in the chairs next to the door. Faces paled.

Dak couldn't take any satisfaction in this surprise knowing Sophie was only a few steps behind Wayne.

"What the fuck do you think you are doing?" Wayne's eyes didn't only stay on King, but moved between him and Dak. It seemed people knew that not only King was in charge.

Dak held himself together as he stepped up beside King. They were partners. Always had been. Only now, the rest of the world knew it.

"Correcting your mistake. Recognize any of them?" Dak cocked his head toward the chairs.

Not only Wayne's eyes pinched as they all studied the faces. Interesting. Dak noted them, realizing they'd joined forces with Wayne.

"It's been brought to our attention that you've all gathered here to discuss me." King dropped his chin and his voice. "Rude I wasn't invited."

"Soft. Weak. Empathetic." Dak listed off the few words used to describe them lately. Gear whipped the chain out to slice at the dead body closest to him. Cole let out a cackle Hendrick would be proud of. King smirked. But Dak mentally reached for the shadows to ground him. He held his breath as he first heard Sophie whimper.

"You think you have the upper hand here? In case you haven't noticed, you're outnumbered."

"Do your research before you make an enemy. This isn't outnumbered." Gear whipped the chain, filleting another body. Cole pulled a gun out with one hand and a knife with the other. They made a show of equality rather than employees of King. That was what made this group deadlier than any other. Sophie would be okay. She had to be with all of them in the room.

"Well, congratulations. You've surprised me, but you don't have the golden ticket anymore." Wayne waved his arm forward. "I do."

The guard holding Sophie stepped forward. A bruise already bloomed below her left eye.

Dak hadn't planned on killing anyone other than Wayne today. But whoever put that bruise on her just made the list.

A NEW ACHE inflamed through Sophie's torso from the manhandling. But that was nothing compared to the throbbing in her twisted ankle or the heat in her face.

She gritted her teeth against each and every whimper. If she didn't, the brute holding her bent her arm hard enough to take her breath away. It wasn't even the same brute that found her at the restaurant.

Archer, true to his word, checked in on her with each

pass during his rounds. This wasn't his fault. That she knew of. Minutes after he checked in with her the third time, one side of the double doors burst open and shut quickly.

"Someone's looking for you." The fist hit her face quicker than she could stand, knocking her out long enough for him to pull her from the restaurant and rid her of the two measly weapons she'd had.

He'd dragged her a block away from the restaurant where they met the guard holding her now. She fought as they passed her between them which was how she'd twisted her ankle.

The blow to the face had left her dizzy and made her movements choppy. She'd tried to get away. With everything she had. Remembering every move they'd all shown her, but she never landed a single one.

"I have her. I could let go of the money. Now that I have her, I can make that money back. In a multitude of ways." Wayne took joy with each word he spewed.

The four faces Sophie knew all had their hard ridged expressions. Normal for them. They showed no surprise or recognition of her. Even Dak. She knew he had to keep it that way. But Sophie was having a harder time holding in her emotions.

Turning her eyes toward the floor, she blocked them all out until she could get a hold of herself.

"She won't be any good to you when you're dead." The chain clinked as Gear swung it in a circle. The silver shone in her peripheral vision.

"I'm not dying today." Wayne chuckled through his words. "But it was kind of you to show up here. Now there's nothing to discuss. We can take you out now."

The buffoon holding Sophie tensed. Fear or anticipation, she couldn't tell. She tuned into his body language, hoping to get a clue for how the rest of the room felt about Wayne's declaration. Feet shuffled on the floor, some moving back, others forward, and the rest only took one step back. Wayne didn't have control over the room like he thought.

Sophie took a mental check of her body. She hurt, but the dizziness had passed. Scrolling through everything they taught her, she tried to come up with the best way to get out of the hold the guy had on her.

With a deep breath to weigh down her emotions, she lifted her head. Everything she felt for Dak slammed into her chest as she set her eyes on him. Then they stomped on her lungs when his eyes met hers. But she held it all back. She had to.

Looking around the room, she discovered she was right. The group of men inched apart into sub-groups. Not everyone agreed with Wayne and his desire to take out *King's Mercenaries.*

Frowns that conveyed a dark wisdom settled on the features of the men toward the side of the room. Red-faced anger filled the rest that stood near Wayne.

Time to get this show on the road. She only had one place she could reach to cause pain to the man holding her. And it was a stretch, but it could be worse. He could be bald. But this man clearly adored his thick, styled locks.

With a quick swing of her arm, she broke the hold he had below her shoulder and kept going to reach behind her. He countered by pulling upward on the arm behind her back, but she ignored the pain. Even if she didn't succeed, she caused a disturbance giving the others a chance to do something.

With a squealing growl escaping through her teeth, she pulled with all her might on a fist full of his hair. She pulled his head down enough that she could smash the back of hers against his nose. The crunch wasn't complete, but it was enough that he let go of the arm behind her.

She readied to launch herself forward, away from him and toward the mercenaries she trusted, but sharp steel flashed in front of her face, stopping her. He angled it so the sharp edge sat against her cheek. If she moved at all, he'd cut her face.

Sophie realized what she should have done. Instead of only launching herself forward, she should have dropped and rolled away from him when he let her arm go. She closed her eyes and backed up until she hit his chest. No one had moved with her distraction.

And Dak thought she could do this. There wasn't room for mistakes like this. She'd just proved him, and herself wrong.

***

It was like a horror film played in front of him. And the scene would live in his nightmares for a long time. Damn, he was so proud of her effort. She almost got away from him. But the knife came out of nowhere. He was fast. Something they needed to keep in mind with their next move.

"She'll lose that fight soon." Wayne looked pleased.

"Don't count on it." Sophie snarled through her teeth, not moving her face at all while she spoke.

"Well, this has gone on long enough." Wayne waved a generic gesture to the summit members. "Secure the mercenaries. And call someone to bring new chairs." He threw the last over his shoulder.

Wilder, who'd moved toward the side of the room, threw his head back and laughed. "You don't command us." Some of the men that stood with Wayne hedged back and forth, from one foot to the other.

"You don't want me as an enemy."

"You're a fool. I don't want the king of mercenaries as an enemy. And I don't think you'll be around much longer to be an enemy to anyone." Wilder's tailored suit stretched as he straightened, crossing his arms over his chest. The other syndicate leaders standing near him mimicked his pose. They'd butted heads with each of them over one thing or another over the years, but at the end of the day they all minded their own business. Dak didn't look forward to the day that changed.

"I'll deal with all of you another time. You may leave." Wayne stood his ground. But no one moved, except those that secured their place next to Wayne.

"Release her." Dak glared at the guard holding the knife flat against Sophie's cheek. He stalked around the table, taking the long way away from King and toward Cole and Gear. Cole matched his pace to cover King.

"You have your payment from her. You control that money I've generously decided to let go. Your business is done. At least it would be if you hadn't turned to the other side as I've suspected. The side of good. Protectors. Disgusting."

"We don't justify ourselves to anyone. But know this, our skills haven't diminished. And when someone attacks a street-side business in broad daylight, they endanger the entire community." King moved away from the head of the table, daring to put his back to Wilder and the others standing with him. Cole moved to stand between them.

"You did what?" Wilder hissed. "They're all yours." They didn't take a stand with them, but they didn't leave either.

The group took a step back and watched. At least it lowered the numbers.

Dak inched his way around the table to stand beside Gear. "As did all the men standing with him. The men sitting in the chairs don't only belong to Wayne."

Wayne's lips twisted. "Duke, remind them who has the upper hand." He flicked his glance over his shoulder to look at Sophie. "Not the face, you fucking idiot."

The second he moved the blade away from her face, Dak roared. "Now, Sophie."

She crumpled to the floor like a ragdoll. Duke reached for her, not seeing the threat coming at him from Gear. The first lash of Gear's chain missed as the guard bent to grab Sophie.

He yanked her up by her hair and slid the knife between her breasts and down her stomach. The sharp blade cut through her clothes and into her skin, deep enough to leave a trickle of blood.

She cried out with a low scream. The cut wouldn't be anything more than a terrible sting, but the sight of her blood filled his vision with the same red colour.

"Sophie!" His emotions broke free.

"Dak!" She matched him as she called back.

The other's moved in, attacking anyone standing with Wayne. Gear and Dak moved as one for the guard holding Sophie. Dak grabbed the wrist holding the knife and twisted. Gear's chain appeared around his neck.

His own preservation of life took control and he released Sophie and the knife. She fell into Dak's chest and the tears sprang forward.

"Not yet, princess. Hold it in and get behind me." Dak waited for her to move and focused on one face only. The others had everyone subdued or killed. It depended on how hard they'd fought back.

King currently toyed with Wayne, waiting for Dak to deal with him. Dak stepped between them and wrapped a hand around his throat. His own knife, jagged, painful, and sharper than the one set against Sophie, flashed in his hand. Before he ended Wayne's life, Dak waited for King to give the final speech.

"I take it the message is clear and that it will reach far and wide after this." King paused. Dak didn't look away from Wayne as King let his words sink in. "I trust we won't have any more foolish actions based on foolish assumptions. We are far from soft or weak."

Dak drove the point home by driving his knife between Wayne's ribs. When he pulled it free, he let go of his neck and sliced from jugular to aorta. His knife didn't leave a clean, easy cut. But an ugly mess, drawing gasps and gags from the room. Some of those men were in the wrong business.

Dak stepped back, relieved knowing the job was done.

"I think it would be foolish of you not to see your own weaknesses." Wilder's voice sounded smooth over the room filled with death. Dak snapped his gaze to the other man, as did King, but Wilder was looking at Sophie.

Dak turned around. Sophie's pale face and wide eyes tried to take in everything in the room at once. He recognized the shock. She'd spread her hands wide over her belly and chest, only covering a small part of the long cut.

Bright blue that had faded to the shade of ice found his. They heaved their breaths to a matching rhythm.

His princess. His weakness.

20

The only things that pierced through Sophie's focus were the blood trickling over her fingers, the warning from the tall, tailored suit across the room, and Dak's eyes.

No one said anything else. At least not that she heard. The floor grew closer until it wasn't the floor beneath her, but Dak's chest and arms. As he wrapped them around her, she realized she was shivering.

She felt as if she was floating as he carried her from the room. They all moved close together as they took the elevator down to the main floor and out the door they'd come in.

She'd watched as death crept into the eyes of Wayne. Like the shadowed figure himself grinned with sin as he grasped hold of the life inside that body. She wondered if that's what her eyes would look like if things had been different. Would the shadowed figure of death smile back at Dak as he watched the life drain from her?

"Dak?" Her voice was full with unshed tears.

"Shh, princess." His lips pressed against her temple.

"You were wrong." Sophie closed her eyes.

When she let herself wake and pay attention, they were in Dak's apartment. He'd laid her out on the couch while he sat on the coffee table. The others held up the walls of the room with glasses of amber liquid that she assumed had some kick to them. Dak's glass sat untouched beside him.

The front door opened and it took a moment before whoever it was entered her view, but none of the others in the room reacted to someone coming in unannounced.

"I haven't seen you guys so much in one week since we were street kids." Thane came in shaking his head until he laid eyes on her. "You poor girl."

She had no response for him. She was a burden that made Dak weak. They'd both broken at the end, and everyone in the room knew she was his. And incapable of defending herself.

Dak peeled away her torn clothing before Thane shoved him out of the way to take his place on the coffee table.

"This is going to sting. I'm sorry." He sounded it, but didn't look it. A professional mask stayed in place over his scruffy features. He poured something on a white cloth and started cleaning the cut.

Sophie's nostrils flared with the full breaths she took to control the sting. But her whimpers still escaped. The room was quiet while the doctor worked. No one willing to make a sound and break the tension.

"You won't need stitches. But I'll tape it closed and you'll keep a bandage on for a couple days. I've got some good stuff to help speed up healing and to keep you from scarring. You'll be just fine, girl."

Her lips trembled as she tried to say her thanks so she pinched them closed and nodded.

"You're welcome." He smiled sideways and taped the cut closed.

Dak moved behind Thane, looking at her over his shoulder.

"I... I'm s...sss..sorry." She couldn't control her speech. Thane's frowning face tilted and cut off her view of Dak. He stared at her, and then looked around him. He spotted Dak's drink still sitting on the table.

"Make her drink that." He nodded at the glass and went back to work. Dak took the glass and settled himself beside her head.

With a strong hand behind her head, he lifted and tipped the glass to her lips. The liquid burned her throat, but was warm once it settled. He forced another sip on her before letting her head rest.

"Why are you sorry, princess."

"I c..couldn't get a...away." The warmth helped ease the words, but didn't yet cure the trembling.

"You did fine." Dak smoothed back her hair.

"How c..can you say th..that? I got caught and then I failed at my escape."

Dak shook his head and picked up the glass again. Forcing her head up, he made her drink.

"Done." Thane moved down toward her feet. He took his time examining her ankle. He pulled out a cold pack from his bag. Bending it, something inside it snapped and he placed it over her ankle. "Just twisted. Keep it up. I'll leave pain killers and an ointment to go under the bandage. Two days at least for the bandage. Change it once a day." Thane looked between her and Dak. He cleaned up his stuff and moved to stand next to King who handed him a glass of the same drink as everyone else.

"You can't fail at something you weren't ready to do." Dak took her hand and held it in one of his. Gear brought him a new drink.

"Think we'll have any more problems with attacks at the front door?" Cole rolled his neck as he sat down in a chair across the room.

"No," said King. "I could be wrong. We need a system in place if it happens again, but it won't happen any time soon. The message was loud and clear." His inflection didn't settle, the 'but' dropping hard in the room.

"They have something else to go after." Dak spoke over his shoulder.

"Me. And Ember." Sophie whispered, but they all turned to her. Dak never had a weakness until she showed up. Ember was well on her way to becoming a fierce match to the mercenary she lived with. Soon, no one would consider going after her as they'd never go directly after King.

But Sophie? She'd be the one to bring them all down.

Fingers pressed on her cheek, turning her head. "Say it." Dak leaned in, his face inches from her. "Say it, princess. I dare you."

"I need to..."

"Not that." His growl cut her off. "You aren't allowed to say those words. There are three specific words I want. Ones I've said, but you haven't. Give them to me."

"If I say them, I can't leave." But he wasn't going to let her leave anyway.

"That's right. Now, say them."

Their audience faded out of her focus. They were still there, watching her lay herself bare. She gave her love too fast the last time. And she feared she was about to do the same, but there were so many differences between her past self and now.

"Sophie." Her name carried uncertainty, hope, and a demand.

"I love you, Dak." Her hushed declaration was for his

ears only. He took her mouth in a soft, soul possessing kiss, sealing her fate and her future. As his.

———

FLAYED open and vulnerable for the first time since he was a child on the streets, Dak breathed in Sophie through the kiss. As the minutes passed, he eased his lips until she calmed beneath him.

She sighed as he let her go. Not quite asleep, but her lashes fluttered against the tops of her cheeks.

Dak stood and turned to the others who still waited. "We've done what we needed. There's no threat right now."

"There might not ever be one." King pushed off the wall. "People have heard that Ember isn't an easy target. They'll learn the same of Sophie soon enough. As we all know, sometimes a threat is just a threat."

"It may have only been a reminder. Wilder made it clear he doesn't want to go up against us." Gear emptied his drink and took his glass to the sink.

"You could be right, but we'll always be ready." King followed him with his empty glass. Thane and Cole also finished.

"Roen is asking if it's safe to bring her parents back." Cole stopped beside the couch.

"Yes. But to a safehouse here and hire out security guards. Just until we know if anyone is taking Wayne's place and will hold the same grudge as him."

Cole nodded and knelt beside Sophie. "Get better soon, Sophie." He squeezed her wrist and left.

Gear took his place, nudging Dak out of the way. "You did good." He emphasized each word and captured her gaze, holding it until she nodded her agreement. He nodded back then stood. "I'll go check on Hendrick."

"Call if you need anything." Thane patted her knee and gave a finger salute to Dak.

King strolled over once the door closed. "Sophie. You and Ember are not our weaknesses."

Dak retook his place sitting on the coffee table. "You make us even more dangerous."

"People have already tried to use Ember against me."

"The mistake they make is they think threatening Ember, threatening you, will control us." Dak ran his thumb over her bottom lip that still had a slight tremble. He suspected it was no longer shock, but the raw emotions that he forced her to expose.

"It only makes us uncontrollable, even by ourselves. We'd burn the world to get either of you back and if they harm you, we burn them."

"Do you understand, princess?" She was a strength Dak didn't know he needed. But now that he had her, he was never going to let her go.

"Yes."

"Good." King ran his hand over her head. "Make sure he takes care of you." King stalked past them. "I need my wife." He left.

"Time to tell me what happened at the restaurant." Dak ran his thumb over the back of her hand.

"Archer checked on me for the third time, but a few minutes later, someone barged in the room. The only thing they said was someone was looking for me. I don't know who he was or how he knew I was there. He reached me before I could get away or draw the knife or gun. He knocked me out and the next thing I knew, we were a block away meeting the guy that had me at the summit. I was too dizzy to get away from them."

"Do you think Archer had anything to do with it?" Cole had assured Dak of Archer. If he betrayed them, Cole knew nothing about it and he'd have to get in line to kill the guy.

"I don't know. I don't think so."

"Wayne must have had spies in there." Dak would deal with it later. He slid his arms beneath Sophie and lifted her against his chest. He set her down in the bathroom and started the water in the sink, pushing the plug down and adding a few drops of bath soap. With the fresh bandage on her chest, he couldn't put her in the shower or the bath. But a proper sponge bath wasn't out of the question.

While the water heated from the tap, he peeled her pants and panties from her body and set her on the counter.

"You don't have to do this."

"Yes, I do." Dunking a cloth, he wrung it out before running it over her face and down her neck. He wet it often to keep the cloth, and her, warm. He was gentle near the cut and determined around her breasts, thumbing her nipples and cupping each as he washed them. His attention didn't waver no matter what part of her body he washed. By the time he reached between her legs, she was panting. But he only washed her.

"Dak. You're so sure I belong with you. I'm not."

"You will be. I'll give you everything and more. But there is one thing I can't."

Her breath paused. Dak lifted her from the counter and carried her to the bed.

"I don't exist. I don't have a last name to give you."

Sophie struggled to sit up on the bed. When she didn't stop as she winced with each movement, Dak caved and helped her up. "Why the hell would that matter?"

Dak's jaw dropped.

"I don't need your name. I don't need a wedding. A wedding means nothing. It's a pretty party with no substance. It's the marriage and the relationship that matter. If I've learned nothing else the past three years, it's that."

"Princess." She'd left him stunned. "I guess if I asked you to marry me, you'd say no?"

"I'd say when we do, it's only us. No one around. No legal papers. No officiant or witnesses. Just us."

Dak eased her back on the bed and she let him. "We're alone now." He kissed her until she was breathless.

"We are."

Dak ran his tongue along her jaw and flicked it over the sensitive spots down her neck. "Don't move, princess." He murmured against her breast. His intent was to drive her mad with his tongue. It was all he could do, and it was all he needed.

Down her body and back up the other side. His name left her lips, hushed, loud, begging, and everything in between.

Reaching into the nightstand, he pulled out the same rope he'd already used. He tied one end around her left wrist and started the other around his right and held it in front of her. "Tie it."

She kept her gaze on his while she tied the rope. It wasn't tight and would be easy to slip out of, but that wasn't the point.

"You're mine. And I'm yours." He moved back down her body and settled between her legs. After a slow circle around her clit that made her gasp, he looked up. "I'll protect you. I'll teach you. I'll support you." Another three circles. "I'll love you with everything I have and more." He latched onto her clit and sucked before dropping to dip his tongue in her entrance. "Your turn."

"I'll stand beside you. Rarely behind you." Her lips lifted into a half smile. "I'll support you. I'll love you with everything I have and more."

Dak thrust two fingers into her heat. "Mine. My wife. My princess."

"Yours." The climax fluttered at the edge. Her walls clamped around his fingers.

"Come for me, princess. Then tell me the rest." Dak curled his fingers and worked her clit with his tongue. They grasped the hands that were tied together. Knuckles white, they held onto each other while he pulled her orgasm from her.

"Dak." She cried out and threw her head back, disappearing into the pillows.

He moved up her body, bringing their bound hands up beside her head. "Say the rest."

"Your wife." She pulled in a breath. "Your princess. And you?"

"Your husband." Dak kissed her. He kissed the light that pushed away his shadows. Or did he pull her into his shadows? Neither. They worked together. Shadows didn't exist with the light.

EPILOGUE

Hendrick hobbled to the wooden targets he'd set up in the gym to place the sticker in the centre. Thane expected him to continue to use his crutches, but they got in the way. However, Hendrick wasn't insane enough to put too much weight on his leg. He liked his job and planned to be here for as long as possible.

He retook his position on his stool next to Sophie and Ember.

"That's the target? That teeny tiny orange dot?" Ember stared, slack-jawed, at the wood. She was overdue for a lesson on throwing knives.

"Yes, Ember. That's the target." Hendrick adjusted himself so he could lift his sore leg higher. The ache ran deeper the longer he was on it.

Sophie had been the one to ask him to teach them how to throw knives. She glared at the dot like it was her mortal enemy.

"Aim small, miss small," Hendrick reminded them. Ember looked skeptical, but Sophie nodded, looking more determined than she had when slamming her fist into his groin.

"Why are we standing so close? Won't this be harder?" Sophie set her feet in the stance he'd already shown them.

"Depends on how you throw. There are different techniques that all have different results. From here, you're going to throw from your side." Hendrick demonstrated the motion while sitting on the stool, keeping his hand at elbow height and whipping it around in a half circle to release in front of him.

He'd set each of the girls up with their own leg sheath and set of beginner knives. Dull, but tapered enough to stick with a proper throw. He'd test each one himself before presenting them with their wrapped gifts.

"Isn't it supposed to spin? There isn't enough room between us and the target." Ember turned on him.

"There can be no spin, a half spin, or a full spin. Now, face the target." He had to take a breath to push the ache in his leg away. If he let it consume him, he'd become short-tempered. Neither of the women deserved that. Ember was still healing from her own stab wound. Luckily, not as bad as his. She was under strict orders from King to practice for no more than twenty minutes. "For this technique and distance, you're going to hold the knife by the handle."

"Like this?" Sophie slipped a knife from her sheath and held it up, gripping the sides of the handle.

"Exactly." Hendrick narrowed his eyes. He hadn't shown them that yet.

"I've been watching." Sophie set her shoulders back.

"So you have. Let's see what you've got then."

Sophie swung, but the knife hit flat and clanged, dropping to the floor. She muttered under her breath as she pulled out the next knife. Ember lifted her knife and took a deep breath before swinging. Hers sunk into the wood at the bottom of the target.

For the next several minutes, Hendrick only corrected them on their form and let them get the feel for the knives themselves. While Ember hadn't thrown knives before, she had used them several times over the past year. But Sophie was as green as she could be. Her jaw clenched harder with every miss.

"Relax, Sophie. You aren't doing yourself any favours."

"You relax." The small blonde snapped back before making her best throw yet. The blade landed hard in the wood about eight inches away from the target.

But she didn't get a chance to try again before Cole entered the gym, interrupting them.

"Lowell's sent a message." Cole passed an envelope to King, who sat beside Dak at the back of the gym. The two men had remained quiet and hidden for the lesson, but Hendrick had no doubt the women knew they were there.

King opened the envelope and frowned. "I don't understand. This is for me?" He frowned.

Cole shrugged. "Jacob said he was told to deliver it to *King's Mercenaries.*"

King passed the note to Dak who had the same reaction but read it aloud. "For Kit. Shane is dead."

Hendrick's first instinct had him gripping the hilt of his own knife strapped to his thigh. Shane is dead? He'd been the most levelheaded of them all. If anyone could have survived that job, it should have been Shane.

"Who is Kit?" Dak stared at the paper like it would answer him. Hendrick turned his attention back to the women. After all these years, it was easy for him not to react to the name.

"Try again, Sophie. This time, take a deep breath before

you throw." He took a deep breath of his own. He wondered when it had happened and if that was why Shane never showed up at their last meeting. They didn't meet regularly to fill each other in on information and secrets. They met regularly because Shane was the only person from his past that Hendrick couldn't let go.

"Hendrick." King stepped forward, eying his wife while he asked. "Do the names Kit or Shane ring a bell?"

"That's like asking, do you know Bob from Saskatchewan." And to let off a little of his frustration without it showing, Hendrick pulled a knife from his thigh and used a backhanded throw to knock Ember's knife off the target.

"Asshole." Ember kept her gaze on the target and pulled another knife.

King sighed. "I'll call Jacob." He left, pulling his phone from his pocket as he walked out of the gym.

Hendrick kept the lesson going, moving them back a couple feet. Sophie's knives stuck more often than not and Ember's crept closer to the dot. He wanted to stop. Grief was one of the hardest things to hide. But he did.

He could only guess who the note was from. There was one who would send the message as a warning. Or there was another who'd send it because they knew the pain he'd be in. The latter wouldn't have been so blunt. The one who sent that was hoping Hendrick would come to heel.

Not a fucking chance. His hands burned as if he held the very flames he was going to use against whoever killed Shane. He was going to enter his past and set it on fire, grinning as he walked through the flames.

The mercenaries mention Jacob Lowell and Lowell's bar a few times in Shades of Cruelty and in Shades of Savage. Jacob has his own novella that is only available to those on my newsletter. To get this free book, and to receive special content, the most up to date information on releases, and special promotions, join my newsletter using the link below.
https://bit.ly/sarahurq

Also, visit my website at...
http://www.authorsarahurquhart.com
...to see my full book list.
Also in the King's Mercenaries series...

Shades Of Chaos, King's Mercenaries Book Three releases Spring of 2023.

Also in the King's Mercenaries Series . . .

Shades of Cruelty, King's Mercenaries Book One. To find King and Ember's story go to...
https://books2read.com/kings1

FOLLOW SARAH ON HER SOCIAL MEDIA

https://www.instagram.com/authorsarahu/
https://www.facebook.com/groups/sarahswildones
https://www.facebook.com/authorsarahu
https://www.bookbub.com/profile/sarah-urquhart